As It Is, When It Was

Also by Brandon Pomeroy

In My Time of Need
Grace Upon Grace

As It Is, When It Was

Brandon Pomeroy

Elpida Press
Kansas City

Thanks to Sofia Pomeroy for help with editing. Any mistakes that remain are mine.

-B.P

Scriptures taken from the *Holy Bible, New International Version®, NIV®*. Copyright © 1973, 1978, 1984, 2011 by Biblica, Inc.™ Used by permission of Zondervan. All rights reserved worldwide. www.zondervan.com The "NIV" and "New International Version" are trademarks registered in the United States Patent and Trademark Office by Biblica, Inc.™

Published by Elpida Press.
Elpidapresskc@gmail.com

Cover design by Sandip Sonawane.

The characters in this book are fictitious, and any resemblance to actual persons is coincidental.

ISBN: 978-0692885482
ISBN-10: 069288548X

Dedicated to all the bands that played the songs that kept me alive.

1

It had been a quiet but blessedly uneventful drive. Ten hours from Kansas City to Fort Worth. A little over five hundred miles with only two short stops. Once to get gas and McDonalds in El Dorado, Kansas, and once more for fuel and Dairy Queen in Ardmore, Oklahoma. Ardmore was just beyond the Arbuckle Mountains, a misnomer if there ever was one. Ben's dad kept the speedometer at sixty, five miles over the excruciatingly slow speed limit.

They spent the night in a Best Western near the school, Ben and his two little sisters thankful to finally get away from each other. They were anxious to cease defending the imaginary but vitally important lines in the backseat. Ben went to check out the pool while the girls watched television on their bed, getting under the scratchy comforter.

The station wagon was tightly packed with everything Ben and his parents thought he needed for college. Not only the back of the car but the roof top carrier as well. Every inch was full from floor to ceiling. After swimming a little he peeked in the windows, checking that the doors were locked and the windows rolled up before returning to the crowded hotel room.

It was after eleven when he pulled a blanket off a shelf and tossed a pillow on the floor. He pushed everything up against the wall, listening to his parents softly snoring in one bed, while his sisters were silently sleeping in the other. He lay on his back remembering the day and trying to picture the next one. Pretty soon he was asleep.

The next morning they pulled up to the all male Tom Brown dormitory. Full of caffeine and pancake syrup from the motel breakfast bar, Ben quickly found the resident advisor for his floor. Brad was at least six foot four and weighed well over two hundred fifty pounds, but any intimidation Ben might have felt was softened by Brad's gentle manner and pronounced lisp.

"Benedict! We finally meet! Oh, I've been wondering what you would look like. I pictured more of a male pattern baldness, thick moustache, cardigan sweater wearing kind of person, or maybe a long black habit and a rope belt, but I guess you'll do. Come, come, let me show you to your suite."

Brad turned right from the entrance and led the way down the hall to the last door on the left.

Addressing Ben's parents he reassured, "Now, I'm right across the hall," Pointing to the open door. "I'll be here to answer any questions, and to keep young Benedict safe and sound. I'm always here. Seriously. I have no social life at all.

"Tom Brown is a great dorm. Not wild like some of the others. I survived my freshman year and my job is to make sure that Benedict does also."

"Ben," Ben said.

"Really? Such a shame. I was afraid of that though. Benedict is such a wonderful name. Doesn't anyone call you that?"

"Well, my mom does when she's mad."

"I guess you'll have to think of me as your mom now. So, I'm glad that's settled. Now Benedict I want you to meet your roommates. They're down here in the common room."

He turned back to the center of the building, to a large room with couches, a microwave, two small tables, and a sink.

"Roommates?" said Ben, following his new, very tall RA and vaguely wondering why he had used the plural form of the word. The information that he had read had clearly indicated that all of the freshman rooms were double occupancy.

"Yes, you lucky boy, you get two roommates. Admission rates were higher than expected so quite a few freshmen are going to be a little cozier. At least for the first semester. People will drop out or transfer and chances are you'll get to stretch out after the first of the year."

Two boys were sitting with their fathers at one of the common room tables. They looked up when Ben and Brad entered the room. Both boys were small, wore tight fitting shorts and Garanimal type shirts. Tube socks and Sears brand shoes completed their looks, it was a match made in heaven.

"Are you guys cousins or something?" Ben asked as he looked back and forth at the pair.

At the same moment the boys and their fathers were looking at Ben. With his pink Polo, green shorts, and gold hoop in his left ear, they were wondering what their sons were getting into.

"Nope, we just met. I'm Tim, From New Jersey." He said with an accent that was clearly neither Texan nor Kansan.

"Nice to meet you," Ben said, shaking Tim's soft, damp hand.

"And I'm Brian, from Denton."

"Didn't we drive through Denton on the way here?"

"You did," said Brian's dad. "Just north of here about thirty minutes. There's a good college in Denton but Brian has always wanted to come to TCU. He's worked hard to be here. Just like you and Tim."

"Yeah well…" Ben's voice faded out as the two dads and the two boys continued to look at him, wheels turning, all trying to figure him out. Whether he was going to be a good or a troublesome influence.

In fact Ben felt like he hadn't worked very hard to be there. School had always come easy. He had been a swimmer for nearly ten years. Two practices a day didn't leave much time for homework. He ended up resting during school. Sleeping, staring off into space, reading, thinking, and planning was how he spent most classes. It was no wonder he didn't have many friends in high school. And yet he somehow ended up with straight A's, an improbably high SAT score, and eventually an offer to attend TCU tuition free. So, no, he wasn't sure he deserved to be there. He hadn't studied and worked hard like Tim and Brian.

His first impression was that they were nice kids. They seemed eager to become friends and Ben certainly could use a friend or two. He knew exactly no one at TCU, or in Fort Worth, or in any of the surrounding communities. His closest contact was an uncle who lived in San Antonio two hundred seventy miles further down I-35. In fact that was where his family was headed after Ben got checked in and settled. As excited as he was to get away from Kansas he couldn't help being nervous. At home he had always been busy. Swim practice, school, sleep, swim meets, his summer job… there was always something to do, very little down time. That was what scared him more than anything- the eighteen to twenty hours a day when he wouldn't be in class.

"Hey, have you guys unpacked yet? Which bed do I get?" Ben finally said as brightly as he could muster.

"We've started. Here I'll show you," said Brian, rising to go back down the hall to their room. Ben's parents stayed to socialize with the other parents while Brad wandered off to help other new freshmen, Ben's sisters tagging along behind the boys.

There were bunk beds against one wall and a single bed under the window. Three desks were squeezed in, as well as a small refrigerator that belonged to Brian. After a brief discussion it was determined that Ben would get the top bunk. Tim would sleep below him and Brian would be on his own. They rearranged the furniture, trying to find a configuration that gave the most floor space. With each arrangement it seemed even more crowded. There was simply a lot of furniture packed into a tiny room made for two people.

About the time they were finished with the fourth or fifth furniture pattern their parents came in with boxes and bags from the cars.

"Just tell us where you want these things," Ben's dad said, dumping his load on Ben's bed.

"Well, that spot seems perfect. Can you help me carry in my stereo?"

"Sure, let's get it next."

It took several trips to bring in the speakers, all of the components packed in their original boxes, the shelves and rolling stand, two plastic cartons of records and a smaller one of cassettes. Tim and Brian's eyes widened as this was all carried in and scattered around the room.

"Wow, I guess I won't be needing this," Brian said, holding up his small boom box cassette player.

"It's up to you, but you're welcome to use mine," Ben laughed.

Besides the stereo and music, there was very little to unpack. A few changes of clothes, some toiletries, sheets, a pillow, a blanket, and posters of October- era U2 and the Clash's Sandinista album. He had left most of his books at home, assuming he would find plenty to read in the school library. His mom had optimistically packed the Bible that was given to him by his pastor at his fifth grade baptism ceremony.

When the station wagon was empty Ben's family came in one last time to say goodbye. "We'll see you in five days. On the way back from seeing Larry."

"Ok, sounds good. You all have a good time. Whoops, I mean y'all."

"His mom laughed and hugged him tight and then they left, leaving the three boys alone in the room.

"Have you found the cafeteria yet?" Ben asked.

"Yeah, come on. We can show you."

The new roommates locked the door behind them and went out into the hot Texas sun.

It was after eleven when his roommates finally went to bed, everything unpacked, posters on the wall, stomachs full, the excitement of the day faded into exhaustion. However Ben was still up. He had reassembled the stereo cabinet and had all of the components stacked inside. The turntable was on top, then the receiver, then the dual cassette player. At the very bottom was the new compact disc player, a graduation gift from his parents.

He was not convinced that he even liked CDs. They sounded a little too smooth. The sound was missing something. He preferred the fuller sound of vinyl, the snaps and pops adding to the experience, not diminishing it. Not to mention the expense, the shiny discs often costing twice as much as a record.

Over the past few years his taste in music had evolved. Following a short metal phase, listening to the likes of Rush, Black Sabbath, early Van Halen and Blackfoot, he had discovered the Clash. And then Generation X and U2 and the Ramones. At the same time he was listening to early New Wave like Romeo Void and Missing Persons.

His first concert had been to see Rush in 1982. It was in a big arena. He had been seated towards the top where it was difficult to see the stage through the haze of cigarette and pot smoke. He remembered the long Neil Peart drum solo. Or were there multiple solos? Even in junior high he knew that drum solos on kits that had more than four drums, a hi hat and a crash weren't something that he wanted to listen to. Not on a record and certainly not at a concert. It felt like he was sitting in a dentist's chair for those minutes.

He would never dispute that Neil Peart was a great drummer. Probably one of the best, although he wasn't one to judge. But now, in 1986, he would take Grant Hart or Larry Mullen any day over intricate, interminable solos.

Ben's first show in a smaller venue, what he considered his first real show, was to see Talk Talk and the Psychedelic Furs. That show was a revelation. No stoners in those three quarter sleeve concert t-shirts. The ones that were white on the chest but had the black sleeves that start kind of at the neck. Who first came up with that idea? And why was that style of shirt nearly always emblazoned with some lame 70's band? The sleeves were uncomfortable and the whole look was one that was worn mainly by the kids that hung out in the smoker's area at Ben's high school. The kids that never took off their jackets and hurried outside between classes to light up. He had never seen a Hüsker Dü shirt in that style. He decided it was sort of a dividing line between good and boring music.

No, as far as he could tell there was none of that style of t-shirt at the Furs concert. Just loud New Wave music, electronic drums, short, catchy songs, and lots of happy people. People in interesting, creative clothing. Boys with dark eyeliner and hats. Girls with ratted up air, costume jewelry and layers of clothing that appeared much more complicated than what Ben ever saw at school. It was a great night. He expected to see much cooler bands in even smaller venues, but it was a start.

Ben decided to leave his records, cassettes, and the few CDs packed away for the first night. He strung speaker wire across the south wall and positioned the big JBL speakers in each corner, trying not to awaken his roommates. Plugging in his headphones, he turned everything on and tried to find an interesting radio station, one that played independent music, but was unsuccessful. It was Fort Worth after all, he reasoned. He wasn't ready to give up hope though and decided to try again the next day, maybe ask around to see if anyone knew of anything.

Finally crawling up to bed, careful to not awaken Tim, he fell asleep suddenly, marking the end of his first day at college.

The next morning there were several activities. Brad made sure everyone was up and knew the schedule. Ben and his roommates took showers down the hall, talking a little as they got ready. They waited for each other before going outside to cross the lawn to the cafeteria. Although Ben wasn't convinced that these guys would become his best friends, it was nice to have someone to walk with. And at least they didn't snore loudly. It had been possible to request roommates in advance but since Ben didn't know anyone, he had only the luck of the draw.

A fairly large percentage of students entered the Greek system. So within a week those kids already had the beginnings of some strong friendships, having gone through rush together.

Others played a sport and if they were on scholarship they could stay in the athletic dorm. Ben had swum competitively for years but at that point wasn't interested in continuing the sport in college. He would see how things went and possibly walk on later. Most of the freshmen that weren't athletes or pledging a fraternity lived at Tom Brown.

Ben's parents had purchased the least expensive meal plan possible. Even eating a modest amount of food of the cheapest quality, he knew the money wouldn't last long. There would be no splurging on pizza at the basement snack bar. There was a little grocery store down there as well with airport terminal prices. He had checked it out the day before and knew that he would do best to stay away. Coffee, hot oatmeal and toast with free jam seemed like a good start. His new friends were in the same boat. Although the school had the reputation of having a fair number of rich kids, these three were going to have to be frugal.

"Me too, I am seriously worried about money. My dad said he would kick my ass if I called home asking for more before Thanksgiving," said Tim as they went over the state of their meager finances.

"Wow, that's pretty harsh. But at least you know where you stand," said Ben. "My parents are more of the 'we aren't going to talk about money but you'd better not mess up' variety. I mean they didn't want me to come here in the first place."

"Yeah, to be honest, my parents have really been saving to get me here. I worked as much as I could at a pizza place as well. The scholarship helped of course."

"You got a scholarship too? That's awesome!"

"It isn't a full ride like yours but it's going to help. I want to be a journalist. There are so many great papers in New York. That's my dream- to write for one of them."

"That's great. I think it's important to have a dream. To have something that gets you up in the morning. Getting out of Kansas was one of mine. I really haven't been anywhere. In order to get into a state school in Kansas you have to take the ACTs. I didn't even take them. I knew I was getting out so didn't see the point. I'll admit I'm a little stubborn and probably wasn't the easiest child to raise. But look- it got me here!"

Brian finally put down his fork. "That makes three of us. I worked every job I could, and I had to do really well in school to convince my parents that I should come to TCU instead of North Texas. Hopefully it's worth it. I think it will be. I'm not sure what I want to do yet. Not exactly anyway. I like numbers. Math, statistics… So, what are going to study Ben? I don't think you've told us yet."

"Medicine. I want to be a doctor."

"Oh, cool. That's going to be tough. A lot of years ahead of you."

"Yeah, I try not to think about that. Just take one day at a time. Or one project anyway. Right now this is enough. Eating breakfast on our first real day at college. It's kind of surreal."

"Agreed," Tim said, looking around at the full, lively cafeteria. "Back to money… maybe we can pool our resources. We need a phone at some point for one."

Ben nodded, "Yeah, but do we need it right away? They're so expensive. Brad said we can call collect from the house phone. And we can make free local calls."

"I don't know how much the house phone is used. I have a girlfriend back home and don't want to have to fight with thirty guys for phone time."

"Seriously? A girlfriend in Jersey? How's that going to work?"

"Honestly I'm not sure. It just kind of happened this summer. Believe me it wasn't planned. But I miss Toni already and we both want to make it work."

"Tony?"

"Yeah, Toni. Like Toni Basil. You know, that song Mickey."

"Oh, got it. Cute. So, yeah, we need to look at phones at some point. And yes, it should be a shared expense. You rent phones right? Or maybe you can buy them now. Plus the cost of the phone line plus long distance if any. That could quickly grow into one of our largest expenses. Neither of you guys have a car right?"

"Nope," they both said.

"We'll have to find a way to get around town. There's a grocery store next to us, but for a phone we'll need a ride. I suppose we could figure out the bus system. But ideally we need to meet someone with a car. We should make a list. Number one- find a hot freshman girl with a car."

"Number two- wake up from your daydreaming. Hey, we need to get going," Brian said. "Besides, I'm pretty sure I heard Brad say he'd give us a ride somewhere if we needed one."

"Oh yeah, good point. We'll have to check into that. He can fill us in on our phone options also. All right, I think I'm supposed to go to a science major orientation thing in a bit. I'll catch up with you guys later."

2

As Ben put his dishes and tray on the conveyor belt and stepped out through the front door of the cafeteria, and then out the student center facing Frog Fountain, he could see the dorms that lined the green space and guest parking lots. Boys were housed on the left and girls on the right. The classroom buildings were behind him on both sides of University Drive. He knew all of this from the small map that Brad had given to everyone, as well as from the brief exploration that he and his roommates had undertaken the day prior.

Coming from out of state, and being admitted with only a paper application, he had never seen the school. It would have been nice to visit it first, but his parents would have laughed at the idea. Besides he had to work, swim and finish up high school. There hadn't been time or money to visit even his top few schools. In fact of the four colleges that he had applied to only one, Johns Hopkins, had a face-to-face interview. And that was with an alum in Kansas City. He had visited no campuses, seen no slide shows, had made his decisions based solely on his high school's college night the year prior and a thick book of colleges he had checked out from the library and read cover to cover.

He wasn't completely sold on the yellowish-cream colored bricks that were used to construct the buildings. He was sure that there was either a practical or aesthetic explanation for them but thus far hadn't heard one. He was partial to normal looking red bricks, and that had surely entered into his decision process. But brick color quickly fell down the list of qualifications when he learned about the scholarship.

The day was quickly heating up. Mid August in north Texas is no joke and even by nine in the morning he could feel the sun beginning to cook his skin. He still had a dark tan from the summer's swim season so wasn't worried about burning. He took a moment to pause on the steps feeling the warmth and trying to be mindful of where he was, and of what was happening all around him. He heard doors slamming, people talking, footsteps, a few birds and the sound of a distant diesel engine.

His eyelids were starting to burn and he was wearing what was surely a goofy expression when the sun disappeared from his face and right arm. He opened his eyes to see a boy and a girl standing a few steps below. They were looking at him somewhat impatiently.

"Are you asleep?" said the girl.

"Or on drugs?" said the boy.

"No. Neither. Just resting a minute, enjoying the sun."

"Hmm. Ok," the girl said skeptically. We're heading over to get our mailbox key. Do you know where the post office is?"

"I do! Hey, I need to do that also. Let me show you."

They walked over to the post office to find that nearly every freshman had the same idea that morning.

"Crap. Well, we literally have nothing else to do so I guess we wait."

"Yeah, I suppose you're right. Hey, I'm Denny and this is Anna."

"I'm Ben. Nice to meet you both," he said, shaking their hands. "Where are you all from?"

"Well, I can tell you aren't from Texas. You don't have the 'y'all' down yet. I'm not either. I'm from California. Laguna Beach."

"I have no idea where that is but it sounds fancy."

"It's not too far from LA. South a bit. And it is a little fancy. But I'm not. My dad has a restaurant there."

"Wow. That's cool. Beach. Free food. Sounds like I've solidified my spring break plans," Ben said, laughing.

"It's a deal. Where're you from?"

"Kansas City."

"Well, I have no idea where that is. This is my first time in the middle of the country."

"Straight up. Or north I mean. Go out here. Turn right onto I-30, then left onto I-35, then five hundred miles north. Then it's two more lefts to my house. The brown split-level. You can't miss it."

"I know that drive. I'm from the Midwest too," Anna said. "Omaha."

"Really? That's pretty amazing. We aren't very far from each other. So, did you two know each other before yesterday?"

"No, we just met in line to get our schedules. Did you get yours?"

"I did. Yesterday also. With my two roommates," said Ben.

"Two? What's up with that?"

"My RA said that there are a few of us that have three in a room. Got lucky. So, you guys only have one roommate?"

"I do," said Anna. "Mine's from Texas. Arlington. She seems nice. She has high school friends so that's why I'm not out with her."

"Mine's from Seattle. His parents are still here so he's with them somewhere. I was glad to have met Anna. It's the blind leading the blind but at least I'm not doing it alone."

"Agreed," said Ben. "It's nice to have you guys to stand in line with. So, I'll bet you'll get tired of hearing this and answering it, but what's your major?"

Denny spoke up first. "Biology. I want to be a dentist. No, I don't have a really strong reason why. It's just something that seems interesting to me."

"Is there a dentist in your family?"

"Nope. Maybe it's because I had braces and spent a large portion of my childhood in a dentist office. I like the feel of them. Calming for some reason. And my dentist and the hygienist always seemed happy."

"Those are as good reasons as any. What about you Anna?"

She was kind of nodding and said, "Similar. Pre-med. Biology. My dad's a family doc in Omaha. That's just what I've grown up with and how I see myself. I like the idea of helping people. Making a difference in their lives. And you?"

Ben smiled and said, "You aren't going to believe this but I'm pre-med also. Probably chemistry, although I also like biology. We'll see. Isn't that strange? Or maybe everyone is premed here."

Two kids behind them in line shook their heads and one laughed saying, "Not me. I'm a business major."

"So, just a strange coincidence then. The three of us meeting in the first few hours."

"Why do you want to be a doctor?" asked Anna.

"Good question. I don't have a super concrete answer either. I was seeing an orthopedic surgeon for mild scoliosis in sixth grade. I was really impressed with him. I remember huge piles of patient charts on his desk and even on the floor. He was flipping through one of them in his office and I was amazed that he could read and understand all of that so quickly. The idea of being a surgeon really appeals to me for some reason. The knowledge, the trust involved, the directness of it. You can really help someone in a very tangible way. Anyway, I've been telling people that I want to be a surgeon since I was about ten."

"That's really cool. Is anyone in your family medical?"

"Not really. My great great great grandfather was a doctor in Oklahoma, if that counts."

"Well, it's just amazing that we already met. Hey, aren't we supposed to be at some orientation meeting soon?"

Ben looked at his Timex. It had a cream colored dial and a brown strap, he rarely heard the ticking during the day anymore. At night it occasionally bothered him so he kept it under the clothes he had laid out for the next day.

"Yeah, we're supposed to be there in twenty minutes. What do you think? Come back for our keys or keep waiting?"

Anna said, "I vote that we leave. I want to be sure we find the right building."

They left the line and walked east across campus. Passing an administrative building they crossed University Drive and continued on to the science buildings. The library was to the left, a place that they would get to know very well over the next few weeks. Talking and bonding they began to form those mysterious connections that people develop when their hearts are open.

It had been about three years prior that Ben had first sensed it. An almost physical sensation of his mind opening up. He felt ideas and facts and opinions coalesce and assimilate. The universe seemed to finally make sense. He began to see his parents as real people, fallible and finite. He understood that his teachers had emotions and families and lives outside of their interaction with him.

It was a feeling that carried over to every aspect of his life. A sensation of wholeness and a deeper understanding of people. He was still a child and knew that he wasn't perfect or consistent, but something had definitely changed.

He rarely talked about this sensation but knew that others felt it also. Maybe they couldn't name it or it wasn't something that reached their full consciousness but it was there. A feeling of God all around. Of being one with nature and the fullness of time.

As Ben and his two new friends listened to the professor give an overview of the premed program, as they traded glances with each other, already establishing their own unique and secret language, they knew that it was no accident that they had found each other. Not predestination, not a rigid, unchangeable plan, but a convergence of paths.

The eternal timelines of individuals are not straight. They zig, zag, and turn back on themselves. They are flexible. Lives cross and recross, often without incident or awareness. Someone is seen across a room or sits down next to a friendly face in class or on an airplane. A friend brings along a friend, a new family shows up at church, a work acquaintance appears or a fellow student, a swim team friend, a lunchroom buddy, so many places, so many people.

And then there is college. Open minds and open hearts. Every moment is new and exciting and unique and meaningful. Searching for friends, eager to make connections. Optimistic and full of hope. Lifelines become intertwined in ways that could never happen in a person's younger years nor later in life. Young hearts searching for community, relevance, comfort and meaning. Maybe the bonds aren't perfect, perhaps they wouldn't stand the test of time, but their importance lies in their placement. Existing right at the point of expansiveness and warm liquid emotion, they would never feel this alive again.

By the time Ben's family returned from his uncle's house four days later, their lives had diverged. He had changed and grown and had made new friends. He had experienced things that he couldn't fully explain. It wasn't for lack of trying. His parents invited Denny and Anna to dinner. The most popular Mexican place in town, Joe T. Garcia's was in an old house in the historic stockyards area. Cash only. No menu. Two choices- enchiladas or fajitas. It was simple, fast and the best meal Ben would have in weeks.

"So it's going ok? Classes? Homework?" Ben's mom asked.

"So far so good. It's pretty much all review to this point. A really fast review and I can tell it's about to become more difficult. My chemistry professor said that about a third of us will drop out of pre-med by Christmas. Even more by the end of freshman year."

"Wow. Do you think that's true?"

"Probably. But we'll see. The three of us will make it. Right?"

"If I can get through chemistry. It doesn't come as easily to me," said Anna.

"Yeah, agree," said Denny. "Biology is more my thing."

Ben looked at both of them. "We've already started a study group. We meet after class and go over the notes. Some of us pick up on different things. There've only been two classes but I think it's really going to help. We'll split into multiple groups once we get too large. There were twelve of us last time."

"It's great though," Anna said. "A good way to meet people."

The nachos had come and gone. It was a corn tostado with cheddar cheese and a few chopped jalapeños that had been baked until the cheese melted and the tostada browned. Next came family style rice and beans. The waiter then scooped two smothered enchiladas onto each plate. Some were cheese and onion, some ground beef. The mild salsa and cheese added to the flavor. A container of flour tortillas was placed next to the chips and for the next few minutes everyone concentrated on eating rather than speaking.

Ben's friends were brought into his family with this meal. A common experience and a story to share and remember. His sisters would go back to school telling their friends how cool Denny was, and about Anna's beauty, and about how they couldn't wait until they were able to go to TCU. His parents would proudly and perhaps a little sadly speak of how quickly Ben had found his place.

The next morning Ben once again said goodbye to his family as they began the long, slow drive back north.

"Thanks for the phone Mom."

"Of course honey. Now you don't have an excuse not to call me."

"Every Sunday."

"Starting tomorrow."

"Yes. Starting tomorrow."

"And don't let your roommates call long distance on it okay?"

"I won't. And if they do I'll have them pay their portion."

"Call me collect. Maybe we can figure out how to use one of those new calling cards. I've heard that we can get the cost down to twenty-five cents a minute. That would help. We need to keep our calls to less than fifteen minutes."

"I'll ask around. Maybe Tim can figure it out. I know he wants to call Toni. Those two are really in love. Or in lust. He just mopes around. Really misses her."

"That's too bad. They're so far apart. Well, hopefully it works out for them."

"It will, one way or another. So, ok, I'll call tomorrow about three. I'm sure we can keep it to fifteen minutes this time with no problem."

"Bye Son," she said, holding back tears as she hugged him.

"Bye Mom."

"Bye Buddy. Be good, have a wonderful time but be safe."

"Ok Dad," Ben said as they somewhat awkwardly embraced.

Ben hugged his sisters and then everyone piled into the now nearly empty station wagon. His younger sister, already enjoying being out of the middle and off the hump, rolled down the window and waved.

And then they drove away, leaving an empty finality in the pit of Ben's stomach. A sensation that he hadn't expected and hadn't prepared for. He felt like crying, or sitting on the curb, or running after them, or putting on his headphones and listening to the Replacements or the Cure or Soul Asylum in the corner of his tiny closet, beneath the hanging clothes and up against the bag of dirty laundry, away from everyone else for a little while.

The freedom was invigorating. Simple things like pizza and Coke. Being the oldest child he was late to be allowed certain things. Ben remembered countless evenings lying awake in bed listening to his parents have little parties. As soon as he and his sisters were safely upstairs he heard the *pfft* of the cap coming off the glass Coke bottle. He heard ice in the glasses, chips crunching, and sometimes smelled popcorn popping on the stove. He knew that someday he would be able to do the same. And now the time had come.

Instead of going to the cafeteria one night Ben and his roommates splurged on Dominos pizza and a six pack of new Coke. Pizza delivered to the door was a revelation. Hot and fragrant and there in less than thirty minutes. Instant gratification.

He wasn't completely sold on New Coke yet. Sweeter and less bubbly than the original formula, it was still a big treat. Very little in life is better than a cheesy pizza with greasy tomato sauce, a salty chewy crust and a sweet effervescent drink to wash it all down. Ben, Tim, and Brian enjoyed every bite and every drink of the dinner. Laughing and telling stories, they teased and bragged and grew closer.

"Toni's really coming to visit? When?"

"Two weeks. I just said that."

"Where's she staying? Here?"

"I don't think Brad will let her. I'll figure something out. Maybe she could stay with someone from my journalism program. I've met a couple girls there."

"What about a motel?"

"We don't have that kind of money. Plus transportation issues. No, we have to find somewhere here on campus."

"We'll think of something. I'm happy for you Tim. You two have been racking up the long distance bills."

"Really. Hey, what about you and Anna? Have you asked her out yet?"

"Huh? No, we're just friends. Study buddies. Nothing else going on there."

"Yeah, ok. I see how you two look at each other."

"She's very pretty. But I don't know. Do you think she notices me that way?"

"No doubt. But does she like your music? I know that's a big thing with you."

"She does! I guess Omaha has a good music scene. Who knew? She's seen some bands and it sounds like they have a few great record stores."

"Well, there you go. Because you know we can't stand your music."

"Believe me I know. You both like major label crap. I'll bet you couldn't name a good indie band if your mother's name depended on it."

"Hey, leave our moms out of it."

"Sorry. What do you think of this by the way? Surely you've heard of REM's Murmur. It's like three years old."

Brian said, "I haven't heard it but I do like it. The lyrics are a little muddled though. I wish I could understand them."

"That's what makes them so great. Michael Stipe's mumbled lyrics can mean anything you want them to. You know? Listen to this one." He put on "Shaking Through" and all three of the boys listened thoughtfully for a minute.

"I have no idea what he's saying and I've listened to it over a hundred times. But that's the main reason I can listen to it so much. Once the mystery's gone... Once everyone can sing along to every word and there becomes only one interpretation, well, there's a limited number of times that I can listen to a song like that. That may not be true for everyone but it is for me."

"I see what you mean and maybe I can identify with that a little. But I still like songs I can sing along to. Ones with a catchy melody. Like Elton John or Billy Joel or Air Supply."

"Air Supply?" Ben almost choked out the words.

"Sure, Air Supply. What's wrong with them?"

"Other than that they signify everything that I detest, and are at least in part responsible for the downfall of Western Civilization?"

"Hey, I happen to be a romantic. I like their songs."

"I'm a romantic also. But the Cure is for romantics our age, not Air Supply. Or bands like Modern English or Style Council or even Roxy Music for goodness sake. Try some of these, Mr. Romantic. Toni might even find you a little bit interesting."

Brian was laughing by the point. "Okay you two, let's move on to another subject before you start on each other's mothers again. Are either of you planning to go to the football game tomorrow?"

"You know, I've never seen a football game in my life," said Ben. "Maybe I should go. Just to see what all the excitement is about. Big strong guys smashing into each other, prematurely aging their joints, and developing life long cognition issues. Will there be girls in short skirts and face paint?"

"It's virtually guaranteed."

"Then I'm in."

They finished the pizza as they solidified plans and then took out the trash. Brad had threatened them with bodily harm if they introduced roaches or mice into the dorm by leaving food crumbs and garbage in their rooms.

They finally settled down and went to sleep and the next day both flew by and crawled in the manner that days filled with new things always do. Every moment shining like a new star in the universe. Something to be catalogued and named at a later time.

By Sunday evening Ben had talked to his mom, finished studying for tests in calculus and biology, written a paper for English, eaten dinner with Denny in the cafeteria and now was alone in his room. He couldn't remember where Tim and Brian were. All he knew was that it was very quiet and he was very lonely.

He wasn't prepared for how lonely college would be. He knew that there would be hours with no homework or classes. There was a television in the common room but people rarely gathered there to watch it. At home his parents and sisters were always around, or soon would be. Even when they irritated him, at least they covered over the loneliness, filling the house with something.

He didn't feel secure in his community. Three weeks wasn't enough to be comfortable with the silence. He didn't know with certainty that his roommates or Denny or Anna would be there for him tomorrow or next week. They might find other friends. In fact he was certain that they would. The chances that all five of them had already met the most interesting, compatible people at the school, people that would meet their particular needs... well it seemed pretty unlikely.

Who was to say whether Anna and her Texan roommate or some kid in her English class would become best friends? Or Denny and someone on the swim team. Which, come to think of it, Ben was regretting not joining, as some of the swimmers were becoming his friends.

The point was that he was insecure and homesick and lonely.

So he decided to make a mix tape for Anna.

It was a pretty big leap. From study friend and classmate to the recipient of a personal mix tape. It was about as intimate an act that two people could engage in with their clothes on.

If the songs didn't resonate, if the person didn't get them, couldn't learn more about the giver by listening, then it wouldn't help further a relationship. In fact it could potentially ruin it. And it would often be for the best. It was one thing for one roommate to listen to Air Supply and the other Hüsker Dü. It was quite another for two people slowly moving towards greater intimacy to have mismatched musical tastes.

The tape didn't have to be perfect. Not every song had to be a new favorite. But it had to teach the other person some new songs, or introduce a new band, or provide insight into where the other person finds joy and comfort.

So Ben pulled out a new ninety-minute Maxell tape, cut a square piece of paper from a yellow school flyer and began to make a list. He pulled out cassettes, looked at the small stack of CD's and flipped through his records, all of which were sorted by genre, and then alphabetically by artist, and then by year released.

His habit was to determine the first two or three songs on each side and then add to it on the fly, letting his mood and the music lead him to the perfect mix.

He knew a fair amount about Anna's taste in music and felt pretty comfortable with what she had already heard. Most of his tapes started loudly and then became slower and quieter towards the end of the side. But he didn't want to get too quiet or suggestive. He also needed to be sure that he didn't tip his hand by being too direct with the lyrics.

He started with the Replacements' "Kids Don't Follow" from the Stink EP. It was so classic and perfect and not everyone had heard it. He had discovered over the past three weeks that there wasn't an independent alternative type radio station in Fort Worth. The school's station only played jazz and classical music. There just wasn't a way to hear new music except by buying it at the store. The Village Voice from New York was carried at the library, as was Spin magazine, so reviews of new music were available. Over the past few years Ben had purchased many records based upon recommendations by Marcus Griel and Robert Christgau.

Unless someone had a huge amount of money or an independent station that played new music, most people were reliant on mix tapes and friends to hear indie music.

He didn't like to put two songs by the same artist back to back, so next up was "TV Eye" by the Stooges. That was still one of the rawest, most intense songs he had ever heard, Iggy just howling and yelping. And to think it was already sixteen years old. Next was Hüsker Dü's "Pink Turns to Blue" a tragic love song with drummer Grant Hart singing lead. The rest followed in line until side A looked and sounded right to Ben.

Kids Don't Follow- Replacements
TV Eye- the Stooges
Pink Turns to Blue- Hüsker Dü
A Night Like This- the Cure
If She Knew What She Wants- the Bangles
Two Rivers- Meat Puppets
Little Mascara- Replacements
I'm So Bored With the USA- The Clash
I Hear the Rain- Violent Femmes
Kick in the Eye- Bauhaus
Mystery Plane- The Cramps
Girl in Trouble- Romeo Void
Bizarre Love Triangle- New Order

Zeitgeist was an amazing Austin band. The city had a thriving music scene and this was one of their best. They were one of the bands that Ben had found since arriving at TCU. He'd been given a tape of their album and the title track was amazing. He heard they would be playing in Fort Worth soon and was intent on finding a way to get to the show.

So it made sense to lead off side B off with "Things Don't Change" by Zeitgeist. Then "A Strange Day" from his favorite, although tragically neglected by most people, Cure album, Pornography. Then the arena ready song "Strength" by the Alarm and finally, to mix it up a little, giving the side a little Cowtown flair, "Guitar Town" by Steve Earle.

When he finally finished the flipside well after one in the morning it looked like this:

Things Don't Change- Zeitgeist
A Strange Day- The Cure
Strength- The Alarm
Guitar Town- Steve Earle
This World- Dream Academy
So. Central Rain- REM
She's Like Heroin to Me- The Gun Club
Absolutely Sweet Marie- The Blasters
Horse Nation- The Cult
Gary Floyd – Butthole Surfers
The Ocean- U2
Little Mascara- Replacements
Stranger- Soul Asylum

The final blast of teen angst by Minneapolis band Soul Asylum was the perfect ending. At least Ben thought so as he carefully filed away all of his records and crawled quietly to bed, his roommates long ago having returned and fallen asleep. As he nodded off he marveled at the power of music to comfort and inspire. Now he just needed to find the perfect time to give Anna the tape.

3

"I didn't hear any of that." Denny said, half whining and half bored.

He was sitting with Ben and Anna at a table in the back of the top floor of the library. They were going over biology class notes and having a small difference of opinion. A package of off-brand Oreos was open on the table and their teeth had telltale signs that they all had been sharing the cookies.

"That's why we're here Denny," Ben reminded him. "Because we don't all hear everything. That's why someone takes notes and why we get together to discuss them. We can't take in everything he says. He talks too fast and that monotone would put the most wired person alive into a coma."

"I know all that. I'm just saying that I don't even remember him covering the phospholipid bilayer at all. There's no way I slept through the whole thing."

"Actually I think you did. It's not high school where we spend a week on it. All the different transport mechanisms, the proteins and enzymes. No, he sped right through. Some of the stuff is new though. To me anyway. Most of it's in the book. Let's just all settle down and take a look."

Denny suddenly got up, scraping his chair across the wood floor.

"No, I think I'm done."

"Come on Denny, give it a chance."

"I have given it a chance. I just don't like biology. It turns out that it's worse than chemistry. Seriously, it's terrible. I just want to be a dentist. You know, pull teeth, fill teeth, straighten teeth, maybe if I'm feeling really crazy even whiten them. There has got to be a way to do that without learning about active transport across lipid bilayers. I'm fairly certain that teeth don't have a lipid bilayer."

"You may be right. Tongues and gums and cheeks probably do though, to be fair."

"You aren't helping Ben. And you know what I mean. I'm just sick of it. College is supposed to be fun. Yes, it's great sitting here with you two making goo-goo eyes at each other. But, let's go have some actual fun. Get some beer and cheap tacos or something."

When Ben hesitated, Anna looked at both of them and said, "Why don't you two go? I want to stay here and study some more. We didn't really get very far and the test is coming up."

Ben said, "I'm going to stay here also. I need to do well on this first big test. We all do. You too Denny. We can go out

Friday night, after the week is done. Do you really want to get in the habit of partying on a Tuesday night?"

"Perfect. And yes, in fact I do want to get in that habit Ben. I want to make it a very ingrained habit. I want to repeat it and repeat it until Tuesday night drinking becomes one of the most important of my defining characteristics. Until, when my epitaph is written and my eulogy is read the first and most notable fact of my life is 'He drank on Tuesday nights,' what of it?"

"Hmm. I can see that you are thinking quite clearly now. Ok, well, have fun. See you tomorrow I guess."

"Yeah, I guess." Denny scooped up his books and papers and shoved them hastily into his backpack. Without looking back he left his friends wondering what they could have done differently.

"Is he going to be alright?" Anna asked. "I'm a little worried."

"About his drinking?"

"Yes, but everything else too. I'm getting a little worried and frustrated also about biology and chemistry, but it makes me want to study more, not less. It can't be a good sign that he's giving up."

"He may not be giving up. He might just need a break. He's plenty smart and he could still pull through. I'm going to get up and walk around for a minute okay? Then I'll be back and see if I can push through until the library closes."

"That sounds good. I'm going to go outside and get some fresh air before starting again."

When Anna went through the library, down the stairs to the first floor, then outside and down more stairs to the sidewalk she found Denny sitting on a concrete bench. His eyes appeared to be focused on a small maple tree whose leaves were green but fading.

Denny spoke first.

"People say that looking at a tree for five minutes can decrease a person's stress level. Even looking at one out a window is better than being inside."

"Well?"

"Well what?"

"Is it working? Are you feeling less stressed than you were five minutes ago?"

"Yeah, actually I am a little."

"Mind if I try?"

"Be my guest," Denny said, moving over slightly to make room for Anna.

"Thanks."

They sat in silence for what seemed like a really long time and yet it wasn't uncomfortable. It was early September and the humidity had begun to drop a bit. The cicadas were less deafening than they had been two weeks earlier and there was a light breeze. It was late enough in the evening that there were only a few students on the sidewalks, walking alone or in pairs.

"This is actually a very nice tree. I like how the trunk splits about halfway up and how the two smaller branches are symmetric. It's very graceful and yet appears solid."

"Kind of like you then."

"I think that's a compliment... although ladies don't necessarily like to be called solid. It's too close to stocky. Or sturdy. It sounds a lot like formless and fat."

"Oh, sorry. Just the graceful part then."

"Thank you. And I agree, this is relaxing. Much better than studying and it does put things in perspective."

"How so?"

"Well, just that studying constantly may not be the only factor in getting us to where we want to be in life. We have to take time to relax and look around sometimes."

"Agreed."

"So no drinking tonight?"

"I haven't decided yet."

"No?"

"No. I got out here and noticed that maple. A tree that we've walked by multiple times over the past four weeks and yet I had never taken the time to look at it. To really properly examine and appreciate it. So I just sat down here and kind of spaced out and then you appeared. So, no, I haven't decided about the drinking yet. It still sounds like a good idea. Do you want to come?"

"No, I'm not convinced that it's a good idea. Plus Ben is still in there. I don't want to leave him alone. We know he isn't going to come out."

"Yeah, you're probably right. Not on a Tuesday, He made that very clear."

"The guy has his principles. I'll give him that."

A few seconds passed as they watched and waited for a couple to walk by. They were talking and didn't seem to notice the two on the bench.

"Yeah, I don't think I'm going either," Denny said.

"Really? Why not?"

"Well, sitting out here with you, and thinking about Ben inside studying and waiting… It makes me realize that my friends are here. I don't have the energy to socialize with strangers. Or people that I barely know. Not tonight anyway."

"Okay, well, that makes me happy. Why don't you come back into the library with me then? You could study some more."

"No, I'm finished for the night. I'm certain of that."

"I'm not going to force you to study. Just come in and hang out near us nerds then. You can read a magazine or newspaper or something."

"I might be able to do that. You know, I just can't study like you two. Not all the time. Hour after hour. To be honest, I'm not sure I have what it takes."

"You can't be serious. You're so smart. You can't let one night get you down."

"It isn't one night. It's been this way from the beginning. I really don't like science that much. I mean I did okay in high school but it's not my favorite. And apparently it's kind of important to do well in the sciences to get into dental school."

"Yes, I'd imagine that is the case. But can't you fake it for a few years? You aren't going to be asked biology or chemistry questions on a daily basis in your real job. I mean, you wanted to be a dentist for a reason right?"

"I'm not sure they were good reasons. I know they make a good living. I doubt they have to worry too much about money after they're established for a few years. I don't think I've ever heard of an unemployed dentist. The job itself seems fairly interesting and not super stressful. Surely there aren't too many dental emergencies that require getting out of bed at night."

"That sounds about right."

"Yeah, also I like the idea of being home. Not having a job that requires travel. Go to the office, do my work, and then come home while the sun is still up. Maybe time to go to the beach before or after work. Catch some waves."

"I forgot you're a surfer dude."

"Yeah, you know, me and Spicoli... 'All I need are some tasty waves, a cool buzz, and I'm fine.'"

"Gnarly dude. Hey, the stability, the predictability of being a dentist. I wonder if it has anything to do with your father. The fact that he's in the restaurant business."

"You're very insightful. Absolutely it does. He's always at the restaurant. He leaves home at maybe nine and isn't back until midnight or even later. That's seven days a week. If I want to see my dad I have to go to him and try to catch him in between meetings and running around.

"And that's when things are going well. When the place was struggling it was worse. We had no money for anything. No new clothes or records or a Walkman or really anything. I will say we always had food."

"That must have been hard. How's he doing now?"

"Fine, the same. He's always busy. But the restaurant itself is doing well. Good reviews. Popular with tourists. It's a great location. It overlooks an amazing beach. But it isn't something I'm interested in doing long term, running the place."

"I completely understand. Well, let's just take one step at a time for now. We don't have to plan everything out this evening. Come back inside with me. I'm sure that Ben thinks I left him."

Denny stood up, hoisted his backpack from the grass next to the bench up and onto his shoulders. "Ok, let's go. But I'm not studying."

"Right. No studying."

They climbed the steps back into the library and then up two more flights, and then walked to the back where Denny was lost in his notes. He looked up as they approached.

"You're back! Good! I knew you'd come around. We can back up and start the chapter again."

"He's not here to study. He just wants to hang out here until we're finished," Anna said with a stern look.

"Oh. Sure. Okay. That's fine. Well, I'm still glad to see you."

"You don't have to make a big deal about it. I just decided to stay in tonight," Denny said, laying his bag down and walking away, towards the periodical section.

"Don't ask," Anna whispered to Ben's look.

"Later?"

"Maybe. Are we going to learn this stuff or not?"

"We are. Let's get busy."

The two friends pulled out their notes and found the right spot in their books. They picked up where they had left off. Reading, quizzing, laughing, and sharing Oreos. Soon Denny was back with a Sports Illustrated and the latest issue of Surfing Magazine. He settled into a soft chair near the others, reading and occasionally joining in the conversation. And it turned into a perfect night at college.

When the library closed they were the last to leave. They walked home together, crossing University without having to wait for the light. Like the maple tree, they split just past the student center, the boys going left and Anna going right. They were quiet and their heads were full of biology and night air and junk food and good friends.

4

Ben was so excited he could barely stand it. He had nearly worn out the Zeitgeist side of the cassette. Doctor's Mob on the other side had been played nearly as much, but it was side A that he loved more than anything. Kicking off with "Araby," the fast drums, ringing guitars and John Croslin's smooth low voice combined to create a beautiful noise. Later, when Kim Longacre's sweet harmonies came in, the song reached a whole new level. The subtle jazz influence was in the forefront on "She Digs Ornette." The two best songs on the album, "Things Don't Change" and "Translate Slowly", were positioned right in the middle.

It was an unbelievable record and one that had defined and shaped the first few weeks of his college career. It covered all of his moods and feelings. It was new and different. He was sure that no one back home had heard of them and really not very many at TCU were interested. And that was fine with Ben. It meant that he could get in the show and have room to scoot to the front of the stage. The Hi Hat held maybe a hundred people. The stage was about waist high and had just enough room for the four musicians and their instruments. There wasn't much room to move around up there but they didn't seem to mind.

They had been playing larger shows in Austin and had even been featured on a late-night segment on MTV, but like the rest of the Austin scene, Zeitgeist was fairly unknown outside of their town. Denny's swimming friend, the one that had given Ben the tape, was there. He played guitar in a local band and kind of knew John Croslin, who had produced a friend of a friend's album. So, not only was Ben excited to see them play but he felt like he almost knew them. Only three degrees of separation. They were practically family.

The show was as good as he dreamed it would be. People banging their heads and jumping up and down to the pop-tinged, guitar-heavy songs. They played the entire album and mixed some covers in as well. He recognized "Sweet Jane" and the Linus and Lucy theme.

Denny and Anna had decided not to come so it had taken some mental effort on Ben's part to go. Once he was there everything was fine. It did present one problem, however. He didn't want to lose his spot next to the stage and there wasn't anyone to save it for him. He knew that if he left to visit the bathroom there was a chance he wouldn't make it back to that prime location. He had downed two beers in his dorm before arriving, which was much more cost effective than buying alcohol at the Hi Hat. The two cans of Old Style had been a gift from Denny, probably a guilt offering.

So, about an hour into the show the beer had worked its way from his stomach to his head to his kidneys and now finally down to his bladder. He held it as long as he could but knew he was going to have to vacate his spot. He stuck it out through "Translate Slowly" and, the last chords still ringing in his ears, made his way to the back of the club. Unfortunately several other guys had decided to take a break at the same time. There was a line for the two urinals in the dirty, flyer and graffiti covered restroom. One stall had no door and the whole effect was filthy and unhygienic and really rock and roll.

By that point Ben couldn't wait and he looked around for other options. The back door was cracked open and unattended so he slipped out into the warm night. He took three steps to the right into a shadowy part of the alley and finally let it go with a flood of relief, trying his best to keep his shoes dry. After nearly a minute, as Ben zipped up and turned to go back in, he noticed someone standing on the other side of the door. He was startled and let out a "Wha?" sound. The man was watching him with what appeared to be a combination of amusement and disgust.

"Nice," he said.

"Sorry, I didn't know anyone was back here. It was kind of an emergency."

"Yeah, I noticed."

The man appeared to be about thirty but it was hard to be sure. It was dark and he had on a black, tattered trench coat over a flannel shirt. A black stocking cap covered much of the dark stringy hair that hung nearly to his eyes and around his neck. Ben saw a flash of gold and noticed small thick hoops dangling from each ear.

"Were you in there too? Pretty amazing huh?"

"No, I don't go to stupid frat party bands. No way would I waste my money on that shit."

Ben felt his adrenaline kick in. He knew he wouldn't come out the winner in a fight with this guy but that didn't stop his reflex from kicking in.

"What's the matter with you? Why're you standing here if you don't like them?"

"How is that any of your business?"

He had to literally bite his tongue to keep from using a few unkind adjectives. He knew that it wouldn't end well and was proud of himself as he said, "I guess it's not. I'm going back in. Take care."

Ben slipped back through the back door keeping his head down and trying not to make eye contact with the front door bouncer guy. He didn't want to have to pay twice in case he wasn't recognized. The small crowd had closed around his front row space so he just joined in towards the back as Zeitgeist finished up another song. By the time they finished the final song of the night, the Clash cover "Train in Vain," he had almost forgotten about the man in the alley.

It had been the first show of his college career and it was hard to imagine that it could be topped. He stuck around a while to see if he could talk to any of the band members but they had disappeared into a back room somewhere. Denny's swimming friends were heading towards the exit so he went with them. Everyone was excited and fully awake and young and those that lived on campus walked across Berry and up University and then over to their respective dorms. They said goodnight to each other and fell into their beds with a heavenly ringing in their ears.

Ben had trouble with seasonal allergies in Kansas City also. It had been worst at his grandfather's farm in south-central Kansas. Baling hay and then trying to get those rectangular prisms into the pickup was hard work. Grabbing the bale with the hay hook, lifting it off the ground on one end and then taking hold of the lower end, trying to get some momentum to get it off the ground and up and into the pickup. It wasn't an easy job. Some of the straw bales were fairly light but those dense alfalfa ones, they surely weighed eighty pounds. Probably more when still damp.

At least once the truck was loaded he could rest in the pickup as they sped to the three hundred twenty. That's what his grandfather called the main farm, the one with the barn and the small house where they lived. The eighty, the forty and the three twenty. It made sense at the time. They kept the windows down as he rode between his dad and grandfather, one chewing tobacco and the other smoking it, Ben just resting and beginning to sneeze.

He did all right when he was outside working in the heat. But in the cab of the pickup, as he cooled off, the sneezing started. His eyes and nose ran and his eyelids began to swell. And once they arrived at the barn it only got worse. That dusty, moldy old barn was teeming with allergens. The sunlight streamed in through the big open door and the very sight of dust particles glittering and dancing in the air was enough to cause Ben to feel his throat swell shut.

At that point he usually asked if he could take a break.

"Oh sure. Go in with the ladies. Those allergies are sure a convenient excuse," his grandfather would say. His dad wouldn't defend him. He would only snort and keep working.

"Traitor," Ben thought, his teenage pride wounded. But he knew he needed to get out of the barn. Once he was in the fresh air, his breathing slowed and his eyes began to clear. His grandmother would have him wash his hands and face and rest at the table. She would give him red Kool-Aid prepared with half of the recommended sugar to save money or his teeth and at least two of those pink sugar wafer cookies. He would sit and listen to his mom and grandmother gossip about extended family or neighbors or some miscreant cow that had escaped again.

Pretty soon one of them would hear the pickup engine start and he would go outside for the ride back to the eighty to get more bales out of that seemingly endless field.

Those summer days had been bad at the time, but the intervening months had already begun to soften the edges. He couldn't imagine that his symptoms had been any worse than they were that early September day in Fort Worth. He literally couldn't see. His nose was red and clogged, his sinuses were painfully congested and fluid was seeping out of his eyes and nose.

Anna had seen him at breakfast and could sense the misery that he was in. She walked with him to the small pharmacy around the corner on Berry to buy him some Benadryl. What he needed more than anything that morning was for someone to take charge. He had no money and didn't know what to do in a situation like this. Finding a drugstore and buying a medication hadn't even entered his mind as a possibility.

She made him take one on the way to chemistry and within ten minutes he started feeling better. The itching began to ease and his nose began to dry up.

They found their usual spots at the back of the class. Denny was already there.

"Dude, what's up with you? You look terrible. Like some old alcoholic that got in a fight and can't stop crying about it."

"Thanks," Ben sniffed. "Good morning to you too."

"Seriously, you look awful."

"I know. It's just allergies. I'm not contagious or anything. And I'm starting to feel a little better. Anna is a real friend. Instead of kicking me when I'm down she actually did something about it. The medicine is already starting to help."

"Well, sorry, your face just startled me."

"Again, thank you."

By that time the professor had begun teaching and people were turning around, giving the trio irritated looks so they settled down, got out their notebooks and began to listen.

Within the next ten minutes, the Benadryl was in full effect. Not only were Ben's eyes, nose and sinuses feeling better, he was sleeping like a baby. One of the antihistamine's side effects was drowsiness, and it had hit Ben hard. He was slumped down in the seat, his neck stretched back and to the right.

Chemistry was held in one of the big lecture halls. The professor spoke from the bottom of the auditorium. There were about twenty rows of seats and the three friends were in row seventeen, the last ones were empty behind them.

As Ben drifted deeper into a carefree, comfortable sleep his breathing became more heavy and distracting. Denny shook him at one point, which helped for about five seconds. But when he settled back down again he began to snore. A loud, nasal, honking snore.

The professor should be given credit for trying to ignore the slumped, sleeping student, maybe even the heavy breathing, the sound of which carried down thirty-four steps and disrupted his flow. He had been a teacher for a long time and had put up with all kinds of students. And although he didn't know Ben well, he did at least know that his first test had resulted in an A, so he tried to be patient.

The snore was the final straw though. With the noise still echoing in the auditorium he picked up an eraser and threw it with surprising accuracy, hitting Ben in the left shoulder. While everyone else was fully alert now, Ben didn't budge.

"Wake up, you son of a bitch!" the professor hollered. "Wake up or get out of my class!"

That did it. His shouts startled Denny into action. He shook Ben until he was completely awake, the eyes of the entire class on him. He brushed at the chalk mark on his left shoulder, trying to remember why that was there. He sat up straight in his chair, got out his pen and notebook and gave a little embarrassed smile to the teacher.

When everything settled back down, when the other students were turned back around and facing front, when the professor was back on track, and when his two friends were once again taking notes, Ben put his head down on his desk and promptly fell back into a quiet, contented sleep.

"I'm allergic to this place. It's not good."

"It's not going to be forever. It must be something in the air this time of year. When it freezes…"

"Freezes? When does that even happen here? Does it happen? Even if it does it'll be in like three months. I can't take it that long."

Ben was walking with Anna to the library to study for a few minutes before their next class. It was warm and windy and he felt like there were spores and pollen and every kind of allergen flying up his nose and into his mouth as he walked.

"I am seriously allergic to the world. You know? Just not made for this place. Some people are and some aren't. I should just go live in a bubble somewhere. Maybe in the Arctic, although I really detest cold weather."

"Please. Stop being so dramatic."

"Am I? Look at me. I'm grotesque. I know that I look nearly as bad as I feel. And there is really no end in sight. And I can't take Benadryl. I'll sleep through the whole semester."

"Why don't we just get into the library? Into the nice filtered, air conditioned, somewhat stagnant, atmosphere of the second floor. You'll feel better up there I promise."

"Yeah, you're right. I need to stop whining. There are a lot of people worse off than me. Like that guy outside the Hi Hat the other night. Did I tell you about him?"

"Yeah, you did. Weird huh? Who do you think he was?"

"I don't know but he had a wild look in his eyes. Crazy or on drugs or both. I don't think he goes to TCU."

"Probably not, from what you said."

"Maybe he was just a local guy that didn't feel like paying the cover, but I just had this feeling that something was wrong. That maybe he didn't have anywhere to go."

"You think he's homeless? Are there homeless people around here?"

"Sure, why not? I mean, I guess. I've seen them in Kansas City so why not here? Texas is quite a bit warmer. I could be wrong about him though. He might just be a really dirty guy with a bad haircut that wears extremely worn out clothing. It is kind of a style now I guess."

"Well, from now on you should use the bathrooms. This isn't your granddad's farm where you can just let it go anytime you want."

"Hey, thanks for the reminder. I could actually use a pee right about now. Hold on a minute."

Ben went behind the maple in front of the library as Anna warned, "Don't you dare Benedict. You're going to get an eraser thrown at your head and arrested for indecent exposure in one day. What would your mother say?"

"All right, you win. I'll only do that under the cover of darkness. Let's go study."

5

Ben wasn't in his room much anymore. He spent the day in class or the library or the cafeteria or in Denny's dorm. For the most part he let his roommates have the room. Tim and Brian had become friends with each other and used it to study and hang out. Ben's music was in there though, and now and then he liked to listen to it.

It was a Thursday afternoon and he had been reading a little and listening to some records when his roommates got back home.

"Oh hey guys, how's it going?" Ben said as he got off the top bunk to turn down the volume of side A of the Cure's *Head on the Door* album.

"Good," said Tim. "How about you? What're you up to tonight?"

"I'm not sure. Maybe just stay in if that's okay. What about you guys?"

"We were going to try and study a little. We can go down to the common area though."

"No, it's cool. I can be quiet. I really should study some also. I just don't feel like it right now. Here, let me turn this off though."

Ben took the record off the turntable, holding it carefully by the edges and dropped it back into its combination dust cover/lyric sheet. He slid that into the album cover and then refiled it in its spot, right in front of *The Top*. He sorted them alphabetically and then from back to front chronologically so that the newest album for each band came up first.

The plastic lid was closed over the turntable and he turned everything off.

He got his Sony Walkman WM-20 out of a dresser drawer and untangled the headphones. A Christmas present from last year, it was light and had great sound. The over the ear headphones were also lightweight and so far worked perfectly.

Ben much preferred listening to music from the big speakers rather than headphones. Something about sound waves traveling through open air, interacting with the environment, picking up the ambient noise of a passing truck or someone slamming a door in the hallway or roommates talking or opening and closing drawers or even his own voice singing along, all of that added to the experience.

Especially the singing along. It wasn't something that anyone should do with headphones on. Not unless they wanted to be branded an eccentric weirdo. But when the music is loud, when it's just pouring out of the speakers and filling in all of the spaces in the room, an added voice only seemed to make the song more full and rich.

And then there was the whole cassette versus record thing. Cassettes were fine. He didn't have very many prerecorded ones. They were mainly dubbed from his records or given to him by other people. So, the sound quality was diminished from the recording process and then from the multiple plays. Listening to a cassette felt like an approximation of the way the music should sound but certainly wasn't an exact replica.

And don't even get Ben started on Compact Discs. He had a few but only from specific genres. He liked the digitally recorded classical ones and owned some Mozart and Chopin. And he felt like maybe there was a place for electronic music to be played on a CD. Guitars were meant to be imperfect but the music of New Order or Depeche Mode or Pet Shop Boys and other bands like that actually sounded decent when played from the shiny little platters.

But they were entirely too expensive. He had read that they cost the same to produce as vinyl. Less than a dollar each. And yet they were priced at nearly twice as much. Seventeen dollars? Eighteen? At least some artists were starting to record longer records than they could have on vinyl. Nearly a double album would fit on a single CD. So there was that.

He wasn't a fan of the bonus song that had been showing up more and more, ostensibly to drive sales. There was that irritating period of silence at the end of the CD, then finally, after one had nearly given up hope and interest, a lame, under-produced throwaway song would begin to play. It certainly wasn't an improvement for the music industry. It made dubbing difficult and ruined the flow of the record. Instead of simply ending on the high note that the artist had carefully planned, it dwindled away into nothing.

He didn't appreciate feeling manipulated by the record companies, being fed the unnecessarily higher priced format. And having to wait a week or two after the vinyl and cassette release date to find the CD. And discovering that most of the music he liked wasn't even available that way. Independent labels hadn't begun to distribute their music on CD, and that was fine with Ben.

He wasn't able to record onto Compact Disc and he couldn't listen to them on the go. He knew that the players were starting to show up in boomboxes and cars and that Walkman even had a portable player, but getting the player for his component system was expensive enough. He just wasn't that committed to it at this point.

No, only vinyl sounded right. The full rich sound. The snaps and crackles from the needle hitting scratches or dust particles. The undiluted intravenous injection of pure noise that makes a person feel like they are present in the studio or on the stage at the time the tracks are being laid down. It's something that a cassette or a CD could never replicate.

There was also the big cover art, the full lyric sheets and credits on the sleeve. Even the occasional cryptic comments on the inside part of the vinyl itself. He loved everything about them.

But for now, a Walkman and headset and a cassette of Sonic Youth's EVOL would have to do. The first Sonic Youth record Ben had owned, it felt a little dark and dangerous and well outside of the mainstream. From the opening chord of "Tom Violence" to the endless locked groove of "Expressway to Yr. Skull", it created a perfect atmosphere of sinister confusion and urban excitement.

Ben laid back on his top bunk, head resting on two pillows, fingers interlocked over his stomach as he drifted off with the music. He floated and glided in his mind and nearly fell asleep until the cassette clicked over to the other side, and the Gun

Club's Las Vegas Story snapped him out of his somnolent state. The band's West Coast psychobilly sound was a completely different but welcome vibe. He looked around to see that Tim and Brian were still studying.

"Hey, you guys want to go out tonight?"

"Not me," said Tim. "I'm kind of tired already. I don't think I'd be much fun."

"Agreed, me too."

"Okay, but we have to someday all right? I mean, this college adventure will be over before we know it. You guys need to live a little."

"We will, for sure. You have fun though."

"I need to find something to do first. I haven't heard from Denny since class this morning and Anna is going to dinner with her roommate. Hey, can you hand me the phone Tim?"

Tim grabbed the heavy tan rotary phone and handed it up to Ben. He dialed the seven numbers, the dial making a satisfying clicking sound after each number as it rotated back to its starting point. He waited while it rang. And rang. Ben hung up after about ten rings.

"No answer. I'll just go over there and see if anyone knows where he is."

Ben went down the hallway, out the front door and turned left towards Milton Daniel dorm. It was where the male athletes lived. He went in the first doorway, up the stairs to the second floor and knocked on the second door on the left. No one answered. He listened and didn't hear anyone. The next-door neighbor's door was open. Ben peeked inside and saw a guy he knew. He was lying on his bed, watching TV and tossing a tennis ball up and catching it. Named JD, he was the swimmer who had introduced him to Zeitgeist a few weeks back. Ben asked him if he had seen Denny.

"Yeah, he was here earlier. Left maybe an hour ago. He said he was going to the Pub."

"Oh, okay cool. Did anyone go with him?"

"No, I don't think so. He tried to get me to go but I wanted to stay in and watch Cheers and Hill Street. You know, just relax a little."

"Yeah, I can understand that. Well, see you later."

"Take it easy."

Ben decided to head over to the Pub and see if he was still there. He checked his watch. Only eight thirty. He walked back past his dorm and the student center. Across the lawn and University Drive, turning right to walk up the sidewalk to the Pub.

This was the nearest, cheapest, and most popular of the TCU hangouts. It would be unusual to not recognize someone he knew on a Thursday, Friday or Saturday night here. A swimmer or someone from his floor in the dorm or from his pre-med classes. There was no cover. It was small, loud, dark, dirty and sticky. Ben thought it was pretty perfect in most ways.

In general he didn't really appreciate big crowds but here, as long as he knew one or two people, he felt okay. And although it was a bit of a gamble to just walk in by himself, he knew he could walk right back out if Denny wasn't there.

He was.

"Hey Ben! You found me!" Denny was standing in the back at the pool table. A cue cradled in his armpit and a mug of beer in his hand. There weren't many people gathered around the table. Thursday nights weren't nearly as crowded as Fridays. He recognized a few of them, including Denny's opponent. He was a tennis player and someone he had talked to before in the athletic dorm. He was probably a senior.

"It wasn't much of a search. You were in the second place I looked. Notice that the library wasn't in my top two guesses."

"You are so freakin' smart. That's why I love you so," he said, putting his arm and beer around Ben, nearly spilling it in the process.

"Yeah okay. So how's it going? Are you stripes or solids?" Ben said as he carefully removed Denny's arm, managing to stay dry. There was one solid remaining and four stripes.

"You have to ask? Whoops my shot," he said as he laid his beer on a shelf and bent over to line everything up. A gentle well placed tap and the solid green six ball fell into a side pocket. The eight ball followed quickly behind on the next shot and the game was over.

"Won again. I'll take my winnings in Budweiser if you don't mind Carl." Denny drained his mug and handed it to the boy who then drank his and headed to the bar.

"Sure thing. I'll be right back."

"It's a living," Denny said to Ben who was watching with a mixture of awe, amusement and disgust.

"You're a mess. How long have you been here?"

"Not long, why?"

"Just wondering."

"You should get a beer."

"I don't have an ID."

"Oh yeah, right. How did you get in here by the way?" said Denny.

"The door guy let me in but not without the black X."

"Oh, yeah, that sucks. Yeah, this new law really blows. Seriously. Twenty-one? Who's twenty-one at this school? Practically no one that's who."

"Yeah, it was really bad timing for us huh? The Texas drinking age was nineteen for years and then we all show up and just like that it's twenty-one."

"It isn't going to be good for business here or at any of the other TCU hangouts. Not everyone has access to such an amazing ID maker like I do."

"Yours is pretty incredible. It's basically the real thing. When can I have one like that?"

"I'll get you one for sure. But it'll be easier if you come to Laguna with me for spring break."

"I would love to do that. We could eat at your dad's restaurant right? Hang out at the beach. It would be amazing. Of course that's a long ways off and in the meantime I have to live with a black X on my hand."

"True, true. Lucky for you I've come prepared."

Motioning Ben to come closer, Denny reached into an inside pocket in his Levi's jean jacket. He pulled a pint of Bacardi Gold out just far enough to make Ben's eyes widen.

"You've really come prepared."

"Yep. I can't pay the prices here all night. Go to the bar and get a Coke."

"What if we get caught?"

"Then we get kicked out of a bar that we really shouldn't be in anyway. It isn't a huge loss. We won't though. Just be cool."

"Easy for you to say. I think you're a little more used to breaking the law than I am."

"I resent that remark."

Carl was getting impatient and said, "Hey Denny, are you going to play? If not then stop hogging the cue."

"Oh, I'm still playing. Don't get your hopes up. Who's next?"

While Denny negotiated his next opponent Ben went to the bar to get a soda. He paid, drank it down about a third and stealthily filled it with the rum. He sipped from the glass and choked a little as it went down. It burned more than he remembered. He was not a hard liquor expert by any means, sticking to beer the times he drank. It seemed safer. Easier to measure and keep track of. He knew that was a justification but it worked. But this wasn't too bad. And it was about free. And he didn't have to stand there stone cold sober watching Denny play pool all night.

Pool wasn't something that he really knew how to play. His dad didn't own a restaurant or have a table in the basement or take him to dive bars or even to the back of smoky pizza joints to practice. He had one or two friends that had pool tables but just had never played much. So he wasn't about to challenge Denny to a game. Or even play for fun. Not here.

Escaping to the front of the Pub, he checked out the jukebox. Currently it was playing one of his least favorite songs of all time, "You Belong to the City," by Glenn Frey. Most of the songs by former Eagles members were at the very bottom of tunes he ever wanted to hear again. Oh, and "Life's Been Good" by Joe Walsh was still pretty good, and even Don Henley's first and only decent song, "Boys of Summer." But the rest, no thanks.

The thing that had always bugged him about jukeboxes, and the thing that made them so genius, was that there was no way to tell how many songs were already queued up to play. It could be one or a hundred for all anyone knew. He could be choosing the playlist for the next thirty minutes or a song for the janitor cleaning the place at two in the morning.

It was a gamble and one he usually seemed to lose. He couldn't count the number of times he had managed to talk his dad into giving him a quarter so that he could drop it into the Straw Hat Pizza jukebox. He would carefully read every song title at least twice before making his choice. A Beatles song. Or maybe one from Styx. Or the Carpenters. Or if he was lucky maybe that B-side to Philadelphia Freedom. It was the live version of "I Saw Her Standing There" featuring both Elton John and John Lennon. It was too good to be true for a ten-year-old Beatles lover.

Regardless, he rarely got to hear his song. Their pizza would come and go and none of his selections would have been played. It was as disappointing as the rubber bouncy balls that always disappeared before they were out of the parking lot, or the sea monkeys which were really just tiny dried shrimp from the Great Salt Lake, or the Topps baseball cards that rarely had a Royals player in them. He should have known better but children's thoughts are magical and blessedly optimistic.

So, with the same blind faith he dropped in his quarters and chose the few tolerable songs that he could find. "West End Girls" never seemed to get old. Nor did the Smiths' "How Soon is Now," or The Plimsouls' "A Million Miles Away" or "Should I Stay or Should I Go" by the Clash. It was a good start and hopefully someone else with decent musical taste could pitch in to the cause.

Ben made his way back to the pool table as another painfully terrible song came on, this one by Huey Lewis. He could never understand how that guy became so popular. He was like someone's awkward dad. Ben was literally embarrassed for him although Huey himself seemed to be blissfully unaware of how ridiculous he was.

Denny was running the table with another outclassed competitor. No one was betting against him anymore but that didn't stop him from playing to win. It was mesmerizing in a way.

Ben watched and sipped on his rum and coke, trying to make it last. He was feeling it already and knew he had class tomorrow.

So did Denny but that didn't seem to bother him. He gulped at his beers and when they stopped coming he switched to rum, boldly pouring it into the mug.

The night passed slowly and in a flash, the smoky haze increasing as it became later. Leaning down closer to the pool table, or standing at the back of the bar where the door was cracked, the air was a little fresher. But in the center, and at an altitude of about five feet, the smoke was thick and affected the way everything felt. It was difficult to see from the front of the bar to the back, a distance of only about twenty–five feet. It changed everyone's voices, made them raspy and somewhat breathless. Talking to the smokers was even more difficult as their personal cloud thickened throughout the evening.

Noticing all of that, Ben was surprised to see Denny lighting up an unfiltered Camel.

"Seriously? When did you start smoking?"

"I do when I drink sometimes. It's no big deal."

"Please. You know as well as I do how terrible those things are. It's just a regressive sales tax, keeping the poor down. Hey, maybe we should go."

"You can if you want. I'm going to stay a little longer."

Ben looked at his watch. Eleven thirty.

Denny looked at him pleadingly. "Come on. One more game."

"Okay. One more game then we're going."

Except it wasn't one more game. Or two. At one in the morning, after all of Ben's songs had been played on the jukebox, after nearly everyone had left, after the doors were opened a little more and the smoke began to clear, after Ben had finally finished his rum and coke and Denny had nearly drained the rest of the only marginally secret pint, after the bartender had wiped down the bar and had begun counting the cash, the doorman finally told the boys it was time to go.

Ben guided Denny out the front and then right, towards the school. They crossed over the quiet road and were nearly to the administrative building when Denny said he had to pee.

"Now?" Ben whispered, "You'll be home in less than five minutes."

"Yes, now. Right now. There will be no waiting five minutes."

He began to unzip but Ben was able to get him against the building, in a shadowy area. The stream echoed in the night and went on painfully long as Ben watched for passersby. There were none. He wondered vaguely about whether there were campus police around at night. He hadn't ever seen them on foot but assumed they must be.

When Denny was finished he stepped back onto the sidewalk. They moved forward a few feet and then Denny sat down on a bench. He reached into his jean jacket, pulled the bottle out and took a drink. He offered it to Ben who shook his head.

"There's only backwash in there. And what are you doing? I thought we were going home."

"Did you see her look at me?"

"See who?"

"Sheila."

"Who's Sheila? A girl at the Pub?"

"Yeah. Did you see her eyes? They were so blue. Like the sky on a sunny winter day. And her eyelashes. They were so long and expressive. The bottom ones too. Not enough attention is paid to the bottom lashes in my opinion. The way her eyes looked when she was laughing or smiling, the tiny smile lines. It was all so mesmerizing."

"Okay, we need to get you home."

"No, stay here. Let's talk about Sheila a little more. Isn't that a miracle? I feel like it shouldn't happen that way in nature. Her hair is so dark and her eyes are so blue. She's a beautiful freak of nature."

"Beautiful freak. I'm sure she'd really appreciate that. I have to admit that it would be a cool band name though."

"You're right! Sheila would have to be in the band. She could be our vocalist. Or maybe she can't sing. Then she could be our bass player. Yeah, I'll sing and you can play drums or something. Imagine that lovely hair bouncing and swaying as she played bass next to me, looking over sometimes and smiling suggestively."

"You are seriously sick. And drunk. And what makes you think I can't play guitar? I can you know. Not well but maybe if I had a couple pedals..." Ben stood up and demonstrated his technique. Air guitar slung low, he played fast and emotionally, stepping on the imaginary pedals as he kicked off the chorus.

Denny laughed, "Okay, you can try out for guitar. But rhythm though. I'm lead."

"We'll see. So did you even talk to this Sheila? Who is she?"

"A little bit. She's a junior. She was there with three of her Pi Phi sisters for one of their birthdays. You saw them back there right?"

"Yeah but I never saw you talking to them. They were in their own little world. I did notice Sheila. And you're right about the dark hair/ blue eyes combination. She was very striking."

"Ha! That's the understatement of the year. She's magnificent and I am helplessly and hopelessly in love with her. In fact we should go down to the Pi Phi house right this very minute so that I can tell her that."

"That is a terrible idea."

"What? It's the best idea I've had all week. In fact if there were a Nobel Prize for amazing ideas that were created after midnight by college students it would be a shoe in to win. Let's go."

"No way. We aren't going down there. You don't even know that she lives there. She could have an apartment. She is a junior, after all."

"Oh yeah, good point. But she might live there. And if not, someone will know where her apartment is."

"Yeah maybe so. And I'm sure they would be thrilled to have some drunken guy banging on their door asking for directions to one of their sisters. No, they would probably call the police. And the police will find you and detect the pee on your shoes and trace that back to the pee on Sadler Hall and you will be arrested and deported to California."

"Ben, you are a supreme party pooper that has no comprehension of the depths of my love for Sheila of the blue eyes and black hair."

"That may be true. But mainly I think your love is magnified by the rum. Plus she's probably already in bed. Besides, you may think differently in the morning. Ever hear of beer goggles? It's a thing. How about we go home? We have class tomorrow and the night is quickly passing us by."

"Yeah, okay. I guess you're right. Sheila may not be the romantic that I am. At least I can dream of her."

"Sure, let's go."

They finally started back to the dorms. The air was calm and fresh and they felt young and alive and full of hope. The band idea, Sheila's eyes and laugh, the music from the jukebox, the smoky Pub and leaning for hours on the wall by the pool table all jumbled together into a pleasant mixture of shared experiences. A night to remember someday when they were older. Or possibly not but it felt formative and important nonetheless.

"Hey Ben?"

"Yeah?"

"I don't like science very much."

"Yeah, I know Denny. You've told me that before."

"No I mean I really don't like it. To the point that I don't know if I want to be a dentist anymore."

"Hey, let's not make any decisions tonight."

"Yeah okay, but I'll bet I think the same thing tomorrow."

"When you're hungover... yep, I'll bet you're right. Here we are, can you make it up to your room?"

"Sure I can."

"And you won't drunk dial Sheila?"

"I don't even have her number."

"Thank God for small favors. I'll see you bright and early."

"Sounds good. Goodnight."

"Goodnight."

Denny was able to unlock the door to his dorm and stumble up the stairs. Once Ben was sure that he was safely inside he backtracked to Tom Brown and let himself in. The common room was empty but the TV was on, a televangelist was pleading and crying for cash and souls. He turned it off and went down the hallway to his room, finished with another long day.

6

Morning came very early. Ben's alarm surely had gone off but he never heard it. He woke to the sounds of Brian's electric razor and Phil Collins on a transistor radio. Had there ever been a more irritating song than "Sussudio"? And now it would be playing in the back of Ben's mind all day long. That awful refrain…

Well, he was up anyway and only about twenty minutes late. He had plenty of time to get ready for class. On the way to breakfast he noticed that his allergies were a little better. Maybe the late night, smoky bar, and rum helped. Or perhaps the pollen counts were beginning to fall. Either way he was thankful for the fresh air coming through his left nostril. Something that hadn't happened in a very long time.

He grabbed a tray and waited in line in the cafeteria. He never talked to the ladies but the one that served the hot meals knew what he wanted by now. Biscuits and gravy and two slices of bacon. It was fairly inexpensive and quite filling. Coffee and apple juice rounded out the meal. He took the tray to his usual table where Anna was waiting for him.

"You're late," she said, smiling and looking up from her biology notes. "And you look like you could have used a few more hours of sleep."

"Thanks a lot! You on the other hand look as radiant as ever."

And she did. Her light brown hair was pulled back into a ponytail revealing silver earrings that dangled and shined. Blue eye shadow complemented her pale blue eyes. Her shirt was unbuttoned at the top, revealing a thin gold chain with a simple cross just below the notch of her sternum. Her cheekbones were high in the way that would help her face remain stunning for decades. She looked rested and vibrant, and at that moment Ben wanted to tell her how he felt. He wanted her to think of him as more than a study friend. He wasn't sure what she thought about him and was too fearful to find out.

"Thank you. I went right to bed after we got back from dinner last night. You'll be proud. I didn't even study."

"Good job. And yes your assessment was right. I was up entirely too late."

Ben filled Anna in on the previous night's events.

"Wow. Okay, that was pretty exciting for a Thursday night. Sorry I missed it. Or maybe not. Sounds like Denny was pretty wasted. At least you didn't let him try to track down this Sheila girl."

"Yeah, he was pretty determined. I'm hoping that he won't remember her this morning."

"Have you seen him yet? Do you think he'll make it to class?"

"Nope and no idea."

"Well, thank you for taking care of him. Getting him home safely and all. You're a good friend."

They finished their breakfast, talking about the weather and what they ate for breakfast at home and what that guy was wearing over in the corner and which cafeteria workers were their favorites and pretty soon it was time to go. As they pulled on their backpacks and got up from the table, they simultaneously saw Denny hurrying in for coffee. He was moving quickly but carefully. Ray-Bans, dark sweatshirt and torn jeans with Reebok Phase 1's, he was cool but casual as he tried to sneak through the line.

"Hey Denny, how're you feeling?"

Startled, he looked over at Ben. "Oh, hey, pretty good. You?"

"I'm good. So you're coming to class?"

"I am. Wait up okay?"

Anna didn't want to be late to class so she said she would save them seats and went on as Denny worked his way through the line.

"I'm surprised you're up. You were pretty hammered last night."

"I'm fine. A little tired I guess. Here, just let me get some sugar."

He tore open and poured in six packets of sugar, two at a time, and stirred them in.

"That should do it. Let's go," he said, sipping on the sugary, creamy, vaguely coffee flavored concoction.

"No food?"

"Nah, I'm good."

They made it to class just as the professor began speaking, slipping in on either side of Anna who had her notebook open on her desk and a serious expression on her face.

71

After a few minutes, when their attention began to wane, Denny leaned up to whisper to Ben, "So, what do you think? Should I call her?"

"Call who?"

"You know who. Sheila. From last night."

"What? No. You shouldn't call her. Do you even have her number?"

"I'm sure I can get it. I'm pretty resourceful."

"Do not call that poor girl."

"But I think I have to."

"No you do not have to. What you have to do is stop obsessing about someone that you don't even know, that you haven't actually talked to, and that isn't interested in you."

Anna gave them a look and they leaned back in their seats and began to take notes. She glanced over at Denny quizzically but when he looked like he was going to say something she shook her head and went back to her note taking.

Denny eventually dozed off peacefully and quietly in his seat. When Anna looked at his paper she found that he had only written the date at the top and then "Sheila" in several different fonts and designs scattered across the page.

Thirty minutes later she shook him awake, telling him it was time to go.

"C'mon Denny, you can't sleep here all day. Let's go."

"But I'm so comfy here," he said, stretching and yawning. "Fifteen more minutes."

"Okay sure, see you later." She and Ben had gathered their things and began exiting the row the other direction.

"Seriously?" He hastily put everything away and followed them out.

Several other classmates looked at Denny and smiled as everyone made their way up the stairs and into the bright morning.

"Hey, was I snoring? People are looking at me funny," he asked Ben once everyone had begun to scatter.

"Just breathing hard. You're lucky you didn't get an eraser thrown at you. Do you want to come to the library with us? We're going to try to study a little before biology."

"Ugh, if I have to learn about one more polypeptide I'm going to lose it."

"I think they're kind of elegant."

"You would. No, I probably should eat something. Maybe they have some leftover sausage. Greasy sounds good. Something to mop up the last of the alcohol. I'm still a little queasy. I'll see you in class though."

"That sounds like a really good idea. And don't call her. Let it sit for a day or two. Maybe ask around and make sure she isn't already involved with someone. I just don't want you to embarrass yourself."

"Yeah, you're probably right. It's starting to seem a little dreamlike now. Maybe I was reading a little too much into the situation."

"You think?"

"Hey, go easy on me. I'm weak and tired. And I haven't completely given up yet. I'm just agreeing that I won't stalk her this morning."

"It's a start. But I do understand. Those late night, alcohol-fueled emotions feel so real. They seem more intense than what we feel during the day. And the way it carries over into the next day…it's like a vivid dream. The kind where you feel this deep connection with someone. And then you see them at school or swim practice or wherever and it seems like they should have had the same dream. But they didn't. It's just this weird, one-sided thing. And even though you have this new appreciation for them- like you shared something special- you really haven't. She just dreamed about a room full of kittens or being chased by an old lady in a creepy house or vacationing in the panhandle of Oklahoma or whatever."

"I've had a few of those dreams," Denny said. "There was this one where a fairly random girl at my high school and I were making out at dinner. We were at Gloria Estefan's house. I'm not sure if the rest of the Sound Machine was there but she was very cool about the whole thing. She just kept on eating. It was a fancy meal. Anyway this girl and I were just really going at it. The next day at school I saw her and just like you said, it still felt so fresh and vivid and exciting. It was so hard to act cool. It was like we really shared something."

"Exactly. Did you ever tell her?"

"No, she wasn't someone I knew like that. But it's weird. Whenever I think about girls I've liked or dated or whatever, I always include her. It was that real."

"Yeah, I don't understand that feeling. I'm not sure anyone does. Love. Attraction. Maybe we'll learn about it in med school or something. It's partly a series of chemical reactions right? Hormones and enzymes and neural connections in the brain. How they all interact and are reinforced and become something real. Honestly I don't think it has a scientific explanation, though. It's a mystery, and much more than the sum of its parts."

"This is getting pretty deep for me. But I'm with you. It's a mystery. Thanks for the talk. Now I'm convinced that my love for Sheila is real. Whatever caused it, those hormones and neurons and enzymes were all on fire last night. Maybe I'll track her number down. We have Pi Phi's in biology right?"

"Whoa! That is not what I said at all. Remember? You didn't talk to your Gloria Estefan dream date girl. And you should definitely not talk to Sheila."

Denny laughed and started walking away. "I'll think about it."

"You do that."

Ben turned back towards the library. It was a clear sunny day. The humidity was lower and he noticed that he was breathing better. Several monarch butterflies were flitting around the zinnias that had been planted along the sidewalk. It was always an amazing thought, how far the fragile appearing butterflies travel. These same insects may have been in Kansas City a week earlier. Always on the move, if successful they would arrive in Mexico in another week or so. Of course many die along the way and even if they make the entire journey, very few survive to start back in the spring.

But this morning, Ben was content to watch them rest and refuel on zinnia nectar, astounded by their beauty and single-mindedness. He tried to imagine what he could accomplish if he could focus like that. Eat, fly, eat, fly... for weeks on end, at the expense of health and family and everything else. Maybe he could get straight A's and test out of some classes and become a doctor a year earlier. Maybe he could start a research project with a professor and get an article published by summer. Or finally learn how to play guitar and start a band that played around town. Or join the swim team and really practice intensely every morning and work out with weights at night to make the All Conference team.

There was literally time to do any one of these things and he was certain he could do them. But life and unhelpful negative emotions like loneliness and sadness and lack of self-confidence and motivation held him back. There was still time though. He might never be as focused as a monarch butterfly but he could certainly make some changes.

He went up the stairs of the library to find Anna in her usual spot. She looked up at him and smiled. He smiled back, rubbing her arm lightly as he sat down without speaking. He pulled out his biology notes and text and found the right spot in the chapter.

"How's Denny?"

"He's fine. Waking up a little, although I know he'd rather sleep longer."

"Yeah, it seems like it sometimes. He's really struggling with something isn't he?"

"Aren't we all?"

"Yes, I suppose we are."

They read and took notes and rewrote them and discussed concepts that were difficult but became easier when they said them out loud. They consulted reference books to fill in the gaps and pretty soon the morning had passed and they felt like they understood the chapter.

They stopped for lunch, sitting with several other friends at a big oval table in the cafeteria. Anna made it through the line first but saved a spot for Ben. It made his heart leap a little to see the spot there as he brought his tray to the table of young, shining people. They were talking excitedly and emphatically as if everything was important. And it was. Their eyes were alive, their foreheads lifted, their mouths smiling and laughing, their arms waving for emphasis.

Ben sat back and took it all in. Not really focusing on a particular story but still laughing along with the group, caught up in the joy of the community, thankful for Anna and everyone at the table and in the cafeteria and at the school. He was aware of the gift that he had been given by coming to this university and was living in the moment.

He looked to his right to watch Anna as she talked and laughed and listened and he remembered the mix tape that he had made for her. He had been carrying it around for two weeks but hadn't found the right time to give it to her.

After lunch they went to biology. They both felt like they did well on the quiz. Relieved that it was behind them they made plans to meet at the snack bar for dinner. It was a bit of a splurge as their prices were high, but pizza and fries really shouldn't have to be a luxury and it seemed like they had deserved a break.

"So what do you think? Not terrible?" Anna said as she began eating the crust of the first slice, dipping it in ranch dressing.

"I've definitely had worse. And it's better than eating in the cafeteria. That just feels a little sad on a Friday night."

"I know. Even though we are literally about twenty yards away and one floor below, it is more festive for some reason. And one more thing- cheese fries."

"Cheese fries are the best. I'm embarrassed to say I had never had cheese fries until I came to Texas."

"Really? That's crazy. What else don't they have in Kansas City? Twinkies?"

"I'll have you know that we are the home of Twinkies. Also Ding Dongs and Ho Hos. They're all made right there. That's why everyone is in such good shape."

"Oh, well, pardon me then sir. I had no idea. I'm glad you like the cheese fries, but now I'm going to say something that is going to blow your mind...gravy fries."

"What? Too much beauty. Where can I get these gravy fries of which you speak?"

"I'm not sure about Fort Worth, but there's a place in Omaha that has the best ones ever. Lots of sausage bits, kind of peppery... They're so good. We'll make it a mission to find them here, okay?"

"It's a deal. Do you want any more Coke? I'll get you a refill."

"Sure, thanks."

When he brought back the drinks they talked more about Omaha and Kansas City, about his sisters and her brothers, about swimming and lifeguarding and softball. They talked long enough that other tables of people filled and emptied around them. It was a wonderful time for both, but Ben was stalling a little. He was trying to decide whether it was the right time to give her the mix tape. And then he finally did. Just like that he pulled it out of his back pocket and set it down in front of her.

"Here. I made this for you."

She stopped and looked down at it.

She picked it up and read the songs, at times squinting to decipher his tiny writing.

"Thank you so much Ben, I love it," she finally said, looking up at him and still wearing a sweet and surprised smile.

"You do?"

"Yes! It's amazing. I've heard of most of the bands either from you or just around but I really don't know many of the songs. I see you put the Replacements on there. I know you love them. And Hüsker Dü."

"Yeah, and don't forget Soul Asylum. My three favorite bands right now are all from Minneapolis. Isn't that weird? How cool would that've been to live there two or three years ago when they were all coming up and just starting to get some recognition?"

"I know. Really cool. And you have New Order. I love that song. And REM and the Cure. I haven't heard the Gun Club or

Meat Puppets. Oh and you have a Butthole Surfers song on there. Of course."

"Their music isn't super relaxing or pleasant but maybe that's why I love them. At least the song on your tape is more melodic than most. Not too crazy. Except for Gibby's voice I guess. And they're from Austin. So are Zeitgeist and Doctors' Mob."

"Well, I'm excited to hear it. Do you think we could listen tonight still?"

"Sure! Do you want to come over for a little bit? My roommates may be there but I'll ask them to not act too weird."

"That sounds really nice."

It turned out Tim and Brian weren't in the dorm room. So Ben and Anna played the tape and they listened to the music and talked and relaxed and found comfort in each other. And that night for the first time they kissed. Her lips were thick and soft. Her tongue was shy at first and later bold and generous. It was all a revelation to Ben, at once what he had dreamed of and something he never expected. They kissed and touched and explored, and the mix tape got to the end and flipped and the night was magical and just right. And it was all sweet and lovely and it was right on time.

7

"How do you get away with this again?"

Ben and Anna were at the Texaco station filling the tank and buying snacks inside the store.

"I've told you. My dad doesn't pay close attention to the credit card bills. He gave me this gas card and basically told me to not go crazy. We don't spend much on actual gas since we rarely go anywhere. He doesn't know that I use it for junk food. It works out pretty well."

"Yeah, it's amazing," Ben said as he tried to choose between a plain Hershey's bar and one with almonds. "You have a Gold Card too right? Show me that again. It's so cool."

She laughed, "It's not that big of a deal really. And it's only for emergencies and special occasions. We can't fly to the Bahamas or anything with it."

"Or at least we couldn't do it twice."

"No, we couldn't do it twice. Have you made up your mind yet? Just get both."

"That's very generous of you but that's not it. I'm trying to determine what I think about almonds in chocolate. Do they simply take up room or do they add something meaningful to the experience? Especially in this case. They're almost equally dispersed throughout the bar. And the way I usually eat it is to either take a bite of chocolate or eat an almond. I almost never take a big bite of both. So what is that telling me?"

"That you don't like them mixed together?"

"Exactly. But I do like them separately."

"So what are you going to do? I can hardly stand the suspense. Plus we should get going."

"I think I'll have a Chunky. Is that ok?"

"Sounds perfect. Although, you do know there are nuts in there right?

"Yeah, but they're peanuts and they're really mixed in. Nothing you can do about it. And the raisins act as kind of a buffer."

"Oh I see. It all makes perfect sense." Anna took the candy bar and put it by the cash register.

"How about a Slim Jim? Or is that pushing it?"

"Nope. Perfect, hand it here."

He gave her the meat stick and candy bar and a can of Coke Classic. She paid with the gas card and they got into her beige 1984 Ford Tempo. Anna was in the driver's seat. Ben occasionally drove her car but for the most part they both felt safer this way. In case of an accident or a speeding ticket they assumed it would go over better with her father if she were driving her own car.

"Don't forget I need to stop at the ATM."

"I remember. I need some money also."

Having an ATM card was a new thing for Ben. He had opened an account across the street from school at First National Bank during orientation. He deposited a one thousand dollar cashier's check, which was most of the money he had earned the previous summer loading trucks in Kansas City, Kansas down by the railroad tracks.

That was a difficult job. Forty hours a week loading boxes of paper onto semi tractor trailers. The trucks and the warehouse were stiflingly hot. Sweat just rolled off of him most of the day. He wore through several pairs of leather gloves that summer. The first few weeks his hands were swollen and stiff to the point that he had trouble holding a fork. He complained bitterly about the job to his parents and to anyone who would listen, but in the end some good did come of the experience.

For instance, he learned that unions were important. He was the only nonunion warehouse employee and because of that made much less money than anyone else. They all had guaranteed health care, vacation days, sick leave and maternity leave. If he was hurt or sick he didn't get paid. It wasn't a big deal to an eighteen-year-old boy living with his parents but for someone trying to pay rent those things were a necessity.

There were only eight people in that warehouse but they worked as an efficient team to get the work done. In addition to the manager, there were two forklift drivers, two order checkers, and three people that loaded the trucks. Every employee became his friend by the end of the summer. From the twenty-two year old female order checker with the nine year old son, to the forty-five year old man who still lived with his mom and referenced her in every conversation, to the four hundred pound fork lift driver who cussed and complained and stank and ate more at lunch than Ben had thought was humanly possible. By late July they felt like family.

The warehouse manager, Leroy, was a thick, muscular guy with dark skin and a forearm the size of Ben's thigh. He boasted of sparring with Joe Frazier once and Ben believed it. He was funny and volatile and competitive and secretive and one of the coolest people that Ben had ever met. Sometimes he would race Ben. They would each take an end of a pallet of boxes and compete to see who could stack them into the truck the fastest. Both of them would grab a box and in one smooth movement swing it up and onto its side, slapping it into place, the rows going higher and higher. By the end of the summer they were fairly evenly matched, Leroy's best days well behind him and Ben's well in front.

The last Friday in July he said goodbye to them all, knowing that most would still be working there when he returned next summer.

He was paid four dollars and a nickel per hour, which was above minimum wage but still left Ben with a pitifully small paycheck every two weeks. It was less than half what the lowest paid union worker in the warehouse made. But he rarely spent money, so was able to save most of it for college, resulting in the thousand dollars that he brought with him to Texas.

They pulled up to the bank, parked and went up the steps to the ATM by the front door. Ben had to admit these things were handy since it always seemed to be odd hours that he needed money. He typed in his PIN and withdrew forty dollars. He hoped that would be enough for the day as it was all he could spare. It was certainly a splurge as he usually only withdrew twenty a week. That thousand was going down fast.

They were getting away to Dallas for the day. It was a lazy Saturday in early October. They had taken two on Friday and didn't have much homework in the other classes, nothing that a little cramming on Sunday couldn't handle.

Both of them had wanted to check out Dallas. There was a big multi-level indoor mall that other kids had been talking about and that's where they were headed.

It was another nice day. There was a slight chill in the air that morning and the sun had begun to peek out around the clouds. Ben's allergies had subsided so they drove with the windows down until the car got up to speed on I-30. Neither had been to Dallas before so they had directions from Ben's RA Brad and a map of the area.

Anna put in her cassette of Depeche Mode's Black Celebration. It was a tape that she had nearly worn through in the six months since its release. It also happened to be one of Ben's favorites. Every song was amazing and they both knew all the words. The last time it had been played it had stopped at the end of "Fly on the Windscreen" which was perfect. They were able to sing "A Question of Lust" at the top of their lungs just as the car was leaving Fort Worth. Their voices exquisitely harmonizing with Martin Gore's, at least in their own minds, the lyrics written deeply into their very beings.

After the song, with windows rolled up, Ben stopped the tape.

"Hey!"

"Wait a minute. I'll put it back in. Let's take a break. That's such an amazing song and I need a moment to collect myself."

"Please. That's ridiculous."

"No, I'm serious. It's such an emotional song. You know what's crazy about this record is how nearly every song is perfect. It's a crime that 'A Question of Lust' is in the middle of side A. Most other bands would lead off with it."

"Most other bands aren't Depeche Mode."

"For real. Don't you think this is their best album yet?"

"I think we've had this discussion before and yes, I do."

Ben continued, "The sound is so much more full and complex. They keep adding layer upon layer. I can't imagine what they're going to do next."

"Yeah, 'Speak and Spell' sounds like an Atari game to me now. I still like the songs but they're so simple."

"It's been a progression for sure. They were getting closer to this sound with Some Great Reward, which still has some of the best songs of all time on it. 'Blasphemous Rumours' of course."

"For sure. One of the best Dave Gahan songs. It still gives me goose bumps when I hear it."

"I love that song. I'm not sure about the theology, but I definitely understand the sentiment."

"Well, God's involvement in our lives is certainly confusing at times."

"That's true but I don't think God laughs at us when we're depressed," said Ben, more serious now.

"No, I don't either. I think Dave is just playing a character. Someone who feels hopeless and confused and doesn't understand why things have worked out the way they have. He's just trying to make sense of things- when nothing actually makes sense. Haven't you ever felt that way?"

"All the time. Why are we so happy right now? Singing and laughing and driving to shop and have fun while people in Ethiopia are starving? Or when someone at school is lonely and suicidal? It's hard to understand. Why the world works this way. I mean, a loving, fair God would give everyone a chance right? Start the playing field level. But it isn't that way is it? Some kids never have a chance. They're born in rural Africa or live in a family with a step dad who abuses them or they have a mental illness or cerebral palsy or something. It's just hard to understand."

"I agree. There's freewill and people do make bad choices, but the situations you're talking about are beyond a person's control."

"It's just sad and confusing. I'm thankful we have bands like Depeche Mode that cause us to feel these deep thoughts and to try to think through some of these issues. That song's helped me empathize better with hurting people."

"That's amazing. Truly. Hey, can we put the tape back in now? And do we have to stop after every song?"

"No, I'm good. I just had a few things to say."

"You always have a few things to say. It's one of your many endearing qualities."

Ben smiled and pushed the cassette into the player in the dash and turned up "Sometimes." They sang along as the car sped towards Dallas. Ben had the map in his lap and a small cassette storage case by his feet. The Coke was balanced between his legs as he tore into the Chunky.

Anna was snacking on the new flavor of Doritos. Cool Ranch. Ben wasn't convinced that they were better than Nacho Cheese but didn't have enough money or snack splurges to really give it a chance. He liked sweet things better anyway. He did take a few when she offered.

"I think they're better."

"Different maybe, not better."

"Okay, I'll go with that."

"And I would rather have actual tortilla chips at a Mexican restaurant with fresh salsa."

"Me too for sure. But we can't always do that. And for those times we have this convenient bag o'chips."

"I agree. Here let me try a few more."

"Ha!" Anna said, handing him the bag.

"We need to be watching for highway one eighty-three. It should be coming up here before too long."

"I see the sign. One mile. North, right?"

"Yeah, north. Then we follow it around to I six thirty-five. Here, take these from me before I eat the whole bag."

"You can put them away. I want to make sure I'm hungry for dinner tonight."

Ben folded the top over and put it down by his feet with everything else. They made the turn onto 183 and continued on, still listening to Depeche Mode.

As they neared the city they saw a brownish haze on the eastern horizon. It was a dome of smog that sat over downtown and spread out for several miles. They stayed outside of it as they drove, discussing the relative merits of Dave Gahan and Martin Gore. They decided that both were important and necessary. The singers provided variety and different perspectives and emotions. It was almost like having two bands in one. When the tape ended they let it reverse back to play again. It seemed to be just the right music for the day and they wanted to continue the mood.

Anna continued on to I-635 heading east. They crossed over the eastern branch of I-35 and eventually made it to the Galleria. The mall was north of downtown and the tall buildings of the city weren't visible from there. They parked and went in to the huge mall.

Opening in 1982, its glass-vaulted ceiling was modeled on the nineteenth century Galleria Vittorio Emanuele II in Milan, Italy. There was a similar mall by the same developer in Houston but this sort of mega-mall was new to the Dallas area. With over a million square feet of retail space, it was much larger than anything that Anna and Ben had seen before.

They entered through Sak's Fifth Avenue, a store that was present in Kansas City but not Omaha. There were multiple levels and the pair explored all of them before exiting on the top floor. From the wide walkway up there they could look down on an ice-skating rink three floors below. They watched several skaters of all skill levels for a while before starting to look at the shops.

Anna tried on hats and belts. She looked at purses and shoes. Ben was mainly along for the ride and was having fun simply watching and hanging out. Being away from school, focusing on each other and on lighter, less stressful matters was enough for this day.

They rode the escalator down to the second floor and continued to look in windows and up and down the aisles of places that interested them. Jewelry, toys, electronics and casual clothes. Many of the brands were new to them. Others were familiar, but the cleanliness and vastness of the mall made them seem more fresh and exciting.

One thing they noticed about the mall was how quiet it was. The gargantuan space and the carpet seemed to swallow noise. There were people everywhere. For an average Saturday in October, they were struck with how crowded it was. But the crowds were calm. Talking was muted and peaceful. People seemed almost anesthetized, very placid. More so than in the smaller malls back home. It certainly wasn't a place to come for wild excitement.

But for a relaxed day away from school it was perfect. After looking at the first floor and the lobby of the Westin Hotel they went down to check out the skating rink. With very limited funds and no natural aptitude for gliding along on ice, Ben wasn't interested in strapping on a pair of skates.

"Come on, why not?"

"I have bad memories of skating."

"So you've done it?"

"Sort of. Enough to know it's not for me. I was invited to a roller skating party when I was about ten years old. I remember slowly working my way around the walls in those heavy shoes, my legs rarely moving in the right direction. One would go straight and the other would head left. It was humiliating and terrifying."

"You never tried again? I doubt anyone gets the hang of it the very first time."

"No. I don't think I did."

"What about ice skates?"

"No. You talk about terrifying. Have you seen how sharp the blades are on those things? I would probably cut off my own fingers."

"I think ice skating is a little easier than roller skating. It's so smooth. You just glide along."

"So, one time I was messing around on the ice on one of the ponds at my granddad's farm."

"Another farm story. Was everything terrifying and miserable there?"

"No. Actually I like it there. It's peaceful and you can kind of do anything you want. Walk around, find things, drive the tractor, look for old arrowheads, burn trash. It's usually nice. You should come with me sometime. It feels real. Unlike this sterile mall."

"You aren't having fun?"

"I didn't mean that. I was simply making a comparison. This place is really amazing in a consumerist sort of way, isn't it? You feel isolated and cut off from reality. Like shopping and buying is the reality. And looking at trees or going for a walk in nature, are far removed from our conscious."

"Yeah, I agree. I wouldn't want to live in here."

"Anyway, I was just messing around on this little frozen pond. I was maybe twelve. My sister was there. I feel like maybe the Olympics had been on and I was trying to emulate those ice skaters. So, I was getting pretty confident. Gliding back and forth in my tennis shoes. Then I decided to try to jump. Maybe it was a spin move. Whatever it was, I slipped and fell and hit my face on a rock. My lip split open and blood just began pouring out."

"Eww. What did you do?"

"Well, I screamed. What else? I screamed and screamed until someone heard me and came to see what I was hollering about."

"So you were super brave. Did you think of holding pressure and going back to the cabin?"

"Nope. I just thought of screaming. And it worked. Remember, I was only twelve. I don't recall much after that. Crying in the back seat of the car all the way to the emergency room in Independence, Kansas. Having six stitches put in. Trying to eat without accidentally biting down on one of the sutures. It was a mess and traumatizing. Here, look at the scar."

Ben pulled down his bottom lip revealing a faint white scar in the mid portion.

"Wow. Impressive."

"I know that voice. You're being sarcastic. Well, I bled a lot. I almost needed a transfusion," Ben said with a slight grin. "So, that's why I'm not going ice-skating. But really you should do it if you want to."

"Oh, come on. You can't live like that. We're too young to give up on something already. Ice skating takes practice like everything else. Do you think Olympic skaters never fell down? And look out there. No rocks."

"Nope, you're right. I just see sorrow and humiliation."

"Ha. We're going and I'm paying. Or my dad is anyway."

"He won't mind?"

"No, this is the kind of thing that he gave me the card for. Having fun every now and then."

"I thought it was for emergencies."

"That too. And this is kind of an emergency. Therapy anyway. We need to help erase and write over those traumatic childhood memories."

Anna presented her American Express Gold Card to the cashier, which always made Ben's jaw drop. She paid for the skate rental and they chose their sizes. They laced them up tightly, securing their ankles, Ben trying to slow his breathing, not focusing on the long steel blade.

As they walked carefully and clumsily to the icy surface Ben said, "Hey, I never asked if you can skate. Probably so huh?"

"Yeah, I spent a fair amount of time at the local skating rink. Ready?"

"No," he said, taking her hand as she stepped out onto the ice.

With one hand on the rail and one hand on Anna they slowly made their way around the rink. After a few minutes, Ben let go of the rail and started to glide as she pulled him along. He began to relax and enjoy himself as he saw others in the same situation. People everywhere were hesitant, falling, laughing. Thirty minutes later he had to admit that he was actually having fun. He slowly scooted around the edges of the rink as Anna skated expertly forward and then backwards. She was graceful and beautiful and Ben felt his heart swell as he watched her.

"See? That wasn't so bad. What do you think? Are you still afraid of skating?"

"Yes! I remain terrified. But it was fun regardless. I'd probably jump off a cliff if you asked me to so I'm not sure it's a fair question."

"You're sweet," she laughed as they took their skates to the desk and retrieved their own shoes.

"I'm getting a little hungry. Are you ready to eat yet?" Ben asked as they rode the elevator up to the ground floor level.

"Famished. But how did we miss this Benetton store? Can we go in for a minute?"

"Sure, be my guest."

They looked at the colorful, oversized sweaters and tried a few on. Benetton hadn't made it to their hometowns yet so they were excited to be there. The warm material was more wishful thinking than necessity in Texas, but they eventually each settled on one. Ben's was on sale. After a short discussion they decided that Anna's dad would be buying dinner and they would both pay for their own sweaters. Ben borrowed some cash from Anna with the promise to pay her back on Monday.

It was an extravagant and uncharacteristic purchase for Ben but he felt good about it. This was a special day and he had worked hard for that money. When they walked out with their sweaters in matching green plastic bags they remembered how hungry they were.

"What do you think?" said Ben. "Italian? Mexican? Bennigans?"

"I saw an Italian place upstairs somewhere. Maybe the third floor? We should have put out breadcrumbs. Or maybe we can find one of those 'You are here' map things."

"I remember it too. Let's just wander around until we find it."

"Spoken like a true man."

"Getting lost is part of the adventure."

It was difficult to get very turned around in the mall and they found the restaurant fairly quickly. Surprisingly intimate, it was memorable in the way that all new things are. The attentive and intuitive waiter, the soft bread, the flavorful lasagna, and the juicy chicken picata, it was accented by the soundtrack playing in the background. Sinatra, Davis, Martin, it all felt simultaneously ironic and authentic.

After the meal Anna presented her magical Gold Card and Ben paid the tip. The mall was nearly empty when they left. They were quiet on the way to the car, the conversation came in shorter bursts, they were content and soaking it all in. The beauty and the grace of the moment.

They took a different way home, wanting to see the Dallas skyline. The big lighted ball of Reunion Tower, the tall green Bank of America silhouette, the interesting shape of the new Allied Bank Tower, Ben imagined he could see beyond the big buildings to Deep Ellum just to the east. It was where all the new bands played. He hoped to visit there soon.

They merged on to I-30 going back west towards Fort Worth. Ben turned the radio knob slowly, trying to find a decent station but gave up. He put in REM's Fables of the Reconstruction. They listened and talked and when they got home they sneaked quietly into Anna's room.

Her roommate was gone for the weekend and they were able to get by the RA's room with no problems. He saw the posters and the make up and the photos from home and the cassettes and he tried not to guess who the guys in the pictures were as they began to kiss and as they moved over to her bottom bunk, pillows and stuffed animals eventually falling to the floor.

And this time they didn't even slow down as they passed their usual stopping point, their excitement and hormones and passion carrying them along on a wave of young love. It felt comfortable and beautiful as they kissed and touched and unzipped and unfastened and unbuttoned.

They whispered to each other, making sure that the other was okay; that they wanted to keep going. And both did. And it was what they expected and nothing like what they expected.

And too quickly it was over. They kissed and whispered some more and then slept soundly and peacefully. And much later the alarm rang, and they woke at four that morning and sleepily kissed one more time as Ben quietly dressed and left the room and the hallway and the building, and happily and dreamily walked in the cool pre-dawn stillness to his dorm.

8

Ben chose his meal and took his tray to a booth at the back of the cafeteria, where he had seen Denny sitting with his chemistry text open.

"Hey Denny, what's with the books?"

"Oh, hey Ben. Yeah, I'm actually studying. Wild huh? I really need to do well on this test. Try to get my grade up to a C at least."

"I'm proud of you, my friend. I can help. We can quiz each other once I understand it better."

"That would be great. Library after lunch?"

"Yep, as always."

"So, how did yesterday go? The big shopping trip. Did you buy lots of makeup and those little scented candles?"

"Ha. No, it was great. We had a really nice time. That mall is gigantic. We ice-skated, had dinner at this little Italian place, just walked around and talked. Oh, I guess we did buy nearly matching sweaters at Benetton. That seems a little weird in retrospect."

"Oh! You both have to wear them to class tomorrow. I can't wait!"

"Don't get your hopes up."

They finished eating and gathered their things to move over to the library. Later Anna joined them, sitting a little closer to Ben at the table than usual. Stealing glances at each other and smiling, Denny finally noticed that something was up.

"Wait. Did you two finally do it?"

They both laughed a little and Ben looked over at Anna. She had a mischievous smile.

"You did! Ohmigod you did!"

"Dude, keep it down. What's the matter with you?" Ben implored, looking left and right.

"So it's official. You're a thing. What's the correct protocol? Do we need to call the editors of the Skiff or something?"

"That would be ideal," said Ben. "But if you'd like I can just write it in the second floor bathroom stalls."

"Sounds great. No, seriously, congratulations, you two. It's about time."

"Thanks. Maybe we should get back to studying now."

It felt differently now to all three and for the same reason. They were at once more comfortable and less comfortable around the big round table but they stuck with it. They read, took notes, looked up information, snacked, stretched their legs, and stared into space. Denny seemed more focused that he had been in weeks. He was awake, sober, and calm.

They studied throughout the day and when they felt like they had learned all they could they went to the cafeteria right before closing. It was Sunday night so it was quiet there. They ate and talked and relaxed. After dinner the boys remembered that the American League baseball playoffs were on. They decided to go watch it in the common room at Denny's dorm. Anna said goodnight and that she would see them the next day.

The room was packed with baseball and football players, swimmers, tennis players and others enjoying the game on a lazy Sunday night. Ben's team, the Kansas City Royals had been disappointing that year. They had won the World Series in 1985 and so anything less felt like a failure. They finished ten games under .500, which was heartbreaking but not completely unexpected. Denny's team was the Dodgers who had also had a terrible year.

It was the Angels that had done well. Although a California team, Denny wasn't particularly interested in them. And they were a rival of the Royals, so ordinarily Ben cheered against them. But neither of them were fans of the Red Sox and they were reasonably happy that it looked like California would wrap it up that night. They began watching in the sixth inning as the Angels continued to pull away. They were up five to two going into the ninth when Don Baylor hit a two run homer for Boston. Another two run homer in the ninth with two outs and two strikes by Dave Henderson put Boston ahead. They eventually won in eleven innings. There were a lot of happy Boston fans in the room. Denny and Ben were only mildly invested in the outcome but it was fun to watch just the same. There is a certain community created when watching sports in a group that is often greater than the sum of its parts.

It was late and people began to disperse when Ben asked Denny the question that had been bothering him all day. Ever since he had seen him studying that morning in the library.

"What's the deal Denny?" Ben finally asked. "It seems like you're actually trying again."

"Wow. That feels a little out of the blue."

"Yeah, sorry. I've just been thinking about it. It took me by surprise, that's all."

"Maybe because I'm actually trying. I realized the other day that I'm here in Fort Worth, spending a huge amount of my parents' hard earned money as my dad continues to work sixteen-hour days trying to keep the restaurant in the black. I've been given this completely unearned gift of an advanced education and the least I can do is to give it a little effort. I could drink and party and sleep and mess around in Laguna. Skip college completely. Maybe teach surfing or be a waiter or bartender or whatever."

"That sounds pretty nice."

"Yeah, it does to me too sometimes. Like when I'm feeling lonely and out of place. Or when I get another low C or D on a test. But you know what? I really want to be a dentist. For all the reasons we talked about the other day. It would be really cool. And it's something I can do if I really try hard. I think I'm smart enough to do it."

"Dude, I know you are."

"Thanks, that means a lot but really it's me that has to believe. Sometimes I do and sometimes I don't."

"Well, it must help when you can put together a good day like today. A ton of studying and then some camaraderie and baseball at the end. It was a banner day."

"For sure it was. And now I'm going to continue with my new found maturity and go to bed before daybreak."

"What? Now that's just crazy. Oh wait. Is that my signal to leave?

"You're quick."

"I'll see you in the morning. Do you want me to call you?"

"No. I'll set my alarm and I'll write a note for my roommate just in case."

They went separate ways and both were tired and slept like eighteen year olds often do.

The next morning Ben went to breakfast with his roommates. Or they left the room together. They didn't associate with each other very much outside of their room, having found their own friends. They went their separate ways in the cafeteria, going to their own table of friends. Anna was there already.

"Have fun last night? Who won?"

"The Red Sox. We were up entirely too late. It went into extra innings."

"Good game though?"

"Yeah, really good. It was fun watching with everyone. There were fans for both sides there."

When Denny didn't show up for breakfast they went to class. They found him already there, doing some last minute cramming. The chemistry test was easier than they thought, or they were better prepared, and they felt like they did reasonably well. The weight of the exam lifted and they could relax the rest of the day. The friends went to lunch and studied a little between classes. Denny left early to watch television in his dorm while Anna and Ben went to the cafeteria for dinner and then back to his room to talk and listen to music.

There was the exciting new sensation of being a couple. Of belonging to each other. They made plans, knowing that they had a companion, someone who would be there to share everything with. It was a natural thing and didn't feel forced by either person.

By ten o'clock Ben's roommates were back. They knew Anna but weren't accustomed to having visitors, especially female ones, so everyone was a little uncomfortable. Ben walked her out and they kissed and said goodnight and both went to sleep happy and content.

The rest of the week had a similar pattern. Anna and Ben ate together, studied together and relaxed together. They even watched the rest of the American League championship together, as Boston won the final two games on Tuesday and Wednesday. It was an exciting series and by the end they were both pulling for the Red Sox as they came back for the win.

On Thursday afternoon, when they were finished with classes they asked Denny if he wanted to come with them to check out a new record store.

"No, that's ok. I'm going to play golf with a couple of the tennis guys. Is it the one on Berry? They just sell CDs right?"

"Yeah, that's what I heard anyway. I'm curious to see what they have there. Someone said it isn't just major label stuff."

"Well, have fun. Tell me about it later."

"Ok, likewise. It's a nice afternoon for golf."

"We'll see. I get pretty frustrated out there."

"Which is exactly why I'm not interested in taking it up. I have enough stress in my life without worrying about the trajectory of a tiny white ball. Catch you later."

Anna and Ben walked towards Berry from the library and then across the street. The record store was a few doors down from the Hi Hat. They couldn't recall what it had been before but it was a small space. Perhaps thirty feet wide and fifteen deep. The guy working there appeared to be about thirty. He had short, thinning hair and a hyper-alert, somewhat nerdy appearance.

"Welcome! Are y'all looking for anything in particular?"

"No, we just wanted to see what you have."

"Excellent, feel free to browse. I have some of the CDs open. Let me know if you want to hear anything and I may be able to play it for you."

"Cool. I will, thanks a lot."

"How'd you y'all hear about us?"

"Some kid told us. I honestly don't remember. So, it looks like you just have CDs, right?

"Yes, with my limited space I thought I could either cram a bunch of records in here in bins or display CDs in an organized fashion and keep any extras in the back. Plus CDs are the future of music. Have fun looking around."

He went back behind the counter and busied himself there. The speakers were playing jazz. Ben didn't know for sure but it sounded like it was from the fifties. Then a few seconds later he saw a CD jewel case propped up near the register with a "Now Playing" tag. And sure enough it was Stan Getz in his pre- Bossa Nova days.

"Do you like this kind of jazz?" he asked Anna.

"It's not my favorite. But to be honest I haven't really listened to it much. My jazz knowledge doesn't go much further back than Kenny G."

"Ugh. Don't even speak that name out loud. The whole smooth jazz thing is nauseating. George Howard or Grover Washington yes. Maybe even a little Bob James. But Kenny G no thanks. I see that they have the new album here. Yuck."

"Hey, maybe he'll play it for us," Anna teased.

"If he does, I'll walk right out that door. Just listen to this though. Stan Getz was an unbelievable sax player. The real thing. There's this other record from about the same time where he plays with Chet Baker. It is unbelievable."

The CDs were all along the walls in small compartments in which they fit just right. They were facing out and there were fifteen rows from the floor to about seven feet high. The largest section was classical, with jazz a close second. They browsed through the entire store, picking up many of them to read the back.

"I think CDs are perfect for classical music. Or vice versa," Ben said.

"It does sound nice if it's recorded well."

"Yeah, there really isn't a lot of use for crackles and pops in classical. Not like there is in punk rock or music with a lot of guitars. It's just distracting. A lot of my mom's old records have so many scratches that I probably wouldn't recognize the music without them. I just know it would sound better with a digital recording played on a CD."

"Same thing for jazz?"

"Well, I guess it depends. If it's old bebop or something then maybe vinyl is still best. But yeah, Grover Washington sounds great on CD, don't you think?" Ben said, smiling suggestively.

"Easy tiger, let's keep looking."

They finally made their way around to the alternative section. It wasn't as large as the others and it seemed to reflect the owner's taste. It was kind of random. There was the brand new Love and Rockets CD. They had heard "Ball of Confusion" already and were interested in hearing what the rest of the record sounded like.

There was the Smithereens album, Especially for You, with the song "Behind the Wall of Sleep." Anna and Ben discussed whether it would sound better on vinyl or CD and the consensus was vinyl. Of course the other thing that entered into the discussion was cost. The CDs in the store were $18.99, which was about ten dollars more than the vinyl at the record store down the road. It would have to sound a lot better to justify that cost.

Next they came to the 4AD section. The owner was obviously a big fan. The 4AD label's best selling song and band was Modern English with "I'll Melt With You" back in 1983. But that was a bit of a fluke, and wasn't really representative of the type of music put out by the label.

No, the most important band for 4AD and the one that set the tone for the others was the Cocteau Twins. Formed in 1981, the Scottish band released their first record the next year. It was completely different than anything else going on at the time. Robin Guthrie's heavily effected guitars and Elizabeth Glaser's nearly indecipherable lyrics and unique way of singing them created a sound that was relaxing and edgy at the same time. It was Goth and Chill Out and Alternative and most listeners felt like they were in a secret club.

Ben was surprised to find so many of the 4AD releases at the shop and when the owner saw him examining the back of the releases he came over again.

"Do you like the Cocteau Twins?"

"I love them! I've played the Pink Opaque until the tape of the cassette is so thin I seriously worry that it's going to snap."

"Cassette? Wow, you're missing a lot if you've only heard it on cassette. Here, I have one open. I'll put it on."

He looked through a drawer, flipping through CDs in thin plastic sleeves until he found the right one. He slid it into the player and there was silence in the room for a few seconds. Then the first restrained drumbeats of "The Spangle Maker" began with Robin's echoing guitar, Elizabeth's voice coming in a few moments later. The sound was so lush and full it gave Ben goose bumps and caused his eyes to water. He looked away from Anna, a little embarrassed. After a minute he smiled at the storeowner and nodded his head.

"This is incredible. It's completely different."

"I know! It's night and day isn't it? Listening to these records on CD completely changes everything. Do you have very many CDs?"

"Very few. I can't afford them."

"Yeah, that's one of the big problems for sure. Hopefully the cost will come down at some point. I'll tell you what. Because you're a fellow fan of the Cocteau Twins I'll give you a three dollar discount on any CD you want. Your friend also. You should both get one."

"That's really cool of you. I might take you up on that. I want to look around a little more."

"Take your time. I'll leave this one on. It's one of my favorites too."

Anna and Ben looked around the store a few more minutes. In the end they decided to go with the new Cocteau Twins CD- Victorialand. Ben couldn't justify spending money on a Thursday, not when he knew there would be some expenses that weekend. Anna wanted to hear it though and they knew they could tape her a copy later. She even used her own money this time, saved from babysitting jobs.

They walked back over to campus and stopped at the cafeteria for dinner. They ate at a table for two and then went back to Ben's room to listen to the new record. His roommates weren't home yet so they were able to relax. The music was amazing. It was inventive and interesting and catchy in an otherworldly way. Elizabeth's voice had continued to evolve as an instrument and Robin's guitar washes and effects created an atmosphere that was perfect for a late night shared between two people in a new relationship.

Ben dubbed the CD onto side A of a new Maxell ninety- minute cassette tape. He wasn't sure what was going onto the other side yet but was happy to have it taped.

When Tim showed up, Anna said goodbye and walked back to her dorm, leaving Ben feeling somewhat empty and alone in a way that he still wasn't used to. He found it odd how quickly his life had changed.

"What was I like before?" he asked Tim.

"Before what?"

"Before Anna and I were dating."

"Um, about the same as now, except more of a loser. I don't know what she sees in you."

"Thanks, that's very reassuring. I just mean- can you tell a difference? Am I more confident? Less mopey? Nicer at all?"

"Well, you're still irritating, but in a new way. Instead of depending on Brian and me to go to breakfast with you, or having to listen to your long stories about nothing, we hardly see you anymore, except for a few seconds at night."

"Yeah, we have been spending a lot of time together."

"You think?"

"Well, she's pretty cool and we have a good time together. And she's better looking than you two."

"All very good arguments I must say. I would probably do the same thing if Toni lived here."

"Right. I know you would. How is she by the way? Are you two still hanging in there with the long distance thing?"

"We are. Only about nine more weeks until Christmas break. I'll get to see her then."

"That sounds like a long time. I'm sorry, it must really suck to have a girlfriend that far away."

"Hey, no problem. I wonder where Brian is?"

"Crap, was it my night to keep track of him?"

"It actually was. Oh well, I'm going to bed. We can go check the hospitals and jails in the morning."

"Great idea. I'm right behind you."

9

The next night after a day of classes and a very small amount of studying Denny invited Ben to go play pool and drink with him at the Pub.

"Dude, it's Friday night! Are you seriously going to stay home with the wife?"

"She's not my wife. And yes, we're going to stay in. I'm not in the mood to go out drinking. We're just going to relax and watch Miami Vice."

"Come out after that. I doubt I'll even go until after ten."

"No, not this week. I will though. Maybe next week. Hey, you aren't stalking Sheila are you? You need to leave that poor girl alone."

Denny smiled. "We had a breakthrough the other night. She was looking at me when I turned around. We made eye contact for a good three seconds."

"She's probably trying to memorize your features to describe them to the police."

"You're hilarious. You just wait, I'm breaking down her defenses a little at a time."

"Okay, well, good luck. Call me tomorrow and maybe we can do something."

"Sure. I'll hold my breath."

That night the Miami Vice episode was one of the best ones they had seen. Ben hadn't missed a show since season one and always looked forward to the Friday nights when a new one aired. Episode four of season three didn't disappoint as Tubbs was put in prison to investigate and break up a drug ring involving the guards. It was tense and stylish and oh so cool. Every commercial gave Anna and Ben a chance to breathe and for their blood pressure to drop as the show built towards the dramatic conclusion. The excitement and music reached a crescendo during the last five minutes as Castillo rescued Tubbs in the prison yard to the music of The Damned's "In Dulce Decorum." They were quiet and pensive for a few minutes after it was over. The few others in the common room in Ben's dorm were also quiet. One of them muted the commercials.

"Unbelievable," Ben finally said. "How does the Damned show up on a national network program?"

"Was that who the last song was by? I hadn't heard it before but it was pretty cool."

"I'm telling you, that show gets better every week. Whoever chooses the music does a great job. I would love to be able to do that. I would be even more obscure but just as appropriate."

"I know you'd be wonderful at it. It seems like that career is taken though. Hey, do you want to play Scrabble?"

"Sure, stay right here. I'll go get it."

Ben brought the game back from his room and they competed and talked and listened to LA Law playing in the background. Anna was a formidable Scrabble opponent and they were fairly evenly matched. They didn't have a dictionary so twice had to resort to asking a guy in the room to mediate on a particularly inventive word.

"We should spring for a dictionary," said Anna. "It might come in handy for other things as well."

"Maybe. Like everything, there's a cost/benefit ratio. I'm so poor right now that buying books is pretty low on my wish list. Right above tickets to the zoo and just below a giant bag of Sixlets."

"You just had Sixlets yesterday!"

"Yeah, they're always on the list. A single package near the top and a huge, Halloween sized bag farther down. They are so much better than M&M's."

"Are we going to do this again? You know that I think that's one of the more absurd ideas that you have. How could a tiny piece of dark colored, chocolate flavored substance covered by a too hard candy shell be better than an M&M? They're perfect. Real chocolate, covered by a thin coating that just happens to melt in one's mouth."

"Woah. First of all, the chocolate that's inside an M&M is no closer to pure chocolate than a Sixlet. It's sugar and milk and oil and who knows what else. I've even heard that Hershey's puts sand in their chocolate to give it a certain texture. The artificial colors and flavors that come from labs and cause cancer and diabetes are in both. The small amount of chocolate that's in them is probably covered in pesticides and harvested by African children working as virtual slaves. Would you like for me to go on?"

The two guys trying to watch LA Law had turned around to see what was happening at the Scrabble table. Anna looked at them and rolled her eyes.

"Okay Ben, if they're such evil products why do you love them so much?"

"That is a very good question. You're exactly right. Yes, I like the taste of Sixlets better than M&M's. Yes, I like the fact that they are small and round and I can just kind of pull them out of the wrapper with my teeth. Yes, they have always been the most exciting things to get in my Halloween bag...."

"You had a Halloween bag?"

"Bag. Plastic pumpkin. Pillowcase. You know what I mean. The point is that we do things that we know are wrong, possibly even harmful to our bodies, harmful for the environment and for other people around the world because we are selfish and shortsighted. Because of advertisers convincing us that it's normal and something we need. I think it's something we should question and not just blindly follow along with the crowd. And yes this means I'm a hypocrite. I still love Sixlets despite knowing all of this."

"Um... maybe we should change the subject."

Ben laughed, "Yeah, who knew that chocolate flavored candies would set me off tonight. It's just something I've been thinking about lately. About trying to line up my beliefs with my actions."

"Well, it's very admirable, although a little annoying."

They continued on for the rest of the night, playing games, talking, getting to know each other, making out when the others finally left the room, and finally saying good night to each other around midnight.

The next day Ben and Anna met for breakfast at the cafeteria. It was Saturday and they didn't have a tremendous amount of homework so the plan was to study until after lunch and then go watch TCU play North Texas. The football team hadn't been having a great year but at least they were heavily favored to win this one. In thirteen prior matchups they had never lost against their Denton neighbor.

"Hey, imagine finding you two together," Denny said as he arrived at the library around ten thirty. "What did I miss?"

"Just stimulating conversation and a fascinating analysis of my English paper. How was last night?"

"Excellent. There were a ton of people out. Too bad you lovebirds couldn't join us."

"Sheila?"

"Sadly no. But I managed. I can't remember every detail but my overall impression was that it was a good night and I didn't do anything too stupid."

"Quite an achievement. Your parents would be proud."

"Actually they might have been. So are you two going to the game later?"

"I'm pretty sure. Are you?"

"Yeah, a lot of the swimmers are going in a group. You can join us if you'd like. We'd let you two sit next to each other."

"Bitterness doesn't look good on you Denny."

"I'm just messing with you. Come along! It'll be fun. We can go over together after we finish studying."

"Okay, that sounds nice. What do you need to work on today?"

"Some history mainly. I'm praying that this is the last time in my life that I'll have to learn about the Revolutionary War."

"It was an interesting time. We only study it from the side of the Colonies. Too bad we can't see the British side. Or even better, from the point of view of Native Americans. Or French. Or Spanish. Or even Scottish. There were a lot of competing interests and cultures and it's much more than a collection of dates and generals."

"Uh oh. Sounds like I've stepped into a lesson."

Anna took that cue to take a bathroom break.

"I'll let you two hash this out. I'll be back."

Ben watched her go then resumed, "No, it just struck a chord when you mentioned it. I've been thinking about the same thing during my class. I'll be thankful when I can take a history elective. Something with a tighter focus and room for more discussion. In the meantime, have you read Howard Zinn's *The People's History of the United States?*"

"I don't read much so the answer to almost any question that begins with 'Have you read...' is going to be no. Unless it's 'Have you read the latest Sports Illustrated issue?' Although I guess it's never phrased that way. It's 'Have you seen...'"

"Okay, point taken. Anyway, you should make an exception for this one. It's what I'm talking about. It looks at history from the bottom up rather than from the top down. The origins of slavery, the slaughter of Native Americans, the way that strikes and labor have been controlled by the rich. It certainly made me think. It opened my eyes so that I'm able to see the world from a completely different angle."

"It sounds heavy to me. I am literally just here to get a diploma and have a little fun and get on with my life."

"Yeah, me too to some degree but what better time to learn about the world? We have books and magazines surrounding us right now, interesting people from around the world- well, ignoring the fact that a majority are from Texas but we've already found a few – classes covering a multitude of mind expanding subjects... this is the critical time to question and discuss and develop our own world views."

"Okay, I can see that. You make a very good point. I have a question for you then."

"Shoot."

"Why are you closing yourself off from everything you've been talking about?"

"What do you mean?"

"You know. Why are you spending more and more time with a single, solitary female person and excluding everyone and everything else? How are you expanding your mind and developing an alternative world view by shopping at a fancy mall, buying Bill Cosby sweaters and watching network television?"

Ben's face fell as what Denny was saying began to sink in. He looked around to be certain no one else was listening. As hypocritical and ridiculous as the question was, coming from an anti- intellectual drunk-in-training, he was still speechless for a moment.

"Where did this come from? Just because I wouldn't go to the Pub with you last night?"

"It is absolutely not that. I'm sorry but it's true. It's not healthy."

Ben was ready to protest when Anna came around the stacks saying, "Okay you two, stop gossiping about Sheila and get back to work."

Ben laughed, saying, "You know us so well."

And with that the subject was dropped. But Ben had trouble concentrating with Denny's words still reverberating through his brain. There were certainly advantages to having a strong, exclusive relationship. The built-in companionship, the feeling of contentment. He didn't have to worry that he would spend an evening alone, or walk into a bar or record store or cafeteria alone. He wasn't obsessing about an elusive woman like Denny's

Sheila. Not to mention the fact that Anna was so incredibly attractive and appealed to him on that level.

But Denny did have a point. It was very early in his college experience and he hadn't met anyone new in the past two weeks. In fact with the exception of his California friend, even the people he did know had kind of faded out of his life.

He watched Anna reading until she noticed.

"What?"

"Nothing. What time should we go?"

"Are we all going together?"

"Yeah let's do it. The three of us haven't done anything except study for a while."

"Fine with me. I want to change and put on some makeup. How about we meet at your dorm in an hour?"

"Perfect."

They gathered their things and left. That night the Horned Frogs did something that no one thought was possible. They lost to North Texas, breaking a string going back seventy years. It was shocking and disheartening, even to casual fans like the three friends. They went to a swimmer's apartment for a party but no one felt like celebrating. There was drinking and subdued conversations on couches and on porch steps and eventually Anna and Ben slipped away to her dorm.

Over the next week the Mets beat Boston in the seventh game to win the World Series. Ben and Anna watched the games together. They also studied, went to class, and ate three meals a day together.

On Saturday they went to Ol' South Pancake House for lunch before the Baylor game, one that they were predicted to lose.

"Hey, thanks for this. I could never have afforded to come here," said Ben as he added more sugar to his coffee.

"No problem. It's pretty good huh? Old fashioned but comforting. I like the way it smells in here. Do you want to taste my pancakes? That's what they're famous for, you know."

"Sure, I'll try a bite. I have to tell you though, I'm not a big fan of pancakes. I feel like they're just filler. Like dinner rolls or potatoes or tortilla chips. Just something to fill your stomach. Like if you're starving and have to get something in fast."

"That's absurd. There isn't much better than warm fluffy pancakes with melted butter syrup."

"You do realize that what you're putting on there isn't maple syrup, right?"

"I don't think I've had real maple syrup. Have you?"

"Just once. It is so good! Completely different from the thick sticky stuff that we're used to. The flavor is so subtle and clean. It's too good for pancakes though."

"There you go again. Mister patty melt."

"I happen to love patty melts. Something about eating an open faced hamburger with a fork. It makes me feel like I'm a hobo from the thirties. Sitting up at the lunch counter, I tell the lady I just have a nickel and she tells me it's alright, that I have a nice face and as long as I don't tell my friends she'll take care of me. She pours me coffee, slides an open-faced hamburger with grilled onions to me, and later more coffee and a slice of cherry pie. She takes the nickel with a wink and I hop on the next boxcar that goes by with a full stomach and a light heart."

"You are a very strange boy. But I like you anyway."

"Hey thanks. By the way, I wonder if they have cherry pie here."

"Let's ask."

It was moments like this that Ben loved. Fun and relaxing. But there were others, when boredom or jealousy or short tempers or perhaps just too much togetherness began to occur, that he began to picture life without Anna. It terrified him to think of being on his own again. And that thought terrified him even more. He knew he would have to make a decision before much longer. They had become very close very quickly and he wasn't sure whether it was what he truly wanted.

She paid and they left full and happy and went to watch the first half of the football game. It was another nice day, but one in which they didn't interact with anyone else. A wave and a short quip was the extent of it.

That night, after they made love and Anna was sleeping soundly, Ben sat in a chair and thought and even prayed for some clarity and direction. He was still up when she awoke at three in the morning.

10

"Why are you up already?" Anna whispered to Ben, as he sat in her desk chair, his back to the bunk beds.

"I couldn't sleep."

"Why not? Too much caffeine?"

"That's part of it, I'm sure."

She sat up in bed, trying to wake up, her voice changing slightly. "What else? Is something wrong?"

"I'm not sure…Anna, do you think everything is okay?"

"With us? Ben, what's going on? Come over here and tell me what you're thinking about. Did something happen? Did I say or do something?"

"No, it's nothing like that. It's just…" He paused and looked down, trying to decide if this was the time or the place. Wouldn't it be better to do this in the daytime, when both of them were thinking clearly? But he felt like he was on a one-way train now.

One with no brakes and flying down the other side of the Arbuckle mountains. Maybe that wasn't dramatic enough. Maybe the Zambezi Zinger at Worlds of Fun. That first big drop. Only not fun at all. No, he couldn't stop himself now.

"I was thinking that maybe we need a break."

"A break?" Anna said and then was quiet. She was staring at a spot to the left of his head. There was a framed picture of Anna and her two brothers in that general area, but Ben couldn't tell if she was looking at it or through it.

He started to reach for his jeans. "Maybe I should…"

"Yeah… maybe you should," she said, leaning down and flipping them to him, coins clanking onto the rugs and floor.

"I'm sorry."

"You are? Then explain what's going on. This feels really out of the blue. Why tonight? Who is she?"

"There's no one else. You can't be serious. When would I have had time to meet anyone else? We're together twenty-four hours a day."

He wished that he could take that back. The hurt in her eyes was visible even with the dim light. There was finally something real, something tangible that she could hold onto. And he wasn't sure that he even wanted to do this. He regretted the fact that he hadn't simply stayed in bed, waited until morning, given himself some more time to think it all through. What was he doing, throwing this away? Their relationship was barely a month old. How could he know that she wasn't the love of his life? His perfect soul mate?

He couldn't. But now that the words were out, still lingering in the air, there was no way to take them back.

Anna took a long time to say anything. And Ben had frozen in place, waiting, not daring to move or to say another word.

"So that's it. We've been together too much. You want space. Maybe want to see who else is out there? It's okay, I get it. Maybe I do too. We have something pretty great though Ben. And you had me fooled. I thought you were happy."

He started to say something but she stopped him.

"No, you can only make it worse by speaking. Just go."

He finished getting dressed and moved to the door. He stopped before turning the knob and looked back at her.

"I'm really sorry Anna. This feels like a gigantic mistake right now. You're right, we've had so much fun. And you're amazing. You've never done anything wrong. Not one thing. The whole thing sounds so idiotic right now. How about if we talk more in the morning? When we're awake and thinking clearly."

"No, I may not understand the reason but your intent is loud and clear. What does Denny think? Was this his idea? This is what you two were talking about when I walked up yesterday, wasn't it?"

"No, he doesn't know. And no we weren't talking about this. Not exactly anyway."

"Okay, get out. And no, I don't want to talk in the morning. I'll find a new spot to study. Don't try to find me."

Feeling nauseated and alone, Ben finally left her room. He walked softly down the hallway and out into the cool air. His steps echoed as he made his way across the lawn and the asphalt to his dorm. He had trouble unlocking the door to his room and Brian finally came to open it with an irritated expression. Neither said a word as Tim continued to sleep softly.

Ben dropped his pants to the floor and climbed up to his bunk, thankful for the people around him. Even though they weren't extremely close, even though neither had any idea what was going on, simply the fact that they were his roommates was comforting. It was over thirty minutes before his mind slowed down enough and the pain in his abdomen lessened enough that he could drift off to sleep.

He slept until ten, which was very unusual. When he awakened both roommates were gone. He looked around in the brightly lit room, trying to get his bearings when he remembered what had happened with Anna. He groaned and fell back on the pillow.

An hour later he awoke to the sound of knocking. He got up and answered the door. Denny was standing there wearing a goofy grin and a Skynyrd shirt.

"Oh thank God, I thought you were dead."

"What?"

"I heard what happened with Anna and when you didn't show up for breakfast or to study... well, I started to worry. Then I ran into Tim. Or was it Brian? Anyway, one of them. And he said he thought you were still asleep. That you didn't move while he was banging around in the room this morning. It didn't cross his mind that you were dead even though I have never known you to sleep past seven. What kind of roommates do you have anyway?"

"Nice ones that let me sleep. Here, come in. Let me take a shower and get dressed. And then we can talk."

He grabbed a towel and a clean shirt and left Denny in the room looking at his records. When he returned he found his friend lounging on the floor listening to Ozzy Osbourne's Diary of a Madman.

"Out of all my music that's what you choose?"

"I hadn't heard this one. It's not bad. A little bit disturbing. I think you've been keeping the fact that you're a metalhead secret from me. I found some Blackfoot, Blue Öyster Cult, lots of Rush, even Van Halen II. As you may have heard, I'm more of a

Skynyrd fan but I certainly appreciate this stuff. Reminds me of my uncle's collection."

"Funny, I have one of those uncles also. Yeah, Ozzy is great but have you listened to this before?" Ben asked, pulling out Blue Öyster Cult's Secret Treaties album.

"I haven't. I'm afraid that I know two songs of theirs. Like most people."

"I'll bet you know three. 'Don't Fear the Reaper,' 'I'm Burning For You,' and 'Godzilla.'"

"I forgot about 'Godzilla.' What was up with that? So, what's this one like?"

"It's just really cool. Their best album by far. It's psychedelic, amazing guitars, cool synths, dramatic vocals. You know, all that is wonderful and terrible about seventies rock. Everything that the Sex Pistols and all the New York bands began to dismantle about two years later. Check it out though. I still appreciate this sometimes. It might be good Sunday morning music."

He put on the third song, "Dominance and Submission." It was not what Denny had expected at all. Pretty soon he was playing air guitar to the solo while Ben was singing into his shampoo bottle with just the right amount of melodrama.

They ended up listening to the rest of the first side.

"That's amazing. How have I never heard that?"

"There is so much good music out there. We can't buy it all and the radio can only play what most people want. I'll tape it for you. I'll put a Rush album on the other side. Which one don't you have? Farewell to Kings?"

"How about Hemispheres? I love that song 'Trees' but don't have it anywhere."

"Perfect. That was their last album from the seventies. They were completely different by the time Permanent Waves came out. I'll make it for you tonight. Looks like I'll have some extra time on my hands."

"Stop moping. It's not going to be easy but I know you'll be glad this happened today rather than six months from now."

"Maybe. But it's going to be a tough day and week. On one hand I don't know if I want to see her. On the other that's all I want to do. Man, I'm really a mess."

"You are. And you will be. Let's go get some food. An early lunch I guess. Do you need to study today?"

"Sounds good. I'm actually really hungry. And yes I do need to study. What should we do about that? Anna is your friend too. Do we sit at our old table? Or study somewhere besides the library?"

"Let's check out our spot and see what's going on there, then decide. One step at a time, my friend."

They went to the cafeteria and found a group of swimmers to eat with. There were eight people gathered around the table sharing Saturday night exploits and Sunday morning dreams. It was warm there and smelled like bacon and coffee and toast and college. They included Ben in their stories and didn't ask any questions about Anna. It was the perfect first meal. And although he found himself looking at the door every time someone walked in, he felt content.

They didn't see Anna at the library. Ben had a strong urge to go look for her. To make sure everything was okay. Denny assured him that it was and to not try to find her. Give her time to begin to heal. They ended up getting a lot done. Ben quizzed Denny and helped him understand some concepts that had been tricky for him.

The next morning they had breakfast together and still no Anna. They finally saw her in Chemistry. She was already there when they arrived. Sitting up towards the front with a girl they didn't know well but thought she lived on the same floor as Anna.

Ben couldn't concentrate on what the professor was saying. His eyes were fixed on the back of Anna's head. Her light brown curls were the focus of his universe that hour. He felt sick. Heartbroken was the perfect term for it. Not injured or wounded, but completely broken.

He waited for her to turn around, to see if he was still in his spot. He planned to smile and maybe give a slight nod or wave. Something subtle. But she never looked back. Not once. And when the class was over, while he paused to see if he could catch her eye, she walked up the stairs facing her friend and avoided looking at him.

So it was official. Real. He'd lost not only his girlfriend but also his best friend. His dining companion and study partner. He went through the rest of the day in a haze, attempting to simply keep moving. He studied, ate, and watched television in the common room with the other lonely dorm dwellers. Denny had offered to come over and hang out but Ben wanted to try to get through this on his own. He didn't want to become dependent on Denny the way he had on Anna. He talked to the guys as they watched TV. He eventually got through the evening and went to bed.

The next day was a repeat. Classes, studying in the library, eating, and sleeping. And the next day was the same. And the one after that. He was physically ill. That knot in his stomach, the heavy sensation on his shoulders and in his chest. The hopeless grey that seemed to cover everything that he saw, heard, or smelled. He kept waiting for the feelings to lessen but they seemed to be intensifying. Sleeping was difficult and not satisfying. He felt isolated and had lost what little confidence he had. He thought that junkies must have a similar sensation when they try to quit heroin, or alcoholics as they lay down the bottle. The relationship with Anna had infiltrated every cell of his body and whatever was fighting for control of his hopefulness and optimism and will to move forward, it seemed to be losing.

He wanted things to return to the way they had been. Not the claustrophobic parts but the easy, friendly parts. But he knew it wasn't going to happen. He was able to finally get a mildly sarcastic, "Hey," from Anna as they awkwardly left biology together. His mouth tried but couldn't form any words. She kept walking with her new friend just as Ben finally said, "Hey," to her back. He sadly turned and went the other way.

"You're coming."
"I don't feel like socializing."
"You never do, but trust me you need this."
"Will I know anyone?"
"You'll know me. And yes, you'll know several people for sure. Swimmers. And that's the point. You need to be around some other people. Widen your circle. You can't just hang out with the weirdos in your dorm. This'll be fun. Trust me."
"I happen to like weirdos."

He stayed for two hours. He and Denny had split a six-pack of Bud Light before going to the off campus apartment. They had caught a ride with JD. The place was in an area of town that Ben wasn't familiar with. It was residential and much nicer than what he was used to. It belonged to a senior but there was a mixture of ages there. He saw maybe five people that he knew, including Denny and the guy that had driven them. There was beer and big bottles of cheap rum. Some soda, chips and the ubiquitous red Solo cups.

126

For much of that time he felt like he belonged. There is an illusion of contentment, of feeling like one has friends and is wanted and valued. It doesn't seem to be a sensation that can created out of the air. It simply exists. And it can just as easily disappear. A missing invitation to a party, not enough room for another chair in the cafeteria, shifting friendships, misunderstandings, hurt feelings, and suddenly a person is alone on an island. Unable to find a way back to the mainland. Self-esteem vanishes in an instant. Loneliness isn't a big enough word for the gaping emptiness and hopelessness inside.

Something flipped inside Ben as he drank and talked. He did less talking and more drinking. He remembered helping mix a trashcan punch using Everclear and Kool-Aid. He had no idea how many cups of the potent concoction he had. Later he went into the bathroom to pee and had to hold on tightly to the wall as he tried to hit the toilet, which had become a moving target. There was a small Patrick Nagel poster above it and he thought about how tired he was of that artist. That the Duran Duran cover had ruined everything. By the time he had finished in there he was convinced he needed to get home.

He would only have three memories of what came next. One was of the Cameo song, "Word Up" playing and of everyone in the room singing and dancing wildly to it, red Solo cups in the air. It was a song that Ben wouldn't be able to listen to again without getting at least a mild headache.

Another was of a girl named Megan hugging him tightly. He couldn't remember the context. He knew it wasn't sexual. There was no expectation and it wasn't leading to anything. He just remembered how nice it was and how uncharacteristic. He wasn't a hugger by nature. Had he been telling her about Anna? It seemed likely. All he could recall was the beautiful, soft warmth of another human pressed tightly up against him, and it was a magical moment that broke through the haze of the evening.

And the last thing he could remember was walking home. The cool air on his face. The dark night punctuated by streetlights. When and why he left the apartment was lost forever as was most of the journey. But he remembered that each time a car came he would duck behind a tree in someone's yard. Or lay down flat on the ground. Or hold very still. Or take off running in another direction. It was a miracle of luck and, truthfully, his skin color that he wasn't arrested for acting crazy. But somehow he stayed basically on the correct path back to the school, stopping twice to throw up, each time in the cool suburban lawn of an unsuspecting homeowner.

Ninety minutes after leaving the party he was still several blocks from home when Denny spotted him weaving and nearly falling down as he tripped on an uneven sidewalk. There was another man slightly behind him. He was wearing a black trench coat, army boots, and a black stocking cap. The man seemed to be watching Ben, following him.

The man turned up the street and disappeared into the darkness as Denny had JD stop the car so that he could coax a cold and disoriented Ben into the backseat. He wrapped a large beach towel around his shoulders, partly to keep him warm and partly to cover the vomit on the front of his shirt.

Denny got him into the dorm and into the shower after stripping off his clothes. Ben was constantly talking but not making sense, mostly rambling about Megan and Anna and Patrick Nagel and the adventurous hike he had undertaken. After getting him fresh underwear and a t-shirt, Denny had Tim and Brian help get him up into bed where he continued talking until he suddenly began snoring loudly. It was two in the morning and he wouldn't move again for eight hours, awakening with a tremendous headache and a dry mouth.

It was Saturday afternoon before he was sufficiently awake and coherent enough to get to the cafeteria and then to the library.

"You live!" said Denny.

"That's debatable."

"You look terrible. But at least you're upright. How do you feel?"

"As bad as I look I'm sure. I owe you a thank you."

"For what?"

"For getting me home and cleaned up. Brian told me all about it."

"You don't remember?"

"Very little. I just recall walking home and getting into bed. He said you got me in and out of the shower. That's above and beyond man."

"I couldn't let you go to bed smelling like that. It was pretty bad. You still have alcohol breath by the way."

"Well, thanks."

"Hey, who was that guy you were walking with?"

"When?"

"Last night. He was kind of following two steps behind when I spotted you."

"I don't remember anyone. What did he look like? Someone from school?"

"I don't think so. He looked older although I didn't get a great look before he took off. He had an old trench coat, long hair, a stocking cap. He stood out."

"I don't remember him at all. That's weird though- he sounds like the guy I saw outside the Hi Hat. Remember? The one that was out there in the alley when I sneaked out to pee. It's a little spooky that he was following me. I wonder what he wanted."

"Who knows? You shouldn't have left though. What were you thinking?"

"I'm not sure. I guess I was just ready to go. Plus too much trashcan punch."

"Yeah, that stuff is lethal. I stayed away from it for once. You just never know. It could be watered down or it could be like 60% alcohol. It's a really bad idea but those guys aren't known for their good ideas. Did you at least talk to some people?"

"A few. But I don't think I started any great new friendships. Who's Megan by the way?"

"Megan? What did she look like?"

"I don't remember much. Kind of medium I guess. Shorter but straight brown hair. Maybe wearing red."

"That's not very helpful. Who was she with? And why are you asking?"

"I can't picture her with anyone else. Just that we were talking. I'm sure I was pouring my heart out to her. Telling her all my problems. The only clear image I have is that she hugged me. And it was the sweetest, softest, tightest hug I've ever had. It was sincere and healing and was by far the best thing that happened last night."

"So then what happened? Did you take her back to one of the bedrooms?"

"Dude, why do you have to cheapen everything? It wasn't like that at all. It was beautiful."

"I can ask around and find out. You're sure her name was Megan?"

"Pretty sure. And don't bother. It's ok. It's possible that I dreamed it. And really it doesn't matter. I think it was one of those mysterious things that can't be replicated. I really needed that connection and she gave it to me. It's amazing how much we miss being touched without even knowing it."

"Yeah, I miss being touched."

"Your mind's in the gutter again. I'm not talking about that. There is something about touching someone, or being touched. A hug, a pat, even a handshake. They all count. Again, I'm not someone who is comfortable with a lot of physical contact. No one in my family is a hugger, so it isn't something that's conscious. But it's still there."

"My family is very touchy."

"Yeah, I know, and that's a good thing. It's like those studies with babies. The ones in the orphanage that were picked up and snuggled and loved did a lot better than the ones that were left in their crib and fed there. They were emotionally and physically better off."

"Maybe you weren't lifting out of your crib enough. That would explain a lot."

"Funny. No, I think it's the opposite. It's why I'm relatively healthy and intelligent. Because I was the first child born to a lonely young mom. I'm sure I was carried everywhere."

"Lonely?"

"Yeah, my dad wasn't around much when I was little. He traveled a lot more with his job in those years. By the time my sister was born he'd been promoted to a desk job. I'm not complaining, you just asked."

"No, it's cool. Okay, so what next? Do we try to find her or not?"

"No, I think I'd rather leave it as a mystery. Kind of like your Sheila. I don't think the reality will be nearly as healing and comforting as the memory of that moment. If I happen to run into her, fine, but I'm not going to seek her out. Like I said, it's possible that I dreamed the whole thing and Megan will turn out to be my pillow."

"She is nothing like my Sheila then, who is neither a pillow nor a warm, squishy hug. But okay, we'll just see what happens for now. Hey, are we going to study or not?"

"I don't know why I bother talking to you. Seriously. Yeah, I'm ready to get started."

11

It was no surprise to Ben that the party didn't help his mood. He still felt alone. He still worried that he would run into Anna in the library or the cafeteria or on the sidewalk, the three places that both of them traveled everyday. Or used to. But he needn't have worried, he didn't see her all weekend.

On Sunday evening he made his weekly collect call to his mom. Fifteen minutes. They both watched the clock carefully. It was an expensive call and that was all they required to catch up on each other's news. He didn't tell her everything of course. And of course she didn't tell him everything either. They stayed within parameters that were unstated but understood. Discussions about weather, homework, general health and diet were fine. Much else wasn't.

"So, you think you'll have mostly A's for the quarter."

"Yeah, mostly. Calculus is tougher than I expected. There's a slight chance that I'll get it up to an A. But it's a good safe B. And everything else should be okay."

"Well, straight A's would be better but it's your first experience away from home and you're doing fine. You are doing fine right? Eating well?"

"Everything in sight."

"A mix of fruits and vegetables?"

"Yes mom."

"Hey, you know I have to ask that. Don't drink too much pop. It's bad for your teeth and will make you fat."

"I don't. Maybe once a day. Don't worry about my diet mom, I'm good."

"And what about Anna. How is she doing?"

"She's fine. Doing well."

"Is she going home for Thanksgiving? You had talked about bringing her here at one point."

"No, she's going home."

"Driving or flying? Maybe she can stop on the way to Omaha to say hi."

"No she's flying. The break isn't long enough to drive."

"I guess not. Okay, then she can visit on her way home for Christmas. The girls want to see her again."

"Okay sure mom, that's still a long ways off. We can talk about it later."

"All right, well, tell her hi for me."

"I will. It's been fifteen minutes. We'd better go."

"Oh okay, it went too fast today. You have a good week. Your sisters and dad say hi. I love you."

"I love you too mom."

He hung up the phone and sat quietly for several minutes unable to move. He couldn't tell her. Couldn't tell her that Anna was gone and that it was his fault. Couldn't tell her that he wasn't doing well, wasn't eating any fruit and in fact wasn't eating much at all. And couldn't tell her that he was lonely and sick and had drank entirely too much grain alcohol and was worried that he may have killed too many brain cells and that he didn't feel like studying anymore and didn't know when he would be all right.

He finally got up, looked through his records until he found REM's Murmur. He carefully pulled out the sleeve, removed the record by its edges, put it on the turntable, set the needle on the fourth track, lowered the plastic cover and sat on the floor cross-legged precisely between the two speakers. "Talk About the Passion" was what he needed right then. Most of the lyrics were a mystery but the emotion was just right.

He closed his eyes and emptied his mind for those minutes, swept away by Michael Stipe's voice. When it ended, his thoughts drifted during "Moral Kiosk," but when the first keyboard sounds of "Perfect Circle" began, and then the clear nostalgic words, followed by the smooth bass, his thoughts came back to what he had lost. And by the time the full band kicked in with Stipe's rising and falling chorus, Ben was crying. He was finally letting go of what he had been holding on to for so long. He sobbed and mourned and when the song was over he got up and played the same three songs again, repeating the process. And then he did it again. And again. And each time "Perfect Circle" played, he dropped his head and closed his eyes, held his legs and rocked back and forth, feeling the goose bumps rise on his arms, tears falling once again.

And when he was cried out and exhausted, he carefully put the record back in its sleeve and then in the cover, re-filing it with the other REM records. He turned off the light and climbed up onto the top bunk, curled up with his pillow and lay awake but empty until he thought he would never fall asleep again.

The Dallas Observer was Ben's window into life outside of TCU. With no money or transportation, stuck in the center of a city with only small pockets of culture that was mainly related to its history as a cowtown, Ben was thirsty for the wider world of cutting edge bands and art. Of kids that didn't send their Oxford cloth shirts to be laundered with extra starch and their Wranglers with a sharp crease down the leg. He longed to be around mohawks and shaved heads, tattoos and earrings, eyeliner and black clothing.

He found all of that and more in the Dallas Observer. Filled with articles about music and art, about local politics and personalities, it was a smaller, marginally more family friendly version of the Village Voice. Both were weekly newspapers that he read cover to cover on the day they arrived in the library. Both had irreverent cartoons and back pages filled with suggestive ads.

It was in the Dallas Observer that he first learned about the New Bohemians. He found himself looking for pictures of their singer Edie Brickell every week. He learned about her budding relationship with local club owner Jeff Liles, whose amazing hair and overall cool good looks Ben envied. They had played in Fort Worth in September but he missed them. He saw that they were to play a show at 500 Club in Deep Ellum on Tuesday. Ben really wanted to hear them but didn't know how he could get there. Nor how he would pay for it. There was just something about Edie and that band that was enticing although he'd never heard a note of their music.

He also learned about the ongoing love/hate relationship between sometimes competing and sometimes collaborating club owners Russell Hobbs and Jeff Liles. They both had music venues in Deep Ellum on Commerce Street and had started a record label together. However Liles had recently opened a competing venue one street over called Club Dada. Their relationship was like a soap opera. Or a train wreck. Lately there was a rumor that Hobbs had become a born-again Christian and was going to convert the Prophet Bar to an over 21 club that only played Christian rock. It sounded like commercial suicide that would surely destroy any reputation he had built as a scene maker.

There were times when Ben second-guessed his Texas Christian decision. If he had known a year ago what he knew now he would have probably applied to Southern Methodist. It was in Dallas and would have been a much better base for exploring the cool areas of the city. Bands like End Over End, the Buck Pets, Shallow Reign, and Three on a Hill played nearly every night somewhere in town and all seemed to be on the verge of a big national breakthrough. It was painful to read about all the shows that he was missing. He tried to imagine the sounds that they played based solely on the words of Clay McNear and other music editors for the Observer. He knew that his imagination didn't come close.

It was a tiny ad on one of the pages towards the back that listed it. Buck Pets were playing in Fort Worth. It said that Doctors Mob was opening their show this Thursday at the Hop. He knew Doctors Mob and was surprised that they were opening. The Austin band already had a record out and had been playing for several years. Buck Pets on the other hand were young. One of the kids was still in high school. But they had been getting some national attention due to A&R reps that had been hanging around Deep Ellum. Their shows were usually reviewed or at least referenced in the Dallas Observer.

Ben was so excited he couldn't sit still. He carried the paper through the library, illegally removing it from the reference section before anyone could stop him.

"They're coming to Fort Worth!" he was breathless by the time he found Denny who had been taking a break, walking around the second floor.

"What? Who's coming? Jesus? Zeppelin? Skynyrd? What's going on with you?"

"No, better. The Buck Pets. To Fort Worth. The Hop. Thursday."

"They're better than Jesus? Uh, okay. Remind me who they are?"

"An amazing band from Dallas that I've been reading about for the past three months. I'm going for sure. You should come with me."

"Have you even heard them before?"

"No, not technically. But I know that I'm going to love them. You will too. Oh, and Doctors Mob is opening. They play that song, 'There's a Way.' You know it, I've shown you before. Rob and the others from Public Bulletin know them. They're from Austin."

"Okay sure. You don't have to sell it that hard. I'd go even if they sucked. It's a bar and it's music and it's better than studying or watching TV."

"Great. It's a deal. You won't be disappointed, I promise. When they're famous and playing at huge stadiums you can say you saw them at this tiny crappy bar in Fort Worth."

"How did you know that's one of my life goals? Bragging about bands I've seen."

"Okay, point taken. I'll settle down now. I guess I'd better take this back to the reference area before I become publicly shamed over the intercom."

"Good idea. I'm going back and study some more."

"I'll be there in a minute. I've wasted too much time today. Need to get going on math."

He and Anna had still not spoken more than a word at a time for over a week. And they were in three classes together so that was quite an accomplishment. And painful. But that day Ben was walking down the library steps when she was walking up. They prepared to ignore each other once again when Anna stubbed her toe, missed a step and almost fell down. Ben reflexively reached out to catch her and she grabbed his arm to steady herself.

"Thanks. How embarrassing. You saved me."

"No problem. Good timing huh?"

Neither moved. They looked at each other then looked away, both trying to decide whether to say more. Finally Ben spoke first.

"I'm really sorry Anna. What a mess. I have no idea what I'm doing. Why I left that morning…"

"Ben, you don't have to say anything else. You made a decision. You don't have to explain. It'll just make it worse… You hurt me Ben."

A boy walked down the stairs at that point, causing the two to stop talking, awkwardly looking around until he passed.

"This isn't the best place to talk," Ben said. "Can we please go sit down somewhere?"

"No. I don't want to do that. I can't."

"Please."

"No, I need to study."

"Okay, but how about later? We can meet somewhere. Somewhere neutral. The cafeteria. Or the snack bar."

"No. I just can't Ben. I don't have anything to say. Nothing you can tell me is going to make it any better. Whether it's another girl or you're just tired of me or you're in love with Denny. Whatever. It doesn't matter and I just want to move on at this point."

"It isn't another girl or Denny, nor was I tired of you. Maybe you're right, it's impossible to explain. I like you so much, Anna. You've been my best friend and it hurts more than I would have ever imagined being away from you. I miss you Nat. We have to figure out a way to talk, to still be around each other."

She stopped him there. "No, Ben, we don't. I'm sorry, but you gave up all of that. You threw it away for reasons that you can't or won't explain. I'm not going to sit and talk about it. We can't be friends. It just isn't possible. I'm sorry."

Repositioning her backpack and books she continued up the stairs, leaving Ben standing and looking up as she went around the corner. He tried to remember what she was like. How they had been so close, laughing and finishing each other's thoughts less than two weeks ago. She seemed like a stranger. Someone that he had known in the distant past. The auras that were enmeshed, the electron clouds and dark energy that surrounded them had separated. He once again felt a sickness in the pit of his stomach. An ache of loneliness that he didn't know how to fix.

He finally continued down the stairs to take the Observer back to the reference area. By the time he returned to the table Denny had left with all of his things. There was a note that said, "Catch you later."

Ben sat down and began to read his math notes, reworking some of the problems as he wondered where his friend had gone.

It was early evening by the time he had finished studying and he went to the cafeteria alone. Denny hadn't come back to the library and wasn't in their usual spot at dinner. Ben ate and returned to the dorm. Tim and Brian were studying there so he went back to the common room.

There were some guys watching MacGyver so he joined them. The episode was kind of confusing. Something about a botanist and illegal orchids in Central America. Of course, Mac stayed one step ahead of everyone and saves the day. Later they watched Monday Night Football, something that Ben would never have done at home. But he was bored and lonely and felt comfort in watching the game with other people. The LA Rams ended up beating the Bears. By then it was late and Ben said good night to the other guys and went to bed.

Thursday couldn't come fast enough for Ben. Boring and mildly painful days of studying, sleeping, watching television and trying to avoid Anna, the only thing that kept him going was the thought of going to the Hop. So when that night finally arrived he and Denny were among the first people there. The Hop was small. It held perhaps one hundred people if most of the tables were removed. Hop had originally stood for "house of pizza" and Ben thought they probably did still serve pizza but he had neither the money nor the interest in finding out.

He and Denny had already eaten at the cafeteria. Then Denny had shared a contraband six-pack of Bud that a senior swimmer had smuggled to him, the floor's RA looking the other way. They drank it in Milton Daniel as they listened to the Dead Milkmen, singing along to "Filet of Sole" and "Bitchin Camaro" and watching the Cosby Show and Family Ties with the sound turned off. By the time Cheers came on, the beer was gone and they were too antsy to sit anymore.

They walked down University and then to Berry. The Hop had two vans out front, which added to Ben's excitement. Something about traveling around the country, or at least north Texas, in a van, filled with musical equipment, beer and junk food was so romantic. He tried to decide which was the Doctors Mob van and which was Buck Pets' when he saw Steve Collier come out of the one in front. Steve was the singer and songwriter for Doctors Mob. They had a reputation for being kind of a mess. Like early Replacements shows, their motto was to either show up drunk, show up late, or not show up at all.

Ben assumed that the band had chosen the first option as Steve was acting like he had already begun drinking.

It was a great show. They were sloppy and wild and drunk and loud and perfect. Don Lamb with his rock star good looks and incredible guitar solos. Steve with hit and miss vocals that somehow worked due to his experience and comfort on stage. They played all the songs that Ben knew from his cassette. The Hop was nearly full, and even though it was calm around the edges, the guys next to the stage were banging their heads, pumping their fists, and mouthing along with the words. It was something Ben had been dreaming of doing for a long time. Seeing Doctors Mob live, in his own town. It was hard to believe that he was even more excited about the next band.

The stage was too small and probably the payout too low to switch out the drum kit so it didn't take long to get ready for the Buck Pets. They let the anticipation build though. It was nearly an hour before the lights dimmed and they came onstage. They wore faded black jeans and work pants with thin dark t-shirts. They had the appearance of, and carried themselves like seasoned performers, but close up they still looked like kids.

The guitarists plugged in and Tony sat at the drums, adjusting the stool, the cymbals and the toms, preferring everything higher than the previous drummer. Chris stood on the right, his loose black shirt hanging on a thin frame, his thick one-length hair long and dirty blond, black Les Paul slung low, excessively long strings emanating from the peg heads. Andy was in the middle with his lead singer aura and Stratocaster. Chuck, the bassist, was on the left. There was barely room for all of them but they made it work in the same way that Doctors Mob had before.

Chris faced the speakers and tuned his guitar, adjusting dials on the speakers and on the floor monitors and effects pedals. He looked over at Tony and then like a jet engine they took off. It was a wall of sound that was deafening and yet achingly beautiful.

By the middle of the first song Ben had made his way over to the right side of the stage so he could watch Chris Savage. His guitar playing was mesmerizing. Ben couldn't tell if he was shy or stoned or oblivious or a perfectionist or simply lost in the music, but Chris was like no performer he had ever seen before. He would occasionally turn to face the audience, sometimes to sing a few notes with Andy or to play a brief solo. When the music sped up he would bang his head, hair covering his face, and shoulders hunched. But for most of the song, and really for most of the show, he had his back to the crowd. His right hand was moving blindingly fast, all downstrokes, hunched over with the guitar low, right over his thighs. At times he would drop to his knees, continuing to face the speakers. Sometimes leaning forward, other times back, he rarely stopped playing.

Chris watched and even directed Tony at times and then would turn to face Andy, sideways to the crowd as they played simultaneously. Even though he wasn't the lead singer it became apparent that he was in charge in his own quiet yet manic way.

Song after song, the guitar sounded like a chainsaw. Ben had never heard the tunes before so didn't know their names but they immediately embedded themselves into his heart. He lost track of time and of Denny, who had positioned himself somewhere towards the back of the room.

They played for over an hour, sounding like a road-tested band rather than one made up of high school kids and recent graduates. The last song was one that would ring in his ears for days. It was loud and heavy and heartbreaking and tender and filled with all the wonderful things of life. Andy sang, "This is

143

just a note… to say… I'm thinking of you," as the bass thumped low like a dying heart. The feedback from Chris's guitar overtook the primary sound as he sat on his knees, guitar pushed up against the speaker. It sounded like a motor revving, mixed with high pitched squeals.

The effect of the noise with the cheap white spotlights, the air filled with cigarette and sweet clove smoke seemed to continue long after the band had left the stage. Ben sat on it exhausted and smiling, nearly laughing as Denny came over shaking his head.

"Dude, did you like that?"

"That was the best thing I've ever heard. It was the sound of Heaven breaking into our reality."

"Uh, okay. I thought the bass was a little loud. Not to mention, what's up with that guitarist? Did he really think we wanted to look at his saggy ass all night?"

"He was amazing! The sounds that he was able to make come on that guitar! And he's like our age! What have I been doing with my life? I'm such a loser compared to him."

"Well, it's true that you're a loser, but not compared to him. He reminds me of Jackson Pollack or something. Like, really? I could make a sound like that if I had the right pedals."

"No way. I've never heard a sound like that. And everyone has those pedals. Or could get them. Nope, he's a genius. I've read that they're close to signing with someone. I just want to have those songs and be able to listen to them every day. In the meantime, we need to find out when they play again and try to catch them."

"Maybe so. For now we should get going. I've got a couple more beers back in the dorm if you want one."

"I really should get to bed. We have classes tomorrow. But okay, my ears are ringing too much to sleep right now anyway."

They walked home in the cool night. Sweat starting to stick as they made it to campus and over to the sports dorm. Most people were asleep but Denny's roommate was still up watching some black and white western.

"Hey Denny, some guy came by looking for you. Said you had something for him."

"Really? When was that?"

"Maybe two hours ago. Before Letterman started."

"What did he say?"

"Nothing. Said he'd be back sometime."

"Do you know who it was? Did he leave his name or anything?"

"Nope. Just poked his head in and then left."

"Okay, thanks."

Denny pulled two of the four remaining beers from the small refrigerator and handed one to Ben.

"Oh, I borrowed two of those."

"I see that. It's okay. What're we watching?"

"Stagecoach. With John Wayne. It's actually really good. I hadn't seen it before. Directed by John Ford."

"I've seen parts of it. I love the movies from that era. Especially the good ones like this. The way they talk. They had class back then, you know? It's all done so well, so thoughtfully. Mind if we sit with you and watch?"

"Dude, we're roommates. You can do what you want. Just don't talk when it's on. How was the show by the way?"

"Incredible," said Ben. "I'm still buzzing from it."

"Who was it again?"

"The Buck Pets. From Dallas."

"Stupid name. What's it even mean?"

"No idea. But their music makes up it."

"Do they play anything I've heard?"

"No. They have a demo out but I haven't heard it. Hopefully they'll print more. I'd give my sister for one."

"Hey, how old's your sister? Maybe we can work something out."

"Not likely. And she's only fourteen by the way. A tad young."

"Shoot, well okay. Hey, it's on, remember our agreement."

While they were talking, Denny had been rummaging around in his closet. Looking under a pile of clothes, behind a stack of books and then into a small container with a padlock on it. He opened it, moved some things around in it then put everything back.

"What's up? Everything okay?" asked Ben.

"Yeah, everything's great, why?"

"You seemed a little shook up when he told you about that guy. Who was it?"

"I don't know. No one."

"Okay, you don't have to tell me."

"Hey girls, remember our deal? No talking during the movie."

"Whoops, sorry chief. Won't happen again."

They lounged on the beds and on the chairs and watched the tale unfold. Ringo Kid fell for a prostitute as they made their way across Apache country. It was suspenseful, well-paced and funny. The three boys sipped their beer and soon forgot about what was going on around them. It was nearly two before Ben finally stumbled home, exhausted, his head filled with John Wayne and ringing guitars.

12

Ben made it through Friday. Luckily it was a day that he didn't have to pay close attention to anything. One in which he was able to float. No tests, nothing too heavy in class, he managed to stay awake and avoid flying erasers.

He didn't notice when Anna came up alongside as he walked towards the cafeteria.

"Hey Ben, how's it going?"

He looked over, surprised to see her there.

"Are you all right? You seem kind of out of it today."

"Sorry, I'm fine. You caught me off guard. Daydreaming. I had a late night…"

"That's what Denny said."

"You talked to Denny?"

"Yeah, sure. He said you all saw a good show. That you liked it more than he did."

"It was amazing. The Buck Pets."

"Oh, you finally got to see them! That's great. So, everything you dreamed of?"

"Yeah. And more. Really. Ugh. I should have told you about it. You would've loved them. They were incredible. Loud and beautiful. And then we stayed up watching some John Wayne movie. That was a waste. Anyway, I'm fine. Just tired."

"Okay good."

"Hey, do you want to get lunch?"

"Oh, I'm sorry. I can't. I'm meeting someone at the snack bar."

Ben's heart sank and that old familiar tightness above his pancreas returned.

"A guy?"

"Ben, we shouldn't talk about this. Let's keep it light."

"Sure, you're right. I'm sorry. It's none of my business…"

He really didn't want to talk about it. Really didn't want to think about it, picture it, or hear about it. The whole idea of Anna with another person made him nauseated and angry and tearful and so very regretful. And yet he couldn't just walk away. It was like he couldn't control his mouth.

"I mean it's really not, but can I ask who it is? Do I know him? I mean did you know…?"

He stopped again as she shook her head.

"No Ben, we shouldn't do this. It's too soon."

"Too soon? Too soon for what? It's too soon to talk about us? How can that be? It obviously isn't too soon to move on."

"Ben, stop. I'm not having this conversation with you. It's none of your business what I do and who I do it with. You did this. You broke up with me, remember? And you even had a chance to change your mind. To at least try to fix things. And you chose not to. So, now I need you to let me live my life. To be able to move on. I'm not going to sit around and mope and miss out on my college experience. I gave you everything, Ben. My whole heart. And we had a good time. And I'm thankful for those times. But now we both need to heal and remember that we are eighteen and have our whole lives ahead of us. I really hope that we can become friends again. You're a great guy. And I'll always love you. But for now, I think it's best that we stay away from each other."

Ben was standing and listening. Trying to understand what she was saying. Other kids were walking by behind and in front of them. Some looked at them as they passed. One junior swimmer gave him a little half wave and a grin, like he'd been there before.

When she was finished speaking some of the heaviness had lifted. Hearing it laid out that way was helpful. Knowing where Anna stood and being reminded of her caring ways helped. She looked like a stranger to him now. A pleasant, somewhat emotional, beautiful stranger.

"You're absolutely right. I completely overstepped. I'm sorry. I want to be friends too. I'm just really lonely right now. Obviously it's self-induced but that probably makes it worse."

"Well, me too. Love is hard. I don't think it's meant to be easy. Hey, I need to get going. But hang in there, Ben. We're going to be all right in the long run you know? It'll be a win-win. It has to be."

"Yeah, I know. I mean I hope so. Okay, see you around."

Anna went down the stairs towards the snack bar and Ben went to the cafeteria, her mind shifted to her lunch date while his continued to dwell on what he had lost. He knew that what she said was right, they had to move on. And he did in fact feel a little less nausea and crushing sadness so maybe his heart was beginning to heal.

He knew this was going to be a bit of a boring weekend. He'd spent money at the show the night prior and Denny had said he had some things going on and wouldn't be around. So with no money and no friends he planned to walk down to the record shop and take a look around at the new releases as his main source of entertainment. And rather than putting it off until Saturday, he decided to go ahead and do it right then.

After dropping his books in his dorm and trying to pry Brian away from his nap to come along, he left in the direction of University and then down to Berry.

The big Sound Warehouse was there. It had a huge amount of music and although much of it was mainstream major label stuff that Ben wasn't interested in, they had plenty of alternative and small labels as well. He liked the idea of that smaller CD store but they were too expensive and didn't have nearly the selection. The CDs that were on sale at Sound Warehouse were at least five dollars cheaper than the other place. He wasn't looking for anything in particular. Mainly he was killing time and rewarding himself for another week completed without a major catastrophe.

Ben had heard about a big record store in Dallas called Bill's. They mainly sold used but had some new as well. It was supposedly as big as this place but so much more tightly packed with rare and interesting records from all genres. One of the swimmers had said that they had everything he could imagine. Tiny labels, limited editions, demos, everything.

That sounded like a place where Ben could lose himself for years, but he had no way of getting there. Not yet. He would have to work on his friend circle over the next month or two. Another reason that he needed to branch out some. Not simply for his mental health but for transportation. He knew that sounded a little cold but it was true. He was stuck within a small perimeter. Maybe a mile or so in radius. There may have been some places two miles away that were worth walking to but he wasn't sure and he wasn't going to walk four-miles round-trip to find out.

He cut through the parking lot of the bank next door, avoided a car that was backing out of a spot in the music store's parking lot, and entered the store. It wasn't busy and he didn't immediately recognize anyone there. The floor manager was in the middle, standing on a small elevated platform sorting some cassette holders. He nodded at Ben as he walked in.

He looked at the top twenty records of the week display. Nothing good there. And a lot of bad. The number one record was Boston's Third Stage. Yes the song "Amanda" was pretty catchy, but that whole genre of heavily produced, studio wankery was something that Ben worked hard to avoid. It felt like a lifetime ago that he had listened to the first album nonstop at swim meets under the big tent. All of the kids stayed under the covering, avoiding the hot sun, playing cards and eating Jello straight out of the box, or trying to get a turn playing with someone's Mattel Electronic Football game.

Only a couple of the luckiest kids had that game which consisted of staring at a small red light and trying to avoid the dimmer small red lights while staving off thumb cramps and eyestrain. It was great fun and way too expensive for Ben's family. So he never became an expert. It was hard to believe that only a few years later he would be playing Punch-Out at a pizza place with Denny, the amazing graphics making the fighting feel almost real. Or the incredibly detailed Zelda game he had watched some nerdy guys play on their Nintendo back at the dorm. Ben was more of a pinball guy himself. He liked the excitement and reality of metal balls being influenced by gravity and magnets and skill.

He shook himself out of his daydream and saw that the rest of the top twenty was equally lame. Bon Jovi, Huey Lewis, Lionel Richie... Worst of all was that slab of war propaganda, Top Gun. He couldn't look at the cover without feeling a little nauseated. The way the movie glorified the military, glossing over the death, destruction and pain. Forgetting that the US was involved in so many questionable conflicts throughout the world, mostly to protect the interests of the rich and powerful. It had nothing to do with freedom and everything to do with profits and power. He had no desire to see the movie nor to hear Berlin's sell-out song one more time.

There was nothing interesting in the top twenty so he moved on to the new release section. Kim Wilde, Elton John, The Pretenders, Roxette. Nothing caught his eye. He had heard the song from the Big Audio Dynamite record, an offshoot of the disbanded Clash, it was pretty good but he wasn't convinced he needed to buy the record yet. Same with the Housemartins. He had heard great things about them but wasn't prepared to get the record.

The new Kate Bush was out. The Whole Story was a compilation and had "Running Up That Hill," which he loved. It was haunting and hypnotic and mysterious. His cousin Debbie liked Kate Bush. He took a copy of it to carry around as he continued to look. It wasn't what he had in mind when he walked in there but that was part of the fun of record shopping. And he had heard people talk about her first single, "Wuthering Heights" and wanted to hear it.

He flipped through every single record in the store, avoiding the country section. He had seen most of the covers many times and not many seemed interesting today. After the initial desire to buy them passed, after he had looked at the cover, read the back, thought about it, and calculated the cost multiple times, it became increasingly unlikely that he would buy a particular album.

When he got to the S's he continued to flip through quickly and when he saw the Soul Asylum records he paused to look at each one. He already had their first record and had looked at the next one many times. "Made to be Broken" had come out the previous year and it wasn't something he had heard on the radio or seen on MTV. But he had recently seen a mention of them in the Village Voice, something about their upcoming new record. And the coolness of Dave Pirner and the fact that the band was from Minneapolis like the Replacements and Hüsker Dü- it all combined to feel like destiny.

He picked up the record, the weird egg picture covering over Kate Bush's face and he looked up to stretch his neck and to think a minute about whether he could afford to buy two records.

Ben was still contemplating his next move, living in a safe and comfortable microcosm of the moment in which determining whether to buy a calming, popular-in-England Kate Bush album or a more aggressive and yet oddly sensitive Soul Asylum record occupied ninety percent of his consciousness, when he felt his world shift. He didn't see her at first but somehow sensed that he was being watched. It's one of the proofs that there is a lot more going on between people than we are able to put into words that we can feel it when someone is looking at us. They can be standing directly behind with absolutely no chance that we've seen them in our peripheral vision and we can still feel it. We are connected and we become connected in ways that transcend the five senses.

So Ben looked to the left, which was in the direction of the entrance. He could see the manager busy in his self-important way in the center of the store. He could see couples and lonely young guys thumbing through records in the "G" and "L" sections. A single older guy looking at the jazz records.

And then he saw her.

She was no longer looking at him but rather listening to her friend. Presumably the friend was expounding on the merits of Madonna based on the fact that she was holding up the True Blue CD box, waving it around and pointing at something on the back cover. But then she sneaked another look. Or maybe he just imagined that it was a sneak. She may have simply been taking a break from her friend's intense gaze.

Regardless, she and Ben locked eyes for perhaps one second, but in that second he felt a jolt. His life would forevermore be divided into two distinct divisions- before and after that look. Even from across a row of records and twenty feet away, in that moment, he could see the deep kindness and the nearly immortal understanding in her eyes. Her eyes searched, found his, and then she smiled tentatively yet warmly. He tried to return the expression but it all happened too fast.

Her friend dropped the Madonna CD back into its place, turned and headed to the front of the store. The girl followed and finally, just as she reached the exit she looked back from the door. Once again she and Ben found each other, but by then they were too far away and he couldn't make out her expression.

And then suddenly she was gone.

13

"Wait, slow down, I'm still catching up. You saw your destiny and your whole life has changed? And you know this because of a glance across a stack of records?"

Ben had gone straight to Denny's dorm after the Sound Warehouse Revelation, as he had already begun to call it. He still had the bag of records in his hand. After the girl left he wasn't able to think clearly. He had walked right up to the door with the albums and the cashier had called him back. He asked if he really thought he could just take them without paying. Too embarrassed to put them back, he bought both then left hastily. Now he was trying to get Denny to understand the importance of what had just happened.

"And aren't you the one that became obsessed for weeks over a tiny inconsequential interaction with Sheila-from-the-pub?"

"I like how you've turned possibly the most important moment of the semester into a German sounding contraction."

"I know. Pretty cool huh? Like *torschlusspanik*. Do you know that one?"

"Nope. My German is a little lacking on actual words."

"It's a great word," Ben said. "It means closing-gate panic. Like when we worry that time's running out. That an opportunity is passing us by. It's similar to what I'm talking about. I saw her and now I feel that things have changed. That I need to find her and see if it was real or if I'm over-reading the situation."

"You think?"

"I guess it's possible."

"Hey, I do remember a relevant German word," Said Denny

"Yeah, what is it?"

"*Backpfeifengesicht.*"

"You just made that one up."

"No, seriously. It's real. It literally means slap-face. It's very appropriate right now. Because that's what you need. A slap-face. Or a cold shower."

"No, I need to find her. Because *torschlusspanik*."

"Okay I'm done."

"It was the weirdest thing. I had just had a surprisingly helpful yet painful talk with Anna, so it was kind of a closure. Or at least the beginning of some kind of healing. I felt lighter and freer than I had in quite a while. I was just minding my own business, flipping through records when I could feel something. A change. It's hard to explain."

"You felt someone looking at you. We've all felt that."

"It was more than that. It was like a sense of peace came over me. Somehow I knew that everything was going to be okay. I looked up and saw her. That look we shared. It's not something I'll forget."

"So she's really hot then?"

"No… I mean yes. I mean, it doesn't matter but yes, quite attractive. But that wasn't it. I don't think you're listening."

"I'm trying, but you're speaking in German again."

"Ha. Okay, maybe you're right. But there was just something about her. About the way we looked at each other. Like there were decades or maybe even centuries of history between us. That we had shared everything and still had eternity to share everything else. If I believed in reincarnation I would be certain that we knew each other in a past life. Can you understand what I'm saying at all?"

"No, not really. I guess I've never felt anything like that before. Your description really makes my Sheila fixation feel like a bad case of beer goggles. There has to be a German word for that by the way. I have this sudden urge to learn German. Don't you?"

"Sure. Let's do that in addition to all the classes we're already taking and worrying about getting into med school and now searching for my needle in the haystack soul mate. You know, I just assume that she goes to TCU. But she may not. Neither of them was wearing purple, come to think of it. Nor sorority clothes or anything else that would give me a clue as to where they're from. They could be visiting from some other school, or might just live in the area…"

"Or from Paschal High."

"Hmmm. Maybe. Although I don't think so. I guess I hadn't thought of that. I hope not, but you know, we'll cross that bridge when we come to it."

"Okay, are we about finished here? I'm hungry. Do you want to go eat?"

"Sure. Although eating seems unimportant right now."

"Ugh. Come on. Oh, and I'm thinking about going to a party tonight. Another swimmer is having one. You probably don't know him but you'll know other people there."

"I think I've had enough swimmer parties for a while."

"You don't have to drink the trashcan punch."

"I don't trust myself."

They picked up trays and chose their food and ate and talked and planned. Ben couldn't help scanning the room periodically. The nauseated despair in his stomach had changed in an instant to an excited impatient hopefulness. He didn't see her and when they finished eating, he and Denny went their separate ways.

"Okay, if you change your mind, give me a call."

"I will. What time are you leaving?"

"Probably eight."

"I'll let you know."

Ben didn't go to the party but heard later that it was a good thing he skipped it. It was another wild one. More trashcan punch with cherry Kool-Aid this time instead of lemonade flavored Crystal Light. And some of it spilled on the carpet. It was a rental and was going to cost a lot more money than college students typically have to clean or replace. There was some controversy about how the punch had spilled so Ben was glad he wasn't around.

Texas Christian was much more Texas than Christian but there was still some religious feeling about it. One religion class was required in order to graduate, but Ben planned to put that off for a year or so.

At home he had attended church his whole life. He had been the president of the youth group, had sung in the youth choir and had been going to Sunday school for years. His church was Protestant and mainline denominational and fairly liberal as far as those things went. He hadn't been forced to memorize scripture or recite creeds or make an abstinence pledge. He felt pretty good about religion and church. It certainly hadn't damaged him in the way that it seemed to have Denny and a few other people that he had met. There were a couple slightly hypocritical religious zealots on the swim team but for the most part, God and spirituality weren't discussed by people he knew.

Even he and Anna had a silent agreement to not mention religion when they were dating.

And he had started to miss it.

There was a certain unexplainable comfort in getting up early on a Sunday, putting on clean-ish clothes, and going to a Sunday School class with church friends. And then resting and sleeping during a peaceful, nonthreatening church service, standing to sing familiar hymns, doodling during the sermon, taking the tiny tic-tac shaped bread thing and washing it down with a micro-shot of grape juice that had been carefully passed down the row, everyone remaining firmly in their seats. And then when the last hymn sounded and the pastor had given the benediction from the back of the sanctuary, everyone filing out, Ben's family usually leaving through the side entrance which was faster because the main pastor was at the center exit, even though they still had to shake the assistant pastor's hand. And then they were finally free and into the fresh air and riding to Denny's or Tippin's or maybe Kentucky Fried Chicken for lunch before getting home about one thirty.

It was something he had done for so long that after a while he had begun to miss it. Maybe it was the routine and the feeling of belonging with the youth group, but on Saturday night he decided he was going to go to church the next day.

University Christian Church had over four thousand members and was numerically the largest "Christian Church (Disciples of Christ)" (the denomination's extremely cumbersome name) in the world. The head of the denomination, William Tucker, was also the Chancellor of TCU. He was forward-thinking and open-minded. The previous year's General Assembly in Des Moines had tackled such topics as the role of women in the leadership of the church, acid rain, sanctuary for Central American refugees, and liberation theology. This was not a repressive, regressive, exclusive environment.

There were probably other Disciples churches in Fort Worth, possibly even within walking distance, but Ben hadn't heard of any. And with University Christian conveniently located on the corner of campus, there was really no other choice. At the time, the senior pastor at University Christian was Reverend Albert Pennybacker. A native of Tennessee, he had recently arrived to take over the reigns.

Ben didn't know any other Disciples at school. His few friends were Catholic and Methodist, so he hadn't talked to anyone that had been to the church before. But the sign outside listed the worship times and he decided to check it out that morning.

Neither Tim nor Brian were interested, so at ten forty-five he walked in the huge front entrance by himself, took a program from the elderly usher and sat in one of the cushioned bottomed, hard backed pews. He sat about halfway up on the left side of the sanctuary on the outside of the row.

About two-thirds of the seats were taken by the time the first hymn began. The beautiful organ and the full choir created a warm feeling deep inside Ben's heart. And as the music continued, and then the welcome remarks were made, and then he shook hands with those standing around him, something inside of him began to thaw. He could feel himself relaxing into his seat, becoming more mindful of what was happening around him.

He took out one of those little golf pencils that was stuck in the back of the pew and took some notes as the sermon began. It was based on Luke 16:19-31, the story of Lazarus at the gate. It was a parable that Ben had heard before but not in this way.

Lazarus is the only named person in any of Jesus' parables which certainly makes him important. In the story he is a poor beggar who waited outside the gate of a rich ruler who dressed in fine linens and feasted splendidly every day. Lazarus dreamed of scraps from the table but he received none. He eventually died and was carried to Sara and Abraham in heaven by angels, while the rich man died and was simply buried. He later ended up in Hades where he could see Lazarus but was separated by an unbridgeable gap.

He was so hot and thirsty there and asked Sara and Abraham to send Lazarus down with some water. It was interesting that the ruler went straight to the top and didn't ask Lazarus himself for help. But the couple said no, that he had enjoyed the best of everything during his life and now it was Lazarus' turn for some peace and love and pampering.

It was a common theme in Christianity and probably in most religions, Ben thought. Pie in the sky by and by. In the end things will work out. The rich and evil will take a fall and the poor will finally get their share. It was comforting or frightening, depending upon which side of the equation one was on.

It was the kind of thing that Ben had heard a million times. It was all through the Old Testament and even some of the New.

And frankly it didn't affect him much as he sat there doodling, trying to stay awake as Dr. Pennybacker continued his message.

Ben took out the pew Bible to read the passage again and this time he saw something different. Verse twenty-seven read, *"The rich person said, "I beg you, then, to send Lazarus to my own house where I have five siblings. Let Lazarus be a warning to them, so they may not end in this place of torment."*

Five siblings? He had read this passage before but that image had never struck him like this. The rich man lived in a huge gated estate with five siblings? He had always pictured Lazarus going from place to place, warning the brothers, but this actually said they all lived together. In community as a family. That meant that there were sisters-in-law, nieces and nephews, possibly even grandchildren. And now that he thought of it, why not aunts, uncles, cousins?

This was a huge estate, filled with his extended family. The parable said it was his place. Ben's image of the man continued to shift. He was rich but shared with his extended family. He wasn't a miser or a loner. He was big and outgoing and loved the beautiful things of life, which he and his family enjoyed to the fullest. The best food, drink, musical entertainment, clothing, schools, lessons, everything.

The problem was that he didn't see Lazarus at his gate. And Sara and Abraham didn't think it would help his brothers to see Lazarus. For apparently they had all read and heard the scriptures. They knew what Moses and the prophets had said. And yet they still didn't see. So, even experiencing a poor, outcast man of lower birth resurrected from the dead wouldn't change their hearts.

They still couldn't see that Lazarus was their sixth brother.

He had a name and was loved by the prophets. In the story he was resting and comfortable and well fed and finally at peace after his death. What was the point of all of this? And why had it struck Ben this morning?

The pastor was wrapping up his sermon, telling people to be good and to care for the poor. But, this parable went much deeper than that. It wasn't saying to merely notice the poor and throw them some scraps. It also wasn't telling the poor that they shouldn't worry because when they die they'll go to heaven and things will be much better then.

It was hard to know for sure as this was one of the parables that Jesus just kind of lays out there with no explanation. But Ben felt like he was saying that Lazarus was a brother. That the rich man had left his own brother, a fellow human, loved by God in every way, as much as every relative in his extended family, left him out in the elements malnourished with festering sores, likely leprosy, eventually to die a painful lonely death.

Understanding the story in this way broke down walls. It tore down the gates of palatial estates. It eliminated political barriers and cultural stigma.

Ben looked around at the congregation. There were a lot of people that looked like him in there. Very pleasant, but the same socioeconomic strata, white... they could be his relatives. What about the African Americans on campus? Or Hispanic or international students? They were obviously part of his family as well. Young, middle-class, highly educated. It was less clear that people outside of his own experience were part of the family. Poor rural Africans or Native Americans- did he consider them sisters and brothers, welcome to eat at his table? Or were they outside of his gates, forgotten and festering and dying?

And what about the homeless?

He suddenly remembered that guy. The one outside the Zeitgiest show who also had been nearby on his long walk home from the party on the other side of town, the man with the long tattered black coat and the unwashed and uncut hair. Ben examined his conscience and discovered that despite his best intentions he separated himself from that man in his mind. He was in a different category, one that included people that were homeless, mentally ill, alcoholic, drug addicted, and felons. He had left him outside the gate, forgotten, marginalized and ignored.

The truth was that the reason that the holocaust could occur, that slavery could continue for hundreds of years, that murder and domestic abuse and the entire sex trade could occur, that war itself could happen was that we envision other humans as less than. Less than us, less than human.

But the thing is, God didn't make any different categories of people. No one is less than. Not Lazarus, not the people in the favelas of Brazil or in the huge Bombay slum Dharavi or in the most violent neighborhoods in Detroit. And not the homeless man moving from place to place somewhere in Fort Worth.

Everyone is the same and is loved and the parable reminded Ben that we have more than five brothers. In fact, we are all sisters and brothers and all are included. The table must be extended and people can squeeze a little tighter and perhaps do with less. Because leaving someone outside the gate only leads to death. Death for the poor and hungry, and a slow spiritual death for the selfish, well-fed, and well-housed.

They were singing now and an offering plate came his way. He dropped in the five dollars that he had remembered to bring at the last minute as it went by. As the final verse ended and they all stood to sing the doxology, Ben was still lost in his thoughts about Lazarus and the poor throughout the world. The local homeless guy personalized the story for him and as everyone sat to prepare for communion he continued to think about what he should do.

He didn't know anything about the man. Not where he lived. Not his name. But he had crossed Ben's path twice and now it felt like an entire sermon was given just for the two of them. He was going to have to do something about this. He didn't know what yet but he felt energized and more alive than he had been in a long time.

Last night the look from the beautiful girl at Sound Warehouse. And now this epiphany. He didn't know what the universe was trying to tell him. His first thought was to tell Denny, but then he remembered how he had perseverated about the record store girl and didn't want to drop this on him also.

It was Sunday, so maybe his mom. But no, fifteen minutes wasn't enough to fully explain this and they really didn't have that kind of relationship. Anna was out of the question. Maybe Tim or Brian. Or even Brad, the RA. He was supposed to be wise right? Ben felt open and expansive and wanted to share but finally decided he would have to do it in less direct ways. With his life's example.

He took communion and they sang the last hymn, then he went up the middle aisle to shake hands with Dr. Pennybacker. The pastor seemed genuinely pleased to meet Ben and invited him to check out some of the activities going on at the church.

Ben felt light and free as he exited the big doors and stepped out into the crisp autumn air.

14

Something had begun to happen as the semester went on. People began to drop out of pre-med. Quite a few had dropped classes following the first two rounds of tests. And others, like Anna and Denny, had begun to spiritually distance themselves from the idea of becoming a doctor or dentist. They knew that if their first semester science classes weren't going well that it was unlikely that they would make it all the way through.

Of course that was one of the purposes of the freshman classes. To weed people out. That's why the entry-level classes were so huge and held in auditoriums. By sophomore year they would revert to regular sized classes.

Ben had heard that Anna's last biology test had gone poorly and he felt bad about that but knew that she was so smart and had a world of options in front of her. As much as she wanted to follow in the footsteps of her father, he knew that her dad would understand and still love his only girl.

Denny also was just kind of bumping along the bottom range of test scores. He talked less about being a dentist and more about football and swimming. He still studied with Ben but not for as long. And often his books just sat on the table for hours while he was wandering around campus or hanging out somewhere else.

And a new group began to form around Ben somewhat organically. Or maybe he infiltrated their group. Either way, a new table had opened up on the second floor of the library and Ben had been spending more time there with three new friends.

Steve was a blond son of a Texas oilman from San Antonio. He drove a new navy blue Jeep that had never had the top on, and had more money at his fingertips that Ben could even begin to fathom. His friend Marti was also from San Antonio. Same high school. She also was blond and outgoing and beautiful. Her 1970's Mercedes was a red convertible. Both of them were intelligent and funny and kind and Ben felt cool when he was around them, even though he didn't logically fit in. That was one of the great things about college- the social rules from middle school and high school didn't always apply.

Silky was from Fort Worth and wasn't rich nor did he have a German luxury car, but what he lacked in liquid funds he made up for in other ways. In addition to doing well in the pre-med classes he could also draw. The doodles that he effortlessly produced while a teacher lectured or while he took a break from Biology or Chemistry were unbelievable. He had a way of drawing cartoonish caricatures of teachers and friends that was genius.

He drew for the school paper. He wasn't the lead cartoonist. That was a tough gig that required many late nights and tight deadlines. But Silky did an occasional special cartoon. And it was always clever and insightful.

The four had begun sharing notes and talking after class and pretty soon they were studying together most days. Sometimes Marti's boyfriend would come by but he seemed to have much less homework as a business major.

So with a new community forming, Ben's mood began to lift. He found himself noticing the nice fall weather and not dreading going to class for fear of running into Anna. He became less dependent on Denny. His own confidence grew which made him a lot more fun to be around.

On Tuesday Steve asked if everyone wanted to go to Angelo's for barbecue. Ben's first thought was that he didn't have any money. His second was what's Angelo's?

"What's Angelo's? It's only the best barbecue in a town that's known for its barbecue."

"Really? I haven't had good barbecue since I got here. Of course all I've had is the cafeteria's poor excuse for brisket. Angelo's is good huh?"

"The best."

"You know I'm from Kansas City right? I'm a pretty hard critic. We have Gates and Bryant's."

"I've never been to Kansas City but I've heard they have some good places up there. I can't guarantee that Angelo's will beat them but it's good. Come check it out with us."

"Okay, I'll come along. I have to tell you that I don't have any money though. I can go to the ATM if we have time."

"Nah, it's my treat. Let's go have some fun. You need to see this place. It's been there forever."

They left their books at the table and found Steve's car in the nearest student lot. It was Ben's first time in a Jeep like this and he couldn't get over the fact that it belonged to an eighteen year old. He wondered how rich a person had to be to buy their son a fully loaded brand new car. He tried to picture the conversations between his friend's parents.

"Hmmm, Steve is going to need a car at school. He obviously can't be expected to walk or to ask someone for a ride. So what should we get him?"

"How about a nice safe functional car that we can get at a used car lot for less than five thousand dollars?"

"Good one honey."

"Yeah, just kidding," his mom probably said, laughing. "I've already scheduled an appointment with Fred down at the dealership. It's on Saturday, right after your golf outing."

"Perfect. What would I do without you?"

"Well, it wasn't actually me. It was Maria. But I'll take the credit."

Ben was still having this imaginary conversation in his mind when Silky, who was sitting next to him in the back seat, leaned up to talk to Steve.

"Hey, what kind of parent buys their kid a new car for college? What would you have done if you'd come home from school and there was an old rusted out Chevy with a big red bow on it?"

"I'd have said, 'Holy crap! A car! Thank you so much.' I didn't actually ask for this one. My dad got it from a friend of his who needed the money or something. It had eight thousand miles on it and was a demo. I can guarantee that there are plenty of people driving around here who paid more for their Chevys and Fords than mine cost."

"Oh, well, that's pretty cool then. I love Jeeps."

"Thanks. I do like it. And it's nice to just have something to get around in. So we can get to places like Angelo's. I'll tell you one thing. We wouldn't all fit in Marti's."

"Hey, leave me out of this. My parents didn't want me carting a bunch of drunk frat boys around."

"Is that really the reason?"

"Maybe. The main reason was that my dad was ready for a new car so I got his old one. Just like most people at this school."

"True. What did he get?"

"Another red convertible Mercedes. He buys a new one every three years. I'm not complaining," she smiled.

"Well, I've got no personal means of transportation so I really appreciate the ride," Ben said.

"Right. I have a communal means of transportation. I'm always driving people around. Let me know if there's something you need to do, I can take you there. I really think that's one of the great things about college. Or it should be anyway. That we can share."

"Yeah, like in Acts four," said Ben.

"Acts four? Uh oh, are you going to preach?"

"No. What you said reminded me of it, that's all. In Acts four a community began to grow and everyone shared what they had. Kind of an early socialism. Only not, because everyone went along and did their thing but then put all of their money and possessions into a common pot. They shared a common goal."

"I like that a lot. Marti, can you toss the keys to your Mercedes into the common pot?" said Silky.

"Sure, no problem. That's the bad thing about my car though. Only two seats."

"Yeah, not the best choice for Ben's new world order."

"I've been planning a coup here at TCU. It seemed the most likely place for a socialist revolution. North Texas."

They all laughed and watched outside as they turned down White Settlement Road and then to the unwieldy parking lot of Angelo's.

"I think I'll park in the neighborhood. That lot looks a little nuts."

He parked on a side street and they walked back, entering the weathered building. They entered the big barn-like interior where a strong voiced woman at the register welcomed them. They ordered slabs of ribs and brisket and slaw and fries and found a good place to sit. It was noisy and smoky and they had to talk loudly to be heard. The food was messy and delicious, and they licked their fingers, sucked the bones and went through a big stack of napkins. Even Marti of the blond hair, privileged upbringing and red Mercedes got her hands dirty and eructed a long satisfied stream of air as she leaned back satisfied and at ease.

"That was good. Thank you for bringing me here. And buying me food. And entertaining me with your wit," Ben said to Steve who was leaning back, looking appreciatively at the pile of cleaned rib bones.

"You are very welcome. Thank you for coming along. Remember our new world order- we share all things in common."

"I love that. In those verses that I was talking about earlier it says that they were all of one mind and one heart. That no one claimed anything as their own but rather they held everything in common. Of course it works out a little better for someone like me than it does someone like you."

"It does? How so?"

"Well, I get more stuff and you get less."

"No, not really. We get the same. That's the point."

"But you have to give up something in order to even things out. And I'm the recipient."

"True. But to me it isn't a problem. I have more than enough. Of course, my dad may not love the idea since it's actually his money."

"No, but you're right and it's interesting to hear you say it. The question is do I share what I have? I also have more than enough clothing, food, even shelter. More than most people in the world I would think."

"I know I do," said Silky. "I really just need this shirt and these jeans."

"Yeah, we've noticed," said Marti.

"Hey, I'm trying to save resources. Less water and detergent usage. You all should be thanking me."

"That's the big question though," Ben said. "How much does each person need? And are there enough resources to provide for everyone in the city, country, and world?"

"I think the answer to that is all yes," said Silky. "That there is enough food, clothing, and resources for shelter for everyone in the world. Maybe enough health care and clean water with some reshuffling of people and a lot of creative thinking. Yeah, I don't think as college kids we have an idea of how much things actually cost. We're pretty sheltered here. Maybe the juniors and seniors have a better feel for it. You know, if they live in an apartment and see the bills. But they're just one or two people. Not a family. Anyway, it's a difficult problem. Maybe the best way is to look at it on a small scale and then ramp it up."

"Are you trying to get my car again?" asked Marti. "It's not going to happen."

"Silky's on to something here. It quickly becomes an overwhelming problem when we only use our own experience. My parents' contribution is on the low end but they do give more than most people in the world make in a year. And the school, or the endowment, subsidizes a huge amount as well."

"Do you have one of those Chancellor scholarships?"

"Yeah, but think about it. There is such inequality in this city, country and world and that's what causes most of the conflict. Some countries and leaders trying to hold on to what they have and some trying to get more. For instance, why are we bombing Libya? And why is our Army in Bolivia? And the crazy expensive Cold War with the Soviet Union... what's that even about anymore? In the last three years we've been involved in armed conflicts in Lebanon, Egypt, Honduras, Chad, Grenada and over the Persian Gulf. What for? I can guarantee it wasn't to fight for long term global equality."

"Wow Ben, how do you know all that?" said Steve who had been listening intently. "I can barely remember what was on my last history test, much less keep up with modern worldwide politics."

"Don't laugh, but Jello Biafra from the Dead Kennedys got me interested in it. Not to simply take things at face value. To question authority and the status quo. It's kind of a college requirement, don't you think?"

"Oh, of course, good old Jello. I often use insane hardcore punk singers as my news sources."

"He's pretty insightful. Their new album just came out and I want to get it but it wasn't at Sound Warehouse this week. It's called Bedtime for Democracy. Anyway, we've fallen way off track. My main point was to say thank you for lunch."

"Oh yeah, that's right," said Steve. "You're welcome. But all this discussion about sharing and reallocating resources has been interesting. It's definitely what we do in college. Like we were talking about in the car. I wonder if it's because it isn't really our money. We haven't earned it so it's easier to share."

"That's probably a lot of it. We hold onto it more loosely. But we still get used to a certain level of comfort and luxury and

174

being able to come to lunch or see a show or buy a new sweater. And if someone said, 'You can't do any of that anymore. Not until every student at this school has a new pair of jeans and a Domino's pizza once a month,' even the most giving person here might balk."

"I agree. People are basically selfish. Or are generous to a point- until they start to feel it. Which I suppose isn't really being generous at all. Hey are you all ready to go?"

Everyone was and they rode back to campus full of barbecue and ideas. They got back in time for afternoon classes. Ben felt a part of something as he sat in his usual place with Denny. His new friends patted him as they passed on the way out.

"So, those are your new friends huh?" asked Denny as they left the classrooms and began heading back to the library.

"Yeah, they're pretty cool. Have you been to Angelo's?"

"Barbecue? No, was it good?"

"It was. Not Kansas City good. I'd take Zarda any day but it was nice to get away and do something different. It's amazing what a little novelty, just doing something out of the ordinary, will do for your spirits."

"For sure. So, are you going to study with them this afternoon?"

"Maybe. What're you going to do? You should come join us. We have that biology project that we need to get started on."

"Yeah, ok. I need to go to my room for a minute. I'll catch up with you later."

"I can go with you."

"No, it's cool, you study."

"Nope, I'm coming with. I could use the walk and I'm not really in the mood. So, are we watching Moonlighting tonight?"

"I can't believe you actually watch that show."

"Hey, it's pretty good."

"Are you serious? What's next? Matlock?"

"Please. Have you ever seen that show? It's really pathetic. I'm not that desperate. What happened to Andy Griffith? Now that was great. Especially the early ones. The black and white episodes when Opie was so tiny and cute. Barney Fife, Gomer Pyle, Aunt Bee. Those were some great characters."

"Not to mention Goober and Floyd the barber. Oh and Otis, the local drunk."

"Andy was such a great cool father figure. Calm, level headed. Never got too out of control or emotional. He had all those goofballs around him. As crazy as everyone was, they all got along somehow. They were more like caricatures of course but think how utopian that place was. The lessons that it taught."

"Like what?"

"Well, like how no one is normal. Or no one except Opie and Andy anyway. They were eccentric and difficult. And yet…"

"And yet they were integrated into the community, adding variety and interest. We have our share of colorful characters in Laguna."

"Yeah, I'll bet you do. I keep forgetting about that. You've got all kinds of homeless and hippies and New Age folks there huh?"

"Yep. And skate punks and surfers and retired starlets and real estate tycoons. You name it and we've got at least two of them."

"And everyone co-exists?"

"Not perfectly. It's not the early sixties. And it isn't primetime TV. But better than you would think. The city council talks about things like public bathrooms and trash receptacles. And it isn't unusual to see wealthy stylish well-dressed people stopping to talk with a homeless guy outside the Safeway. Or a high school group doing beach clean up as a class project."

176

"That's exactly what I've been thinking about lately. About mutual aid. Sharing what we have and appreciating, instead of vilifying differences. If we embrace and learn from the Barney's and Gomer's and even the Otis's we would do much better. Everyone has value. A story. Something to add to the rich tapestry of life."

"Dude what've you been smoking? How did we get here from Moonlighting?"

"Moonlighting, Matlock, Andy Griffith, pastoral anarchism. Seems like a logical progression to me. Truly I seem to get here from every direction lately. I don't know what it is. Part of it's that sermon I heard on Sunday. The pastor didn't take it nearly far enough but it got me thinking. About how we ignore what we can't see, what doesn't directly affect us."

"Out of sight, out of mind."

"Yeah, but sometimes even in sight, out of mind. Like Lazarus in the parable, and like the different folks in Laguna. But as you said, in some instances people interact and care for one another that ordinarily wouldn't in other settings. Like in Mayberry- a small self-contained town. And as in Laguna, which sounds like a kind of Mayberry also. A nineteen eighties, Southern California one."

"Laguna as post-modern Mayberry."

"Exactly. So the trick is to create Mayberry's everywhere. Because it's much easier to care for someone you see every day, someone that you can't avoid, that's a part of your everyday life, that you might even know their name, rather than a number or a statistic or a biased news story."

"Right. People mainly fear what they don't know. What they read about but don't have direct experience with. A lot of people would freak out if the people that I see every day in Laguna came and hung out here on the TCU campus or went to Hulen Mall.

There would probably be police helicopters and a SWAT team surrounding the place."

"Yeah, or if we learned that a bunch of Libyan refugees were moving into Fort Worth. Or Iranian. Or even communist Russian immigrants. It would get ugly. But I can almost guarantee that if a muscular blonde Russian guy or a pretty Libyan girl with giant dark eyes showed up in biology they'd instantly be the most popular kid in class. People would be tripping over each other trying to get to know them."

"So funny when you put it like that."

"You know I'm right. Your mental image changed also, admit it. From an abstract place on a map to an actual person. Meeting or envisioning individual people changes our perception. On the flip side, our governments work hard to dehumanize groups of people in order to justify bombing them or cutting off their food stamps or executing them or imprisoning them. It's a problem that's been around since nations have existed and a difficult one to combat."

"Even this year in history class I've seen cartoons of devilish looking British soldiers and Native Americans. Really awful subhuman pictures."

"So again, the trick is to remember that people are real. That some guy in Ethiopia and I could talk about our lives and have so much in common. Or a girl from the Chicago slums. Or a kid from Cuba or Thailand or Finland. I could meet any nineteen year old from anywhere in the world and we could find a lot more in common at the deepest level than we could ever find differences."

"I'll bet that's true. Hey, I just need to grab something here. Be right back."

They were in the hallway and Denny unlocked his door and slid in, closing the door behind himself. It was a little odd but

Ben assumed he was changing pants or something so he stood in the hall and waited.

It had only been about thirty seconds but felt much longer when someone came around the corner. A tennis player, Ben thought as he leaned on the wall across the hall.

"Is Denny in here?" the guy asked.

"Yeah, but…" he started to say something about the fact that he wanted to be alone or was changing clothes or come up with a reason that he should wait a second, but the guy was too fast and didn't really want an answer. He opened the door and began to go in. Ben was directly across the hall and could see Denny with his little safe. It was out of the closet and open on the bed and there were tiny wads of aluminum foil next to it. He looked up and told the guy to come in and shut the door.

Ben was left out in the hall again, this time with a whole new set of scenarios as to what was going on there. None of them as innocent as changing a shirt or getting some study snacks or listening to an answering machine message. It was another two or three long minutes before both of them came back out.

The tennis guy said, "Catch ya later," to Denny, glanced at Ben, and then walked by, heading down the hall and out the back stairs.

Ben looked at Denny who shook his head with a cautionary expression and led the way to the front of the building, down the stairs and back outside. They were walking quickly on the sidewalk and were just past the cafeteria before Ben finally spoke.

"What was that back there?"

"It's not something you need to worry about."

"Well, I saw it. I can't erase it. So I guess you're going to have to tell me."

"Maybe we should just leave it where it is. You saw something you don't understand but right now you're innocent. It's definitely better that way."

"Denny, if you're doing something that could potentially screw up your life I want to know about it. I'm your friend. Were you selling that guy drugs?"

Denny stopped and looked at Ben. His shoulders slumped and looked around and he moved over next to a big sycamore before speaking again.

"Just remember you asked. And you insisted on coming to my dorm."

"Okay, I'll take that on- it's entirely my fault. So what's going on?"

"Yes, I've been selling a little. Very small amounts. I get no more than three grams of powder at a time. I cut it down into single doses and sell them to a few friends. It's really not a huge deal."

"You're selling crack and you say it's not a big deal?" Ben whispered fiercely.

Denny laughed a little. "It's not crack dumbass. It's speed. There are racist new federal mandatory minimum prison sentences for coke possession so less people are messing with it. Simple possession gets you a long sentence. They're going after poor black men in the ghetto. No, meth is cleaner anyway. A better drug. It's like caffeine."

"Only it's not. It's illegal and addictive and you're an idiot."

"Thanks. Hey, you asked."

"Do you need the money that badly? We were just talking about all of this. About sharing and community. If you need money we can figure something out. This is crazy."

"It's not the money. Although I am accumulating a nice little pile of cash."

"Then why? Wait, are you using it yourself?"

"What is this? Why are you all excited about it? I'm not the only one at school that does this, you know."

"Do you?"

"Yeah, occasionally. It's one of the perks. It's like a pyramid scheme. The guy above me makes a lot of money and gets a lot of free drug. I make a little money and get a little free drug. And the guy I sell it to just has to worry about buying enough for himself. Less risk. I don't do it often. It's expensive and keeps me awake for like twenty-four hours. The timing has to be right."

"Well, that's just great. It makes me really happy that you've found yourself a nice way to make some money and gain extra energy. Why don't you go work at Ol' South? They give you free coffee and you get to keep your tips. And there's no risk that you'll be arrested, thrown in prison for five years and come out with a felony. If you get caught you'll be out about the time I'm starting my clinical rotations at med school. And the only person that will hire you with a felony is your dad. You'll be bussing tables at his restaurant for the rest of your life. It's crazy."

"You're blowing this completely out of proportion. I'm careful. This is something that I did in high school. I'm not going to get caught. And if I do, people like me don't go to prison."

"People like you?"

"Yeah, well maybe it's unfair but it's true. White college students with access to an attorney. I'm going to do a lot better than an inner-city kid."

"There's no guarantee and that is a justification. You have to stop."

"I don't feel too much like studying right now after all. And you need to let this go. Go cool off a little or something. It isn't your business and you're getting yourself all worked up. Just keep it quiet and forget it happened."

"Or what? You'll send someone after me?"

"Or nothing. You've been watching too much Miami Vice. Never mind. I'll catch up with you later."

Denny turned to go back the way he had come while Ben leaned back on the big sycamore and watched him go. His anger and disbelief began to fade and pretty soon he felt completely different emotions- regret, shame, and a deepening sadness.

15

Ben didn't feel like studying either at that point. It seemed like days ago that he'd gone to Angelo's with his new friends. He didn't think he could face them right then. As badly as he wanted to tell someone about Denny he knew that he would have to hold it in for now.

It was time for dinner and even though he was still full of barbecue and French fries he decided to go down to the snack bar and see if they had anything sweet. Maybe a slice of pie or a soft, brown sugary chocolate chip cookie would help. Who needs meth when the world contains such incredible desserts?

When he got down there he saw Brad sitting with a few other sophomores that lived in the dorm. He didn't know them well but decided to take a chance and be social. There happened to be cherry pie and a nice looking cookie so he got both and took them to the round table, sitting next to Brad.

"Hey, Ben, welcome to the popular table. How's your day going?"

"Well, it's been interesting, that's for sure. So this is the popular table? I had no idea. I've been trying to find it the whole semester."

"Yep, right here. And we just happen to have a vacancy. So there you are. We were talking about favorite movies. Have you seen anything good lately?"

"Well, I wouldn't call it my favorite movie but I watched Stagecoach the other night. It was actually really entertaining."

"Can't go wrong with John Wayne," one of the guys said. "Although Stagecoach isn't my favorite. I like the later ones. When he's kind of overweight and rough looking. True Grit. Things like that."

"I'm actually not a huge John Wayne fan. I mean I like him and all but maybe I'm too young to really understand him. I don't watch a lot of old Westerns."

"Okay, then you get another one. What's your favorite movie so far this year?"

"Uh.... I guess it's been Pretty in Pink. John Hughes is amazing. The way he captures what it's like to be young..."

"For sure. We actually just spent fifteen minutes talking about that movie and the music. Some like it, others thought it was a chick flick. You get another try. What else?"

"Okay, I have two then. One that I love and another that I haven't seen yet but really want to. I've heard such incredible things about Blue Velvet. Have any of you all seen it?"

Brad answered for the others. "I saw it last month. It was very weird but really good. Kind of artsy but so suspenseful and creepy. The Dennis Hopper character is terrifying. In fact there are a few old guys in there that I still have nightmares about."

"No spoilers!" Ben said, putting his hands over his ears.

"All right. All right. But you should see it and decide for yourself. Did you see Eraserhead? Or Elephant Man?"

"Nope, neither one. I can talk about music for days but I haven't seen that many movies. I've heard of both of them. Eraserhead is also supposed to be pretty freaky right?"

"Right. Elephant Man was really good but was more mainstream I guess. You should see it though. Eraserhead is a trip. So beautiful and disturbing. It came out in seventy-seven. The same year that all of your punk bands began. It wasn't just the music scene that was exploding then."

"Ok, sold. I need to have a David Lynch marathon someday. The other one was Repo Man. It's been out a few years but I just saw it last summer. That was so amazing. The music, Emilio, Harry Dean Stanton- who by the way is in both Blue Velvet and Pretty in Pink and is one of my favorites- that weird friend of theirs, spaceships, generic food and how life has gotten so messed up."

"Yeah, I've heard you playing that soundtrack."

"Sorry about that. A little loud huh?"

"A tad. And a little scary."

"But it's all a commentary. Even that shootout in the liquor store. The Emilio character is the only one who doesn't have a gun and is the only one that isn't shot. Oh except for the hot thief with the long silver jacket and the Mohawk. Just the absurdity of each person in turn pulling out a gun and shooting someone, and then in turn being shot. Guns never solve anything."

Only one of the guys at the table had seen it but everyone seemed interested. They talked about trying to get a copy to watch sometime. An idea that Ben loved for several reasons. Of course he wanted to evangelize the awesomeness of Repo Man and give himself a chance to see it again. But he also liked the idea of meeting new people and sharing an experience together. Similar to what he was doing right now.

Brad looked at the pie and cookie that Ben had about finished off.

"Nice dinner by the way."

"Yeah, I'm kind of a health nut."

"I can see that."

"Actually I had a huge lunch. Just needed to top it off with some dessert."

"Oh, yep, been there many times. Hey, I need to get going. You'll be okay here?" Brad said as he started piling up the dishes and trash around him. The others did the same.

"Sure, I'm fine, go ahead, I'm right behind you. Thank you for the good conversation. I needed it. And we definitely have to watch Repo Man together. I know that I missed a lot the first time through."

"You got it."

They all departed, leaving Ben sitting by himself. He was thinking about the crazy day he'd had. How life sometimes provides entirely too many ups and downs.

He was taking the last bite of pie, having saved two cherries with plenty of the gooey filling to go with the sliver of browned crust. It turned out to be the best bite, since he had eaten the rest absentmindedly as he talked with Brad and the others. Just when he thought that a moment in time couldn't get any better, when he was silently thanking God for giving people taste buds and the sense of smell and sight that all came together in such a way to make the pie experience so perfect, it happened.

Once again he felt her before he saw her. The air in the room seemed to change. Like the ionization that occurs before a rainstorm. A sense that something electric and powerful is imminent.

He turned and saw her as she neared the bottom of the stairs. She was smiling and talking excitedly with a guy that he didn't recognize. He was tall and dark and had nice hair and was wearing everything Polo, but in a slouchy, cool, "don't care that my dad's a millionaire, but actually I do," kind of way, and Ben loved the guy despite himself but also hated him deeply for walking with her.

The guy was listening and smiling as they walked towards the little store. Ben thought he detected a slight embarrassment, a touch of condescension as he listened to whatever she was telling him.

He hadn't seen her since that day in the record store but she had been in the back of his mind ever since. That life-altering look they had exchanged.

He stayed at the table. He tried to keep his focus forward, on the wall in front of him, rather than to the right where they had passed. His instinct was to get up and get out of there. To not torture himself with the two of them together. She was obviously taken. And the guy was so far out of Ben's league that it wasn't even worth holding on to any hope at all that she would notice him.

They were in there for a while and when they came out Ben was disappointed and relieved to see that they had bought some snacks to go. He didn't know if he would be able to sit and watch them eat and flirt with each other, and yet he couldn't stop himself. It was making him feel nauseated and lonely.

As they passed within four feet of his table she saw him. This moment lasted a fraction of the time as the record store and yet was just as electric. She recognized him and her smiling eyes shone even brighter. The universe narrowed to only the two of them as he quickly tried to think of something, anything, to say. But it was over in a flash and she had passed him and the spell was broken and he was left alone, floating in the depths of his own consciousness once again.

He watched her walk away and it took several minutes for his heart to slow enough and for his mind to clear to the point that he could stand up, return his dishes and slowly walk home, wondering how the moon was still out, the crickets were still singing and that he still had to go to classes the next day.

Brian and Tim were in the room. They were listening to a really lame radio station that was playing a .38 Special song, and after about ten minutes the dissonance became too great. The beautiful memory in Ben's head was being distorted and destroyed by the mediocrity around him. He had to get out of there, so grabbed his button covered jean jacket and left again.

He walked back the way he had come, wishing that the Denny incident had never occurred, that he was still naive about his drug dealing, or that he felt comfortable enough with Steve and Silky that he could talk to them, or even better Anna or Marti or another girl, someone who would understand how important a fleeting glance could be.

But now, in that moment, there wasn't anyone to confide in. He turned away from the library and down University. He walked past the Pub, thought briefly about going in but decided to keep going. He crossed the street and went down Berry, not stopping at either of the two bars he had seen shows in recently. He looked at his watch and decided that Sound Warehouse would still be open. Maybe he would be able to detect a trace of the girl's aura there, a lingering collection of electrons.

Ben was nearly across the parking lot when he saw him. Some movement caught his eye along the dark side of the building near a green dumpster. It was the homeless guy. The man had seen him so he had to make a decision. He could ignore him, or acknowledge him and keep walking, or he could go and talk to him. The last one seemed the least likely and yet his legs had a life of their own as he slightly changed direction, pointing towards the dumpster now.

"Hey, how're you doing?" he heard himself asking as he reached a distance that he could speak without shouting.

The guy looked over at him but didn't say anything.

"I've seen you a couple times around town. Remember? You caught me peeing outside the Hi Hat a while back."

"I remember."

Ben struggled to think of something to say. There was an awkward few seconds and he was about to walk away when the man said, "I guess you made it home okay the other night."

Ben turned back and looked at him.

"What night?"

"I don't remember. A couple weeks back. You were walking up Bellaire, through people's yards. Really drunk."

"You saw me?"

"Yeah."

"Was I pretty bad? I have an annoying habit of leaving places suddenly if I'm bored or upset."

"Which was it that night?"

"Both I think. Although honestly I don't remember much."

"Well, I saw you way back at Hulen and wanted to be sure you made it home. That was pretty stupid of you. It's safe in that area but you could have been hit by a car, or shot by a homeowner."

"So you followed me?

189

"Yeah, for a ways."

"What was I doing? Did I know you were there?"

"Dude, you didn't know anything. You were just tripping and stumbling along. When a car came by you'd hide behind a tree or fall down into the grass. Like some kind of secret agent or something. You peed in a flowerbed in this really nice yard. You were a mess. No judgments though man, believe me I've been there more times than I can count."

"That all sounds pretty embarrassing. Why were you following me though?"

"Well, I was kind of headed in the same direction. But mainly I wanted to be sure you made it home okay."

"That's so nice of you. Thank you."

"Yeah, it's just something I do, I suppose. It happens a lot out on the streets. Someone gets wasted and they're just so vulnerable. They can get hurt or need medical help or someone might try to rob them. It sucks waking up to find your shoes have been stolen."

"Well, thank you. So I guess I made it home all right huh?"

"Yeah, your friend found you and got you into his car. Man, that's a good friend."

"That was Denny. Yeah, he is." Ben was quiet for a minute as he thought about Denny, how he needed to apologize for how judgmental and crazy he had acted that afternoon.

"So, you had the sudden urge to buy a record tonight?"

"What? Oh, yeah, kinda. I just needed to go for a walk. Was feeling cooped up on campus. Thanks again for helping me the other night. What's your name by the way?"

"James. Yours?" he said, offering his right hand.

"Ben. Good to meet you." As they shook hands he said, "Hey, do you need anything? Food? Money?"

"No, I'm good man. Thanks though."

Ben dug into his Levis and found a five. He folded in half with one hand and held it out to James.

"Take this. It isn't much but it's what I have right now. Get something to eat."

James took the bill. "Thanks. Take care of yourself. See you around."

"Yeah you too. Thanks again." Ben hesitated a little then turned back around, deciding to skip the record store. He walked home lost in his thoughts.

16

"Why are you wearing that poncho? Now you literally look like a drug dealer," Ben said to Denny as they walked to the Pub that Friday night.

"Shows what you know. It's a parka, not a poncho. A poncho is just a blanket with a hole cut out in the middle for your head. And this is how you picture drug dealers?"

"Oh sorry, parka. Is that even comfortable? I mean the shape makes it look like it might be. But isn't it all scratchy? And it kind of smells bad. Like a rug on my grandmother's living room floor. And what happens when it rains?"

"Hey I'm not commenting on the fact that you're wearing that shirt for something like the three hundredth time without washing it. Talk about smell."

"Really?" Ben said, smelling his right armpit.

"Actually kidding. You're fine."

"Whew. Not that it'll matter once we get in here and everyone's smoking."

"Seriously."

They got past the doorman and into the bar. It was a fairly good crowd already. They saw some swimmers and golfers and a few people from their science classes.

"So, what's this about becoming a hobo?" asked Denny, bringing over a pitcher and pouring it into two white plastic cups. He handed one to Ben.

"Thanks," he said, taking a sip. "Not a hobo. I'm going to see what it's like to live on the streets of Fort Worth for one night."

"I can tell you what it's going to be like. Cold, miserable and dangerous. I don't understand why you want to do that. You think I've got problems!"

"Well, you know I met that homeless guy named James on Tuesday? I brought him a sandwich last night and we had the most amazing conversation. One of the main points was that a person can't understand homelessness unless they really immerse themselves in it."

"So that's what you're planning to do. I'm sure Brian and Tim will be happy if you're immersed. It'll free up some space in their room"

"It's just for one night. He said we'll meet some people that he knows and just kind of hang out downtown."

"Well, I always knew you were different. This confirms it. But it's pretty cool and I have to say I'm not that surprised. With you, the conversation always seems to come back around to poverty and equality."

"Yeah, I'm not sure why. Then on the other hand I'm not sure why most people aren't interested in helping others. Everyone seems to be only caught up in their day-to-day lives.

Short-term solutions. Throwing a little money, or even worse, a prayer at the problem then moving on. If I learn a single thing about what it's like to be down and out on the streets of Fort Worth, then I'll be happy. I'm not expecting anything life-changing to happen. But hopefully it will be life-affirming."

"Okay, well I'll be interested to hear about it. In the meantime we should play some pinball before it gets super crowded in here."

"Sounds good to me. Do you have any quarters?"

"I've got you covered, my friend."

They worked their way to the front of the bar where two pinball machines were stationed. They chose the usual one. Pin-Bot was the newer, brighter, louder one.. Pinball wasn't the most popular thing to do at the Pub. That would be drinking and hitting on each other. But still, it was rare to find empty machines at ten on a Friday night so they decided to kill some time and some quarters.

They took turns on the machine. Ben shooting first and Denny going as Player two. They each had a few good rounds but nothing spectacular. Slingshots and ramps and scoops that look cool but seemed designed to end the game quickly to get players to feed more money into the slot. Pin-Bot had plenty of all of these. The robot voices mocked them with unintelligible words as ball after ball drained quickly. No extra games, no multi-ball rallies. But it was the third ball of the second game that finally showed how perfect and transcendent pinball could be.

That third ball. The magnets, gravity, and the laws of physics seemed to alter from the time Ben released the plunger. The flippers returned the ball to the playfield time after time. Up the outside orbital ramp on the right once again, dropping targets, keeping the ball moving up and away, bells were ringing and lights were flashing. Ben's focus narrowed to the ball, and at times to several balls as the bonuses racked up. He was oblivious to his surroundings as people began to gather.

Pinball is a great spectator sport. Focused on the ball and the flippers, all the intricate lights, awards, and information are lost on the player. But everyone that watched knew what was happening, they saw the points quickly increase. As Ben continued to play, feeling in sync with the machine, he felt like he was floating, like his fingers and mind and the ball were all one.

When the last ball finally drained, when the spell was broken, when several onlookers began to wander off, he noticed that Denny was still standing there.

"Holy crap, dude. That was the coolest thing I've ever seen. You were on fire. I think you hit every reward, every light on the machine."

Ben looked up at the back box and saw that he now had six games remaining.

"Wow- I won six games. Can you believe that? Someone take a picture or something. Maybe I should quit while I'm ahead, you know? It's not like I'll ever play better than that. That was a once in a lifetime thing." He looked around. There were two guys nearby, kind of watching and kind of ignoring them.

"Hey, do you guys want to play these games?"

"Sure, thanks man. That was an amazing game by the way."

"Thanks. Got really lucky."

As Denny handed Ben the beer that he had been holding for him, one of the guys said, "Hey man, you got a high score. Don't you want to put your name in there?"

"Oh, yeah sure." He pushed the button twice- B, then moved to the next letter and the next. As he walked away he saw his name light up in the top left box. "1: BEN." It looked so cool and he felt like it meant something. That things were really looking up. That it was important in some way that wasn't clear yet but would be if he stayed mindful. And then he took a swallow of beer and joined Denny, who was already deep into conversation with two Tri-Delts.

Three hours later he left Denny behind, certain that although he denied it, his friend was on meth. He was expansive and way too talkative. He was bouncing off the walls with excess energy, concocting plans and scenarios and showing no signs of slowing down. In fact he wanted to move on to a party at a friend of a friend's condo.

There were nights that Ben might have gone along with the scheme but not this one. Three beers had only made him tired and he was a little concerned about sleeping on the streets the next night so decided to be strong and stand up to Denny and tell him no.

But Denny wouldn't take no, which meant Ben had to wait until he was engrossed in a conversation about proper surfboard waxing techniques and then sneak out the back door, giving the bouncer a wink that he hoped wouldn't be misinterpreted.

He had to go back around the buildings and then across University and the familiar sidewalk home, passing a few people sitting on benches but for the most part it was quiet. He was pleased to find both roommates gone. They were finally becoming more social and were going out on weekends more often. He had no idea who they were with, but at that moment didn't care.

Ben took the opportunity to flick through his records to find something that fit his mood. Since breaking up with Anna he hadn't listened to Depeche Mode at all. Nor any of that genre of music. So he passed by Bauhaus and Joy Division and Pet Shop Boys and looked for something with more guitar.

As he looked, it became clear to him that he was going to do what he usually did this late at night- listen to the Replacements. There were four or five songs that he loved when he was tired, maybe a little buzzed, and feeling lonely. And three of them were on a relatively new import EP. It only had eight songs but they were good ones and his favorite wasn't on any other album.

He dropped the needle at the beginning of the third track, "Within Your Reach." It was a simple song from the Hootenany record that for the first three minutes consisted of a ringing guitar that bounced back and forth from one speaker to another, a smooth bass line and a simple, rapid drumbeat. Paul sounded immensely regretful and hopeless as he lamented that he could live without her touch and die within her reach. When the guitar kicked in at the end it was cathartic and difficult to not scream along in his anguish.

The last song on that side wasn't on any other twelve-inch record. The flipside to their first single and fairly rare, it was one of Ben's favorite songs. "If Only You Were Lonely" perfectly captured the feeling of loneliness and sadness and anxious regret at the end of nights like this. It had an immediacy and honesty that helped Ben ask the unanswerable questions he had been carrying around. Why hadn't he and Anna worked out? Why couldn't he find and talk to that girl with the beautiful eyes? Why is he here in Texas, five hundred miles from home and away from everyone he grew up with? He was wasting time here. Alone and sick and missing out on whatever everyone else was doing.

He played the same two songs over and over. Initially he listened to the music and the sad lyrics, but later only to his own thoughts. He was feeling that same nauseated painful lump in the lower part of his stomach, the same hopeless and helpless anxious loneliness that he had felt so many times. The third time through he started to cry. The tears ran and he held his face and he began rocking and sobbing and softly repeating, "Oh my God."

"Oh my God. Oh my God. Oh my God," he whispered and wept and rocked and occasionally let out a louder, wordless moan and his breath was fast and shallow and he felt like he would pass out or his heart would stop. And at that moment he desperately wanted those things to happen or for the world to end or for the earth to swallow him up. "If only you were lonely, I'd go home with you." His sadness felt bottomless and his loneliness felt endless and timeless and he had no idea how to get himself out of the deep dark hole that was suddenly closing in around him. How to slow his breathing and stop weeping and find hope that he would be able to go to sleep and wake up tomorrow to a new day. At that moment even that simple prayer felt foolish and impossible.

And how could that girl be walking around with that guy? And how could Ben be hopelessly in love with her? And was he really or was this just loneliness and existential despair?

He had been through the pair of songs six times when he heard the doorknob jiggle. Brian had put his key in the already unlocked door and opened it and peeked in quietly. When he saw that Ben was awake and that Tim wasn't there and that only a dim table lamp was on, he flipped on the fluorescent room light.

"Hey, what are you doing here in the dark? Are you okay?"

Ben was standing up, keeping his back to Brian as he took the record off the turntable and began sliding it back into its sleeve.

"Hey Brian. Yeah, I'm fine. Just listening to some music. I'm going down the hall to brush my teeth. I'll be back in a minute."

He was able to get into the hallway without Brian noticing his red, swollen eyes and by the time he returned the lights were off and his roommate was in bed. Ben crawled up to his bunk, scooted down between the sheets, pulled the blanket up halfway and rested there, eyes focused upwards on nothing. It had done him good, to release whatever was inside him and as he drifted off he began to focus outward again, to remember his blessings and to realize that Anna, and his family back home, and even the girl with the shining eyes weren't going to be able to save him.

No, it was the tiny spark of spirit that was dimly flickering somewhere in a hidden corner of his created self that was the key. And right then in that moment he could feel it at last and he sensed a physical calm that spread from his core and then outward to his extremities, reaching his fingers and toes and they seemed to tingle and glow. His mind began to relax and his eyes began to close and merciful sleep came at last.

17

"Do you know Deuteronomy eight?" James asked.

"Not off the top of my head, no. What does it say?"

They were sitting behind a building on the far edge of downtown. Ben had asked James to show him what it was like. He wanted a taste of life on the streets. He realized that one afternoon and night wasn't going to make him an expert, but since meeting James he had been trying to visualize how he survived the monotony, the danger, the cold, and the hunger. It was all a mystery and something he felt that he couldn't understand unless he experienced it first hand.

"It's one of the passages in which God warns the people to remember where they came from. He reminds them that they were humbled when God let them go hungry, but then provided them with the unexpected- manna. Their clothes didn't wear out and their feet didn't blister for forty years. Then he said that they were about to experience a land of milk and honey, a place where food was plentiful and building materials weren't lacking. They would be wealthy and comfortable."

"I remember part of that. Then what?"

"He warned them that when they're rich and living in fine homes and have large flocks and piles of gold that they should be careful. They should remember God and all God did for them. Verse 17 reads: *God did all of this so you would never say to yourself, 'I have achieved this wealth with my own strength and energy.'*"

There was silence for a moment as they both reflected on the words.

Ben spoke first. "That's a simple but difficult passage. The natural inclination is to be proud of our accomplishments. I studied hard, went to school, tried to stay on the straight and narrow, so I deserve this."

"But I think you know the problem with that kind of thinking. What if there was someone exactly like you? Same personality, brain function, health, all except one thing. Such as that you were born in Ethiopia to a peasant farmer. Or even born in the US. Even Kansas City but your skin had more melanin. Or your dad split before you were born and your mom smoked crack. You can see now that one factor would change everything, making it extremely unlikely that you would be an A student at TCU. It's not all you."

"Sometimes I know that, but others I forget."

"Yeah, well, that's partly what the passage is about. And it's what I want you to think about as we go around tonight. Try not to judge or diagnose people. Just look at them as human beings like you and me. Or your sisters or dad. Just people."

James said a short prayer asking for safety and guidance as they traveled and then they hoisted their backpacks into place and began walking. James said the immediate plan was to find dinner. There was an organization that delivered food sometime around six if he remembered right. They did it three times a week and he was pretty sure one of the days was Saturday. It was at least three miles away but they had plenty of time.

The weather was nice. About fifty and sunny and pretty soon they both were getting hot so they stripped off the top layer and squeezed them into their backpacks. James saw a few people he recognized but no one that he knew well enough to stop and chat with. As they reached a corner liquor store he saw three familiar faces. A guy came over and smiled and shook James's hand.

"Bobby, I want you to meet a friend of mine. This is Ben. He's new out here. I'm just showing him around."

"Pleasure to meet you Ben. Welcome to the neighborhood. You're in good hands. Just stay close to James. It can get rough out here."

"You got a minute Bobby? Can you sit with us? I'll bet Ben would like to hear some of your story."

"Sure I do. Nothing but time. You got a cigarette?"

James reached into his pocket and brought out a pack of Kools. He shook one out and Bobby took it. James lit it and they began talking.

Ben would discover over the course of the evening that many street people were talkers. Just like anyone, they had opinions on everything. Sports, politics, religion, you name it, they had thought about it and loved to share their insights.

Bobby had seen a play that afternoon put on by a local food ministry. It was street theater about trusting in God and it had made an impact on him. The message was simple but effective. That plus the free bag of food had put him in an expansive mood. He told Ben about the brain aneurysm that he had suffered. Ben couldn't understand how far in the past this had occurred but the near death experience that followed had affected him deeply.

"Man, I died! I mean it! I was looking down at myself and I saw Jesus! His robes were so white it was like he had been drenched in Clorox. For real. And there were these kids by my bed. I didn't know who they were. There was a Chinese one. An African one. Her skin was so dark it was purple. And a Mexican one. Kids from all over the world just gathered around my bed."

"Wow. That's pretty wild. But you woke up."

"Yeah, God was there too. Not as vivid but he was white too and said 'No, he goes back.' He said it real firm. 'He goes back.'" Bobby pointed down emphatically.

"I woke up and looked around. There were forty doctors in my room and I was like, 'What you all looking at? I'm fine. You can all go now.' They didn't know what to do. So I stood up out of bed and they all fell back. I said, 'I'm fine and I'm going home.' Well, they didn't let me go home but they sure left the room in a hurry. They'd never seen anything like it."

"That's quite a story Bobby," James said.

"It's true. Every word. You can believe it. So where y'all going?"

"We're heading down to see if we can get a meal from that Chili van, does it come to sixteenth and Jones?"

"Yeah, I think it does. About six. They might be early and they might be late."

"Okay, well thank you Bobby, it's been nice talking to you. We need to get going."

"It's always a pleasure. Stop by anytime. I don't stray too far from this corner. Where y'all sleeping?"

"I've got a spot picked out."

"Yeah, well be careful man."

"We will, thanks again."

They started on their way, talking about their lives and their families. Where they had been, what they had done. When they came to the corner Bobby had told them about there was no one around and no obvious stopping place for the van. So they walked a few blocks in each direction trying to find someone to ask. There were two guys sitting next to a building in an alley drinking and hanging out. The more sober one was the spokesman.

"They stop right out here. At the end of this alley. If you aren't there they won't stop. Usually around six."

Ben looked at his watch. They had ten minutes so they sat on the curb and waited. Cars drove by but most people didn't look at the two boys sitting there with backpacks and sleeping bags.

They heard a shout from behind and turned to find a guy walking up carrying a small cardboard sign that said "Recently Homeless. Every Little Bit Helps." It was written in black, thick block lettering. He said that a guy had tried to stab him.

"In broad daylight! I couldn't believe it. I saw the knife. It was that guy there. See him?"

They turned to see a man in the next block looking back at them as he walked away.

"With all these witnesses driving by, and he didn't care. Crazy. I've only been here fifteen days and I've had all my stuff stolen. My bike. My sleeping bag. All my money. All I have left is this backpack. If anyone tries to mess with it I'll knife them." He demonstrated his knifing technique at that point.

His name was Florida and he was from, not surprisingly, Florida. He talked a steady stream of (justifiable) paranoia and physical complaints. His left hand was broken. The left side of his face was bruised. His bike had been stolen. He hadn't yet found a safe place to sleep. He drank vodka out of a plastic bottle.

In between rants, as a car drove by he would raise his sign. When the car didn't stop he would complain about Texas, or the economy, or Christians who ignore poverty when it's looking them in the face but sure feel good sending money to feed starving kids in Ethiopia or taking a tax deduction for supporting the Fort Worth Opera or their pastor.

When a family walked by with two little girls, he rummaged around in his backpack and found several small cans of apple juice.

"Would you like some juice?"

"Say no thank you," the mom said as she pushed the girls quickly past.

"Yeah, don't take poisoned juice from the crazy homeless drunk." Florida muttered once they were out of earshot.

He offered one to Ben and James and both accepted. But as the man continued to verbally harass people driving by, James motioned to Ben that they should go back up the alley.

"That guy's making me nervous. He's not ready to listen. He's too new. Still so angry."

As James was saying this the helpful guy from the other alley walked by and said that they needed to be back down by the street because the van usually comes by at six thirty.

The two boys looked at each other and laughed a little because the time kept changing. By six thirty they had about given up hope when they heard a honk and a bell. It was the Chili van. They followed the small crowd that had assembled from nowhere. A volunteer dished what looked like chicken casserole onto Styrofoam plates. There were pickles and jalapenos and hot sauce to add to the meal. They were given plastic spoons and a small bag of Oreos. Another volunteer filled plastic bottles with lemonade.

They took first names as a record of the number of meals served. The side of the van opened up to reveal books, socks, underwear, shirts and pants. Even a few pairs of shoes and toiletry kits.

A very sincere sounding young woman said, "Ben, do you need anything tonight?"

The question caught him off-guard. Did he really look homeless?

"No, thank you, I'm fine."

"Are you sure Ben?"

"Yes, thanks though."

Her concern was surprising and touching to Ben. It was the kindness in her voice and how, after only two hours on the streets, he had really missed that random human-to-human interaction. The feeling of concern. He felt a wall between the homeless world that he had entered and that of the people that were securely housed.

The truck pulled away and they got settled, squatting next to a wall where they ate the meal. It was warm and filling. The hot sauce added a lot of flavor and the cookies were a nice touch. James didn't know the other men and no one spoke to each other.

When they finished the meal they headed into the entertainment district of town just to experience it. They talked briefly with other homeless people, asking how they were doing and getting a feel for the night. They eventually reached an area filled with young, well off, mostly white people. They were spilling out of bars, laughing and carefree as they carried open cups of beer in a way that homeless people wouldn't be able to without giving police a reason to harass them. As they stood and watched, Ben noticed the way the partiers avoided his gaze. After a few minutes a security guard came up and told them they needed to keep moving.

"Why?" asked James. "We're just hanging out here like these people."

"No backpacks," was his answer.

"Okay, well, is it alright if we go through here to the other street?" James said, pointing through the crowd of people.

"Sure, but don't stop. You can't be in there."

Ben was amazed that a style of dress and a backpack was enough to exclude someone from what appeared to be normal activities for people their age. If he had his TCU sweatshirt on or a white shirt with starched, pressed Wranglers he would have been welcomed. They walked through and then turned back around to work their way out of downtown. Going south to Lancaster and then east, they entered the area where many homeless lived and gathered for social services.

It was fairly quiet out but they did stop and talk to a guy that was living in a marginally viable auto repair shop. He knew James and was happy to show him the cast on his leg that was scheduled to come off in two days. He was anxious to get back to work. He had been with GM in Arlington for twenty years, but with health and family problems he was barely scraping by. He lived with his older brother and two others in the shop. They were all sitting and standing near or leaning on the building.

After a few minutes the two new friends continued their journey up Lancaster. Sitting on the steps of the Salvation Army shelter were two guys that James knew. Fred was the older one and Deuce was the younger. James sat down and shared a cigarette with them. Fred had been a hoarder for years. He had a shopping basket completely filled with bulging plastic bags that were carefully tied to the basket. James told him later that this was just one of probably five baskets stationed around the area.

When he was pushed out of one home base he would simply move to another and a basket would already be there set up with clothes and necessities.

James talked to Fred as they sat and smoked.

"Where you staying tonight?" James asked.

Fred gestured behind him to a slab of concrete next to the building. There were blankets laid out, approximating the shape and size of a full mattress. Ben assumed there was cardboard below the blankets.

"They let you sleep here?"

"Yeah, for a night or two. Then I'll have to move along."

"Isn't it too noisy and bright?" asked Ben as a police car raced down the street, lights and sirens on. It was the third one that had been down in the past ten minutes and the sound was deafening.

"Yeah, later, about eleven it seems like there's one a minute."

"Can you sleep through it?"

"No, man. The sound tickles your ears. Like a dog. You know why dogs always bark at sirens? Because it tickles their ears. Ain't no way to sleep through that."

"Why do you think they have to race down there with the sirens on all night? There's not much traffic on this street."

"Just to bother folks. They don't want people to get any rest. That's the truth. Harassment, plain and simple. Hey, there's room for you fellas here if you don't have a place to stay. I can get you a blanket," he pointed at his overfilled basket.

"That's very kind but we've got a place. We're just walking around, getting a feel for the evening," said James. He looked over at Deuce who was just smoking and staring into the street, not involved in the conversation to that point.

Deuce was a contemplative soul. While Fred counted and sorted his ballpoint pens, Deuce talked. His voice was quiet and a little slurred from the beer. Ben asked him what he thought about all of the downtown development. The new stores and the entertainment district. The answers surprised Ben.

"Man, I think development is good. I mean, people need something to do. Like they need people to work on the buildings or in the shops and restaurants right? So more jobs are provided. What's needed is more things for young people to do. Like in St Louis. That zoo and all of the downtown free activities."

"You've been to St Louis?"

"Sure! I've been to everywhere man. Like what if there were movies for people? Free ones. Not dirty movies or any of this violent shit. But like the old ones. Something that people of any age could watch. Just be able to come in off the street and rest and watch a movie."

"I like that idea."

"Sure you do. Look at all of these empty buildings. Why can't people go in there to sleep or get warm? It's a two way street. Developers come into our neighborhood and want to make money. That's fine but they need to give something also. Not just 'green space,' but something real. A game room. Or cheap housing. Or a place to sit and drink and shoot the shit. Somewhere that we aren't constantly getting hassled by the police."

Ben was listening intently, occasionally agreeing or guiding the conversation as Deuce went on with his beautiful vision of a harmonious community. After a while James said they had to get moving. They were supposed to meet a couple friends.

They walked up the street two blocks and ran into the guys. One was carrying a plastic grocery bag completely full of 40's. They were in there haphazardly, like he had just scooped them off the counter and let them fall into the bag. It seemed to Ben that some were empty but most were full. He could barely speak or walk and was surprised to see James.

"Man what you guys doing out here?"

"This is my friend Ben. Remember? We were going to come visit your camp tonight."

"Tonight? I thought that was tomorrow night."

"No, I talked to you this morning remember? Tonight."

The man seemed embarrassed and confused as he stood in the street holding the bag.

"I'm sorry. But you know I didn't think it was tonight and I got all these forties...."

"It's cool man, don't worry. Hey, so what're you two up to tonight?"

The other man spoke at that point. He was on the sidewalk and his words came faster and were less slurred.

"We're just going for a walk. Our women are back there. You should go see them. Man, they would be blessed to see you. Just go talk to them. Say anything. It would be a blessing, for real."

"Anything? Like 'Hi'?"

He laughed, "A blessing! Just go, they're right up at the seven-eleven. Across the street. You'll see them. That's my lady. You know her. We've been together twenty-seven years."

"What? Twenty-seven years?"

"Yes! We're married. Well, we didn't go to the courthouse," he said, gesturing back up Lancaster towards downtown. "But we're married in here," he pointed to his heart.

"That's a long time."

"Yeah, she's stuck with me. Never left. We've been out on these streets for... well, for a long time, but she's never left me. Man, just go talk to her. She's waiting up there. Her leg was hurting so they stopped. We're going to finish a few of these cans then we'll be back. Hey, you're staying with us right? See that cardboard?" He pointed across the street and down a ways towards the Salvation Army. "That's for you guys. We saved it for you."

Ben had been listening closely to the man who spoke with such eloquence and poetry and love, and when he pointed at the cardboard he felt such a surge of gratitude he almost hugged him. Even though the guys had forgotten the day and felt ashamed that they were too drunk to walk around with Ben, they had still set aside some prized bedding material.

James spoke next. "That's very kind of you. I think we're headed in a different direction, but we'll go talk to your ladies first okay?"

"Thank you so much. It will be a blessing to them and to me. Tell them we'll be back before long. Y'all stay safe," he said as he and his friend continued on their way. Deuce had walked up and was looking into the bag of beer. He was negotiating but so far had come up empty handed. The three started towards the Salvation Army as Ben and James turned the corner.

When they made it to the 7-11 they saw two women across the street sitting on concrete slabs and sucking on cans of beer. They recognized James and motioned him over. The larger of the two ladies did the talking while the thinner one smiled and nodded, punctuated by an occasional, "Amen" or "That's right."

"Samuel sent us over here. He said they'd be back in a few."

"Oh I know what they're up to. They ain't fooling me."

"Do you mind if we sit here for a few minutes and talk? This is my friend Ben by the way."

Ben put out his hand but she didn't move to shake it.

"Sure honey. But first could you boys turn around for just a second? You see, this is how I use the restroom."

Before turning Ben noticed that she was in fact carefully balanced on the concrete slab and there was a trickle of fluid that had run down and darkened the dirt. Her jeans were sagged down and her shirt and sweater were pulled over her thighs. Even when he knew what she was doing he had trouble believing how perfect her execution was.

When she was re-situated they sat and talked about the downtown development. Ben was surprised to learn that the conversation was about the same as before. She was more optimistic than he had expected. People seemed to give developers and government planners the benefit of the doubt, even when they appeared to betray that trust over and over.

High on her list of dreams was more public bathrooms. Somewhere to pee for free with dignity. But she also mentioned opening up the vacant buildings to people that needed them. There were plenty of places for people to sleep out of the cold. But the empty buildings sat boarded up and patrolled to keep poor folks out.

Ben and James listened and agreed and encouraged and after a while the two ladies said that they felt rested up and ready to go find their men. While they had been sitting there, a thin, dreadlocked guy came and somewhat stealthily placed a small package of weed up high on the electrical apparatus that the women were sitting on. He stood there for a moment then kind of paced around behind the four. He asked if they wanted to buy a Walkman for two dollars. They said no thanks and then he walked down the road. A few minutes later another guy came up quickly, took the packet and walked on. Ben saw it all but wasn't sure what was going on until James told him. He assumed there was money exchanged but he never saw that happen.

During their journey that night they were offered drugs twice and sex once. And at one house, as they walked along the sidewalk there were six Hispanic teenagers, no older than fifteen. One of them said, "Hey, do you two want a Corona? We have a lot in the house, help yourselves." The other five stared at Ben and James as they walked past, saying, "No thanks, you guys have fun and be careful." It was a little surreal but in the end, no stranger than the rest of the evening.

They talked to several other people that night and simply walked up and down Lancaster for a while longer. Finally, about eleven, James found the place where they would sleep. It was an old memorial of some kind at the end of an out-of-the-way road at the top of a small hill. There were several cars parked in front. Some had two people in them, others mysteriously had only one. Ben and James looked behind a concrete wall and saw a nice grassy area that was cleared of shrubbery. It dropped off quickly into the woods. They set up their sleeping bags and then sat on the ledge talking. James pulled out a sheet of paper and showed it to Ben.

"So, earlier tonight we talked about Deuteronomy eight, remember?"

"Is that what this is? Yeah, it seemed really appropriate. The parts that you quoted before."

"Is it ok if I read the whole thing? I think it might have even more meaning now that we've spent some time on the streets."

James began "*Remember how the Lord your God led you through the wilderness for these forty years, humbling you and testing you to prove your character, and to find out whether or not you would obey God's commands?*"

He continued to read verses two to eighteen, stressing the parts that described how God provided when they were wandering in the desert. And how now they were headed to a land of milk and honey and would have houses and food and iron and copper.

"*Be careful that you do not forget the Lord your God, failing to observe his commands, his laws and his decrees that I am giving you this day. Otherwise, when you eat and are satisfied, when you build fine houses and settle down, and when your herds and flocks grow large and your silver and gold increase and all you have is multiplied, then your heart will become proud and you will forget the Lord your God, who brought you out of Egypt, out of the land of slavery. He led you through the vast and dreadful wilderness, that thirsty and waterless land, with its venomous snakes and scorpions. He brought you water out of hard rock. He gave you manna to eat in the wilderness, something your ancestors had never known, to humble and test you so that in the end it might go well with you. You may say to yourself, "My power and the strength of my hands have produced this wealth for me." But remember the Lord your God, for it is he who gives you the ability to produce wealth, and so confirms his covenant, which he swore to your ancestors, as it is today."*

James put down the paper and was silent. Ben had been watching James read and now looked straight ahead, also silent for a moment as they listened to the wind and watched as one of the cars slowly pulled away.

Finally Ben said, "Thank you for this. For all of it. It's been an amazing night. I have so much to think about."

"That's the point. When you finish college and then medical school and then when you've been in private practice for fifteen years. When you've bought everything that you want to buy, when you've been everywhere, eaten everything, when the novelty is gone... well, I want you to remember these people down here on Lancaster. I want you to remember that we have all been lost in the wilderness. That even you were once lost. I want you to remember that there are people just like you down here. Smart, insightful, caring people who through the luck of birth, circumstance and choice are stuck at the bottom. And I want you to find a way to help them in a tangible way. You know now that throwing money at it doesn't help it. Writing a check is a cop out. Talk with someone. Or even better, listen to us. We have ideas and we know what we need. Listening is how the healing begins."

They prayed together. And it wasn't awkward or strange or unnatural. They took turns praying for the people they had met on their journey, for their health and safety. For the landlords and the developers and the city planners to have softened and creative hearts. For politicians to plan for long-term solutions. And they praised God for the beauty that is found in all of creation and for the wisdom that is carried by the outcast and marginalized. Finally, after a period of silence, they prayed the Lord's Prayer.

And then they crawled into their sleeping bags behind the rock wall. James quickly fell asleep while Ben stared at the stars. He listened to sirens, cars, trains, helicopters, and even some gunshots. There were crickets and frogs and some unidentified sounds. It was the sound of the city and of the earth. He became cold as the night went on. The hard, lumpy earth below drained his body heat. If he lay on his side he could stop shivering but his hip and shoulders quickly became painful from the rocks digging into them. So all night long he moved from back to side to back to side, pulling the sleeping bag over his head and breathing into it to warm up the interior.

But all this time he was never anxious or worried about the discomfort or the lack of sleep. He knew that Sunday he could rest and that he didn't have much homework. He was thankful for the cold earth and the hard dirt and the discomfort. It made him feel that much closer to those that he had met that night. If on a relatively warm night he was so miserable, how did they do it? How did they go on day after day and night after night?

Finally daylight arrived. He unzipped the bag, crawled out and went down the hill a little to pee. He came back and sat against the wall for a few minutes with the bag wrapped around his shoulders until James woke up. When they had packed up their things they walked back to Lancaster and then towards downtown where Ben could catch a bus and eventually get back to campus.

They didn't talk much, both lost in their thoughts that cool, cloudless morning, with the yellow-pink tint causing everything to shine in a warm glow that felt like hope and peace.

Once they were at the bus stop Ben thanked James and they hugged and went their separate ways, promising to meet again soon. The bus eventually brought Ben back to campus. He got off with a cafeteria worker that he recognized, following her in to get coffee and some warm biscuits and gravy. He sat down at an empty table and covered the gravy in black pepper and then, without thinking, shook hot sauce all over everything. Tired, cold, and fuzzy headed, the meal was one of the best he had ever tasted and at that point he was grateful for everything.

18

He finished the meal and went back to the dorm to shower and change. The hot water was a revelation and something that he wouldn't take for granted for days. By the time he was cleaned up it was only ten fifteen so he decided to go to church before starting to study.

The sermon was another good one. This time from Luke 19:1-10. It was about Zacchaeus and that sycamore tree that he climbed to get a better view of Jesus. He was a tax collector and everyone in town knew him as a greedy, mean little man. And yet something changed while he was up that tree. When Jesus saw him there and asked him to come down and that he would like to eat with him that evening, Zacchaeus pledged to give over half of his belongings to the poor.

It reminded Ben of the day before. How he had chosen to go out on the streets to meet people where they live. The streets were his sycamore tree. And James was his Jesus. He had sought out the place where he could see more clearly. Where he could find a different vantage point. Like Zacchaeus he knew that by staying on the ground with everyone else he wasn't ever going to change. He already knew how things looked from where he was. And he was stuck in that understanding and perspective. But by climbing a tree- and Ben tried to imagine the small grown man trying to get up those first branches- or by carrying a sleeping bag and a backpack up and down Lancaster, he was risking change.

And when Zacchaeus came down, he immediately decided to give up half his belongings and to make restitution with everyone that he had cheated. His new outlook led to immediate action. He couldn't live in the same manner. He saw that life wasn't about property or belongings or even prestige or respect. It was service and humility. It was justice and equality.

The story was a powerful one and Ben spent the afternoon reflecting on it and on his own treetop experience. What could he do differently? He didn't have possessions or money. He didn't have influence over groups of people. What he did have was potential. Intelligence. And youth. All very powerful qualities. His thinking began to shift that day. From becoming a doctor with a goal of stability, wealth and prestige to becoming one for the sole purpose of helping others.

He began to think in terms of possibly becoming an Emergency Room physician. Or Infectious Disease. Or Primary Care. He had years to decide and still felt like he wanted to become a surgeon but maybe he would avoid becoming too specialized. He would try to keep from digging himself into a hole in which he could only treat a small subset of patients. He wanted to be able to help everyone.

He was working through these thoughts while attempting to focus on the task at hand. Passing biology. He was actually doing fine in there but the weekend was about to slip away and he had done very little studying. At least he had been trying. That was more than he could say for Denny who finally showed up at the library at four in the afternoon to say he couldn't stay long.

"What? Why not?"

"I've got some things I need to take care of."

"Really? Instead of passing biology? Because I would think that would be a little higher on your to-do list."

"Well, then you would be wrong. And I'm going to pass it, don't worry."

"I'm not worried for me. I'm worried for you. We have a test soon and have you even looked at the material yet? Have you finished the lab that's due this week? I haven't seen you since Friday night. Where have you been?"

"Well, you didn't see me Saturday night because you were wandering around downtown with your new homeless bestie. And this morning because you were at church learning to be more saint-like and patronizing."

"Patronizing? Really? That's what you think? I just care about you and want you to succeed. How is that patronizing?"

"It is. You aren't my dad or my parole officer. I was here studying this morning for like two hours. So maybe I'm farther along than you are. And maybe you should mind your own business."

"Listen, I'm sorry Denny. It's not your fault. I'm just tired. I didn't sleep last night and now I'm worried about this coming week."

"As well you should be. So am I. If I don't do well on this round of tests I'm done here."

"So, stay and study with me then."

"I can't. Not today. I promise I'll be here tomorrow okay?"

Denny's eyes were anxious and clouded. He was in a hurry to get out of there, already repacking his things.

"You just got here. I didn't mean to chase you away already."

"No, it's fine. I need to get going. I didn't have very long and now there's no point in getting started. "

"I'm sorry Denny."

"For what? You've got nothing to be sorry for."

"For being patronizing. About the other day. It isn't any of my business. I know that we're all making our way through life the best way that we know how. I'm not perfect. In fact I'm a raging mess."

"You think?"

"That obvious?"

"You've about gone off the deep end my friend. Sleeping on the streets, obsessed with a girl that you've briefly seen twice… You're the one that needs help, not me. And I'm not even going to mention your music."

"Okay, there you go. See? We're all confused and searching. But again, I'm sorry. This semester has been hard on everyone. None of us have done this before. Been away from home, been forced to find friends, self-motivate, wash our own clothes, get ourselves out of bed, study with no one to nag us. It's not easy. And I'm proud of myself and of you. We've done a pretty good job so far."

"Except that shirt actually hasn't been washed since Kansas."

"Okay, those were just examples. Yeah, I haven't really got the whole washer/dryer thing down yet. Hey, I don't want to keep you. We can talk later if you want, I'll be around."

"Thanks Ben. I may take you up on that. Maybe we can watch Designing Women together."

"You know I never miss an episode."

Denny pulled his backpack over his right shoulder and turned to go. Ben watched him with an unnamed concern and dread, resolving to check on him later that night.

He ended up studying another hour then deciding that he couldn't do anymore. Partly because he felt like he knew the material. But mostly because he was exhausted from the night before and his mind was having trouble focusing on anything except the conversations that had occurred on the streets.

How could he be here, in a quiet, safe library with a clean restroom on every level? How, even with such limited funds, can he have a full stomach and snacks waiting in his backpack? How could he have had that long hot shower this morning? And the soft, comfortable, bug-free bed that he didn't have to stand in line for. He didn't have to show ID, or sit through a church service, or risk getting beat up or knifed if he looked at someone the wrong way. He had it so easy and had taken it for granted.

And not only did he have the comfort and safety, he also had love. As lonely as he felt much of the time he really wasn't alone. He had Brian and Tim and Denny. He had Steve and Marti and Silky. There were people that he talked to in class, said hi to in the cafeteria. He even had the nerds in Tom Brown's common room. There were the kids he talked to at swimmer's parties and at the Pub. He had been taking all of this for granted also. He had complained inwardly that he didn't have anyone when in fact he was surrounded with people.

James was the one that needed a friend. Someone on his side. He was out there struggling day to day, foraging for food, trying to keep warm, looking for bathrooms, keeping his head down so as not to be noticed by police or security guards or fast food employees or mad dogs or angry, schizophrenic, paranoid, drug-addicted people on the streets. His own addictions and depression had brought him there but it wasn't fair that so much had been stripped away. He'd literally lost everything. He had paid for any mistakes so many times over that he had lost count.

Ben didn't know what to do with this feeling. He didn't know how to turn these intense feelings into something useful. He had to finish school. Had to go through the steps, pass the classes, get the degree, then get the other degree, then do a residency, then make some money, then begin to help people with his time and money. Really? Was that the only way to do this?

He felt the pull to go back out there. To find James and... do what? Become homeless too? Just hang out? It was unreasonable and confusing. And in the end he decided to just make James a mixtape. Why not? He had an old Walkman and it wasn't like there were any good radio stations around. Nor could he get in to see shows. It was one small thing that he could do to help his new friend.

Back in his room Tim was there but was headed out.

"So what are you up to tonight?" Tim asked.

"Nothing really, just going to make a tape for a friend. When do you think you'll be back?"

"We don't have any specific plans. But I'll give you a few hours. Unless you plan to put some of my music on there."

"Not a chance buddy."

"Didn't think so. I'll see you later then."

"Sounds good. Thanks for understanding."

"Dude, I'm doing this for myself. Your music sucks," he laughed as he left the room.

Ben got out a pen and paper and started flipping through his records. He had a fairly good idea what kind of music James liked. Some old Blues occasionally. But he also had enjoyed that Zeitgeist show that he was lurking outside of, and liked hardcore punk and newer stuff.

He began putting the records into piles, beginning to make A side and B side stacks. The A side would be loud and aggressive, but he would load the first part with the angry songs and let the emotion soften as the side progressed.

Side B would continue that trend, eliminating the chaos and volume and introducing folk and eventually the blues. He started recording, getting lost in the sounds and in the act of creation. He read the liner notes and studied the front and back covers. Sights, sounds, smells and memories came before his mind with each song. They reminded him of specific times, places and people.

He had carefully recorded the playing time of each song before finalizing the list, attempting to use every bit of the forty-five minutes on each side of the tape. Some songs took more than once to get just right. He dropped the needle in the wrong place, forgot to start the tape, forgot to rewind the tape, waited too long to stop the tape. It ended up taking nearly three hours to get every song just right.

Here's how it looked:

Side A
My War- Black Flag
Retired at 21- Black Flag
I'm So Bored with the USA- the Clash
Banned in D.C. – Bad Brains
Kill the Poor- Dead Kennedys
God Save the Queen- Sex Pistols
Bastards of Young- Replacements
Wichita Cathedral- Butthole Surfers
New Day Rising- Husker Du
Broken Home, Broken Heart- Husker Du
1970- The Stooges

Sonic Reducer- Dead Boys
Suburban Home- Descendants
Killing Us- Public Bulletin

Side B
Up on the Sun- Meat Puppets
Kiss Off- Violent Femmes
To Have and to Have Not- Billy Bragg
Waterfront- Simple Minds
Where Were You Hiding When the Storm Broke? – The Alarm
Charlotte Sometimes- the Cure
Sweet Jane- Velvet Underground
Treatment Bound- Replacements
Sally MacLennane- The Pogues
Green- Public Bulletin
Nine Below Zero- Sonny Boy Williamson
Worried Life Blues- Lightnin' Hopkins
In the Neighborhood- Tom Waits

He put all of the records back in their places and just as he was finishing and beginning to think about getting ready for bed the phone rang. Their phone didn't ring often. There wasn't anyone that he could imagine wanting to talk to but he answered anyway.

"Hey, what're you doing?" said the excited voice on the other end of the line.

"Who is…? Oh, Denny. Hey, what's up?"

"Good, you're home, meet me outside in five minutes."

"Why? What're you up to?"

"What are WE up to? We're going to a party. At Freddy's apartment. It's going to be epic and you're coming."

"Dude, we've got class tomorrow. I was about ready for bed."

"Stop whining and let's go. I'll be there in five. No excuses."

"Alright, alright. I'll be ready. We can't stay out super late though okay? Promise me."

"I promise. Okay bye."

He hung up, changed his shirt, sprayed on some Armani cologne, slipped on his worn out LL Bean leather bluchers and left the room, forgetting to turn out the light.

19

Ben waited outside Tom Brown for five minutes before he realized that Denny might not be coming after all. It was already past ten and he really just wanted to go to bed early and be well rested for Monday morning. He wavered for a few minutes, trying to talk himself into going back inside and climbing into bed. But in the end, with a "dammit" under his breath, he walked next door to Denny's dorm.

The side door was locked at night. He was hoping that somebody had propped it open but no such luck. He decided to go to the main door and talk his way in without alerting Denny that he was there. Something was definitely up with his friend and he was now committed to seeing it through.

Just as he reached the bottom step of the main entrance someone came out the side. It was a tennis player he had talked to before, one who lived on Denny's floor.

"Hey, can you hold that door for me?" Ben said, hurrying over.

"Oh hey sure," the boy said, waiting for him to arrive. "You looking for Denny?"

"Thanks a lot," said Ben, grabbing the door and swinging in. "Yeah, how'd you know?"

"Just a hunch. Man he's flying already. Are y'all coming to the party? I can drive if you hurry. I'll wait here long enough to smoke a cigarette."

Ben felt increasingly uneasy about this whole scenario as he thanked the guy, remembering that his name was Billy as he bounded up the stairs to the second floor and found Denny in the hallway with a beer in one hand and a cordless phone in the other.

"Okay, I'll get it to you tonight. Don't worry. Fifteen minutes," he was saying. "No, fifteen minutes. I've got you my friend. Usual spot."

"Ben!" he said, turning off the phone and tossing it on his bed. "Where the hell have you been, Ben?" He laughed at his joke. "Glad you're here. Hey, I'm going to a party. Wanna go?"

"That's why I'm here dumbass. You were supposed to meet me."

"Oh yeah, sorry. I forgot."

"I see that. Hey, that tennis guy, Billy, is waiting downstairs. Are you ready? And are you sure you should be going out?"

"Huh? What do you mean? Of course I'm sure. I called you, remember?"

"Yeah but I just…"

"It's going to be great. Oh and guess what? I heard Sheila's going to be there."

"Sheila?"

"Yeah, you remember, Sheila... from the Pub. The love of my life."

"Seriously? Is that what this is about? Dude you need a therapist. This is nuts. She isn't interested in you."

"You have no faith, Benedict. I can do this. Tonight's the night. I can feel it. The air is pregnant with possibilities and excitement. Can't you feel it?"

They got to the door and found Billy leaning against the dorm, pulling on the last of his Marlboro Light, he kicked off the wall saying, "Hey Denny, y'all ready?"

"Ready. Oh and shotgun. I get to pick the music. What do you have in there?"

"Okay you can ride up front but I get to choose the music," said Ben. "And wouldn't you know... I have just the thing," He pulled James' mix tape out of his pocket. He had mistakenly grabbed it on the way out the door. He wondered briefly what he was trying to find when he took the tape instead. Wallet? Money? Either way it now seemed like a lucky mistake, as there was no telling what kind of crap Billy listened to.

"I haven't authorized this," said Billy. "Have you all heard of Randy Travis? Storms of Life? We may have to check that out on the way."

"I've heard of him," said Ben. "There've been articles about him and Dwight Yoakum and Steve Earle. The New Traditionalists or something. He's the most country of the three though I think."

"I don't know Steve Earle but Dwight's cool. 'Guitars, Cadillacs' is a great song. Oh and that other one..."

"Heartaches by the Number?"

"Yeah that's it. I think it's an old song but it's really amazing. They play it at some of the honky-tonks around here."

"Uh.... yeah… I don't frequent honky-tonks very often."

"Really? You should. You haven't been to Billy Bob's or the White Elephant? Dude, you have to. How is it that you've been in Fort Worth all semester and have been deprived of that pleasure?"

"Hard to believe huh? In general, country isn't really my thing. There's some country-ish stuff I like. Long Ryders, Flying Burrito Brothers, Dellords, Del Fuegos, the Blasters, even Johnny Cash. And yeah Steve Earle and Dwight are on that list now. I don't know what's happening to me. Maybe I do need to get some boots and Wranglers and get down to Billy Bob's. Ride the mechanical bull. Hell, I am in Fort Worth after all."

Denny finally spoke up as they reached the car. "We aren't going to Billy Bob's. It's lame and depressing and racist. And we aren't listening to any country shit. Billy may be sucking you in with his smooth talk and schoolgirl looks but it's not happening. And anyway, what part of shotgun do you people not understand? Ben, hand over that tape."

Ben climbed in the back of the Accord behind Denny, pushing dirty clothes and a tennis racket to the other side. Mountain Dew cans and tennis balls were on the floor and he had to kick them over the middle hump to make room for his legs.

"Sorry about the mess back there Ben. Wasn't expecting company."

"No problem. I'm excavating out a spot."

Billy backed out as Denny fiddled with the radio, saying, "Hey, where's that tape?" as he ejected George Strait from the cassette player.

"George's case should be down by your feet somewhere," Billy said. "Can you find it?"

"Yeah, I've got it," said Denny, returning George to his holder and putting him away in the center console saying, "Ben, let's see that tape you made. It's for James the homeless guy, right?"

"You made a mix tape for a homeless guy? That's not strange at all. What's he supposed to do with it?"

"He's supposed to listen to it. Homeless doesn't always mean possessionless. He has things. Clothes, a place to sleep, and yeah he even has a Walkman."

"Well, he can't be that poor if he has a Walkman."

"Huh? Do you have any idea what an apartment costs here? Rent and utilities every month. First and last month's rent and a deposit before he even moves in. Transportation. Thousands upon thousands of dollars. Do you know how much a used Walkman costs at a pawnshop or on the street? Not much."

"Okay, sorry. That was a little insensitive. It just surprised me I guess. And he likes your whacked-out music?"

"He likes my diverse and eclectic and creative music? Yes. So I made him a tape."

"How did you meet this James guy?"

"It's kind of a long story but we've crossed paths a few times. And last night I spent the night on the streets with him. I wanted to get a better feel for what life is like out there. It was an eye opener for sure."

Ben proceeded to give a summary of his time on Lancaster with James. It was very brief as Denny had already heard it and quickly became bored with the subject.

Pushing in the tape and cranking up the volume, Greg Ginn's atonal, menacing, distorted and unmistakable guitar sounds kicked in. Small drum rolls helped set the tone and then, thirty seconds in, Henry Rollins let out the first howls of "My War."

Denny began banging his head and playing air guitar and Ben became distracted as he listened, his story fading out.

"Seriously? This is what we're listening to?"

"Come on man, shout along. 'My warrrrrr, you say you're my friend but you're one of themmmm!!" Denny knew this one because Black Flag were from Redondo, not too far up A1A from Laguna. They were huge in California. Or at least as huge as an aggressive hardcore punk band can be with no radio play and no major label support. The song brought back memories of slam dancing with the skate punks back home.

"I can't believe they broke up. It still hasn't really sunk in," said Ben.

"I know! They're so amazing and innovative and awesome. I'm not sure I want to live in a post- Black Flag world."

"Yeah, I think everything will be okay. Everyone will survive. The sun will still rise and set," Billy was saying as he turned down the volume.

"I don't think you understand... Hey, wait, where are we?" We need to go back the other way."

"What, why? The party's this way."

"Can you just turn around? It won't take long. I need to see if someone's home. Check something."

"Okay, but I'm ready to get to the party. You sure this won't take long?" Billy said as he made a U-turn at the next intersection.

"Promise. It'll be quick. It's up here. Turn right at that grey house."

Denny guided him right, then left, then right again to a suburban side street.

"That one. On the right. Pull up to the mailbox," he said, reaching into his jacket pocket to pull out a small foil wrapped package.

When Billy had the car positioned so that the front passenger's window was lined up, Denny reached over to the mailbox, opened it, scooped out a letter sized envelope, peeking inside and then dropped the aluminum foil into the box, shutting the door and saying, "Okay let's go. Take a left up here."

As Billy pulled away he said, "What did I just participate in? I thought you had to meet someone. It feels like I may have been an accessory to a crime."

"Yeah, sorry about that. You'll be fine though. No one saw us."

"Really? How do you know? Have you been to that house before? Who was it? How do you know it wasn't an undercover cop? How do you know this place isn't swarming with them? Someone may be calling them right now. A lot of these streets have neighborhood watch vigilante, Rambo-type people. One could have been in the shadows of their porch writing down my license plate number. What's the matter with you?"

"Dude relax. Everything'll be fine. He's cool. It's not his first time and he has as much to lose as I do if either of us gets busted. Nothing is going to happen."

"Still. Not cool. Don't pull that shit on me again okay?" he said as he worked his way back to Bellaire Drive.

"Sorry. You're right."

Ben was still in shock but tried to defuse the situation as the last strains of Black Flag's "Retired at 21" faded and the Clash kicked in. "Did they make the greatest first album of all time or what?"

"Who is it?" asked Billy. "It sounds familiar but I can't place it. As we've just established, I mainly know country."

"It's the Clash."

"Oh yeah, 'Rock the Casbah'…"

"What? No, that's like their worst song. Made for MTV. No, you know some of their songs. 'Should I Stay or Should I Go' and 'Train in Vain.' Those are bar band standards."

"Not at the bars I go to."

"Both of those are on the jukebox at the Pub. Surely you've heard them there. Anyway, you should check them out. They rock, they sound a little ska at times, and they're political in all the best ways. This is from their first album. I think you can guess the title," he said as the refrain of "I'm so bored with the USA" repeated.

"Yep. Yeah, it would be hard to dislike this. It's pretty catchy."

Denny was bouncing his head around and singing along loudly. The windows were down but it was dark and chilly and no one was outside to hear. As he watched from the back seat Ben once again noticed how wired Denny was. Everything was fifty percent faster, fifty percent louder, and fifty percent more important. He was singing, laughing, dancing and talking. So much talking.

"Have you ever tried it?" he was saying. "I mean have you seen that guy? Robert Tilton, the preacher on late night television? I know it seems crazy but I believe in him. He talks about how if we have faith we'll be successful. Get everything we want. Maybe he's just found a great way to get rich but what if that's not all? What if he's on to something? If we believe and pray and practice positive thinking we can be happy and rich?"

"Is that what you want? To be rich?" Ben said as Denny took a breath.

"Doesn't everyone? I mean really? If we're honest? Money is the most important thing. With money comes freedom. Freedom to live life the way we dream. With money I can go wherever I want. I can surf, buy a house and a dog, buy drugs, go to restaurants, get a Ferrari, live the Miami Vice lifestyle. Seriously how cool would it be to have one of those white suits that Crockett wears? Drive a Testarossa. Have a big contemporary white house with nothing in it except identical suits in a white closet. Never wear socks. A huge TV and a massive sound system. Soft couches. Hot, deeply tanned girls falling all over me. What do you think? Are you in?"

"What are you proposing? No I don't want all that. My fantasies are much different from yours. But how do you suggest we get there? Selling drugs to fellow students? Praying to Robert Tilton that we don't get caught and put away for ten years? All so we can make a fifty dollar profit?"

"First of all, it's much more than fifty dollars. The amount of money would make your head spin. The potential is limitless. Guess how much I made just now. Take a stab at it."

"I just did. Fifty dollars. Obviously it's higher."

"Not even close. Would you believe three hundred? Yep, three hundred bucks profit for five minutes work with little to no risk. It's amazing huh? And I owe it all to God and Robert Tilton."

"Whoa- what?"

"Haven't you been listening? It's Robert Tilton. The man is a genius. A prophet. Don't look at me like that. I'm serious."

"That's why I'm looking at you like this."

"It's true. Haven't you seen him? It's all true. All you have to do is believe. Trust in him. I've been embarrassed to tell you because I knew you'd make fun of me. But as I sit close to the TV and as he tells me to put my hands on his I do it. And I can feel the power right through the glass. I'm telling you it's real. He prays for me and can give me anything I want."

"You touch the television?"

"Yes, of course. You've never watched have you? You have to. Tonight! Or maybe tomorrow night. That's how he does it. It's so real. I can feel his fingers. They're warm and there's energy that courses through me. It's what's protecting me right now. It's why I wasn't worried about getting caught back there. I can be invisible or super small or make others think I'm someone else. I can fake my identity."

"You're literally insane."

"I knew you'd say that. But I don't care anymore. It's self-evident. Look at me. My grades are better. I'm happier. I'm making money. I have so much energy. I can get any girl I want."

"Are you sending him money?"

"Who?"

"You know who. This televangelist."

"Fuck you. You have no idea what you're talking about."

"Are you?"

"It's none of your business. Screw you," Denny said, turning around to face forward.

"You are! How much have you sent?"

"I'm not telling you anything. It isn't much."

"How much? Five hundred?"

"Five hundred won't get me anything. He wouldn't even notice."

"Ha! So you admit it! What do you mean he wouldn't notice?"

"You have to make a vow of a thousand to get the special prayers. More money, more attention. You get out what you put in. Like in life."

"That isn't how life works. Life is about grace and position at birth. Then later it's about hard work and focus. It isn't about paying bribes to a television conman."

"You don't know anything about it. There's nothing more real. Look at me. I'm proof."

"You're proof he's a sham. I can't believe you sent money. And over a thousand!"

"He warned us that people would say that. It doesn't matter though. I thought you were a Christian. I know what I believe and I know he's helping me get closer to God and to my own potential. He's a true prophet. A miracle worker. And he's the reason I'm alive right now talking to you."

Before Ben could protest Brian pulled the car up behind an old Audi on a suburban side street. There were at least fifteen cars lining both sides of the road. He said, "Sorry to interrupt you two psychopaths but here we are. And please don't talk about this shit at the party?"

"No problem. Just point me in the direction of the keg."

20

They walked through a lawn and followed the sound of music and voices until they found the correct backyard. The metal gate had been left open so they walked in and then back to the gathering on the patio. There were probably forty people in various stages of inebriation. Girls with floral dresses and red bows in their hair and girls in t-shirts and running shorts. Boys in frat shirts and boys with spiky mullets and polo shirts.

Ben looked around and didn't immediately see anyone he was interested in talking to. Billy had already gone to join his tennis friends so Ben followed Denny to the keg. It was like a watering hole in a desert oasis. Everyone shared it in relative harmony. People that usually wouldn't speak to each other ended up pumping the keg or holding open the spout over an outstretched cup. It was a beautiful thing and soon the two friends had their own red Solo cups filled to the rim.

Denny had mercifully stopped expounding on his love for his savior Robert Tilton but had moved on to something only slightly less irritating. He was trying to start a conversation about how there should always be sweet snacks at a party.

"This from someone who brought neither salty nor sweet snacks. Nor money," said the swimmer he was talking to.

"I did actually bring money. A pretty large amount of it actually. And I'm happy to run out and get more food if needed. That's not the point. The point is that some people don't like chips. Well some chips. Chocolate chips yes. Potato chips no."

"But I think it's pretty universal that salty goes with beer. When have you ever been to a bar and seen Hershey's Kisses in a little bowl? Never, that's when. When have you ever sat at a bar, taken a sip from a frosty mug and reached over for a handful of M&M's?"

"But why not? I would love to do that. There have certainly been much more idiotic things than that. In fact, the Pub has a jar of pickled eggs."

"Right, salty."

"Yeah, but who's ever eaten one? I've spent hours and hours there and have never once seen the bartender reach in for a pickled hardboiled egg and serve it up to an expectantly waiting frat kid. Have you? I mean how absurd are those things? The giant pickles are weird enough and I've never seen anyone eat those either, but an egg? I'm telling you, sell Kit Kats and bags of M&M's or even big soft chocolate chip cookies with huge chunks of chocolate. Any of those would put the pickled egg vendor out of business so fast. Of course there might not even be a pickled egg vendor at this point. I'm fairly confident that the same jar has been there since at least nineteen fifty-eight."

"So candy. In a bar?"

"Not all candy. Not gummy worms or jawbreakers or anything that takes forever to eat and gets stuck in your teeth. I mean the main activity is still drinking. But yeah chocolate, Pixy Sticks, cookies, maybe apple pie, things that can be eaten quickly. How about sugar cubes? Just lay them out there in a bowl on the bar and let people dig in."

The swimmer shook his head and walked away at that but Denny didn't miss a beat. He immediately started up a new conversation with a girl that had the misfortune of standing too close to him.

"So what do you really think of Gilligan's Island?"

"Huh? I don't."

"No, but if you were to think of it, what would you think?"

"Umm, it's terrible but that I couldn't avoid it when I was growing up. It seemed to be on constantly."

"Yeah, exactly. Terrible and yet provocative."

"No, I said it was on all the time, that doesn't make it provocative."

"I'm reading between the lines here. Consciously or not, you watched it for some reason."

"Because we had three channels and the other two were worse."

"Okay, well, let's take as a given that you watched it when you could've turned it off and done something else. So why? You knew that it would be the same every week. There was a tiny uninteresting mystery, usually a new character. There was the miniscule hope of finally getting off the island. Then less than twenty minutes later we see the special guest star floating away on a boat."

"Yeah it was pretty predictable. Hey, my friend is waiting for this beer," she said slightly raising the red Solo cup in her left hand while she held the right hand cup steady.

Denny wasn't phased by her departure. He continued with another bowhead at the keg.

"What makes us watch it? What is it that makes the show so compelling? It's called Gilligan's Island but I don't think we watch for Gilligan. He's certainly not the most likeable character. He's a goof and he's funny-looking, and not in a good way either. He looks older than the way he dresses. You know? It's like he's some kind of teenager but he's not. He looks like he's in his forties, which I find a little disconcerting. Now Mary Ann, she was the star."

The girl finally spoke up. "Mary Ann? Seriously?"

"Yeah of course."

"How can you say that? What about Ginger or the Captain? Even the Howells are more important than Mary Ann."

"I beg to differ. Mary Ann, who by the way was from Winfield, Kansas…"

"Dawn Wells was from Kansas?"

"No, not the actress, her character. Mary Ann was. Anyway, she was always the calm one. The one who held everything together. Even the professor would get caught up in crazy schemes and plans. But Mary Ann, she could see through everyone and would often catch on the fastest. It didn't hurt that she was the most beautiful."

"Okay, I knew you'd get around to that. You think she's hot."

"Well, yeah, of course. You know, you have a little of that Mary Ann look yourself. Has anyone ever told you that?"

"Oh please," she said, rolling her eyes and walking away.

"Hey, wait!" She ducked behind a football player as Denny turned to another swimmer and continued.

"But really, I think it's the idea of hope. Perpetual and eternal hope. These people are never getting off this island. Never. And yet every week they get back up and try again."

After checking out who was there at the party, Ben had come back to the keg to see what Denny was up to. He saw his friend talking excitedly to someone about Gilligan's Island. He listened off to the side for a bit then jumped in.

"Wait a minute. Hope? How is that hope? I'll admit there's a moment every week where the viewer feels like there's a chance that they'll get off the island. But that feeling fades just as quickly and we know they won't. Not that week and not any week."

"Well, you're a little cynical."

"No, I'm a realist. They don't want off the island. Admit it, every single week you can figure out a way to get out of there. They always go about it all wrong. By the later seasons they've invented so many things but somehow still can't build a boat? Scores of people have visited but they can't convince even one of them to let them hitch a ride? Not one?"

"Did you just say 'scores'?"

"Yep, I did. This rant called for it. No, they didn't have hope. They were scared. It's a metaphor for all of us. Living on that island became their normal. It's where they were comfortable. They did everything imaginable on their little place on earth except try to leave. It's their box, their containment. It makes perfect sense for them to work inside the limits of the box and not be able to see outside of it."

"This whole explanation is going to end up with 'thinking outside the box'? Lame."

"That's part of it, but it's all about fear of change. We all feel it. They'd have to go through a period of uncertainty if they truly wanted out. It's the same thing when someone changes jobs, or gets married, or divorced, or has children, or learns to sky dive, or stops doing drugs. It's terrifying, the unknown that threatens to shake up the status quo."

"Okay, I see that."

"Yeah, one has to move from a nice safe predictable life to a chaotic one in order to change or grow as a person. It's a helluva blind leap but if we can do it, if we can jump into the unknown, there's such unlimited potential. We can go from order to reorder, but first we have to experience disorder. It takes time and there'll be pain but it's the only chance at true life we have."

"I'm not sure we're talking about Gilligan's Island anymore."

"No, I am. They're all scared that their community will break up. That Ginger won't talk to Gilligan anymore. Or the Professor will go back to being a lonely introvert. But they aren't being true to themselves. It's too small a container. It isn't life. So that's why I can't watch it. It's soul crushing to see them sabotage every opportunity they have to get off the island. They're scared and dead inside and by watching them it legitimizes that kind of behavior. It makes it normal to keep doing the same thing over and over."

"You've thought about this entirely too much."

"Well, at least I'm not staring at Mary Ann's chest the whole time."

"Where were you looking then?"

"Her big green eyes of course. And her eyes looked beautiful and yet terrified and achingly sad. And in the end I couldn't watch them anymore. I have enough trouble focusing on the present and experiencing life the way it could be. Open and infinite and beautiful. I don't need Gilligan and the Captain crushing my spirit."

"Wow, ok."

"Hey thanks for letting me get that off my chest, Denny. Another beer?"

"Sure, anytime. And yes. Here, I'll pump and you hold the cups."

"Teamwork."

"Did you see? Sheila's here."

"Yeah, I saw. I was hoping you didn't."

"Seriously? That's rude. You're supposed to be watching out for me. And what about leaping into the void?"

"I am. And you don't need to become obsessed with her again. Have you even spoken to her in the past month?"

"Yes. Not much. But yes. And anyway, who cares? Tonight's the night. "

"Tonight's the night? What makes you think that?"

"Because, tonight I'm irresistible. I could charm Cindy Crawford tonight. She'd be like, 'Yes, Denny, anything you say Denny, you want me to move to Fort Worth? To move in with you? To share your twin bed. I'll do it tomorrow…'"

"So, you're having a manic fantasy about Cindy Crawford and that's supposed to make me think that Sheila, with whom you've shared seven words in the past three months, is going to fall in love with you right here, right now at this ordinary and somewhat lame college party."

"Precisely," Denny said as he left to pursue his dream.

That left Ben to look around at the scene. The party really was somewhat lame. By now he been to quite a few and they were all pretty much the same, but this one had a weird energy. Not a particularly joyful one. Maybe because the weather was cold and gloomy. Maybe because it was a Sunday night and everyone was worried about school the next day. Maybe he was simply tired and starting to get a little drunk and was seeing everything through that filter. He wasn't sure but was glad when Denny left him alone so he could think for a few minutes.

There was a patio with a low stone wall and a small bit of yard behind that, shrubbery encased the yard, creating some privacy from the neighbors. A sliding glass door led into the kitchen, which was brightly lit, but fairly devoid of people. Nearly everyone was on the patio, either gathered near the keg or the table that was covered in chips and pretzels and salsa, or sitting on or standing near the rock wall.

Denny was now on the lawn trying to infiltrate a small group of girls that included the famous Sheila. As Ben sat down on the stones a little away from everyone else he watched their interaction. Sheila was a pretty girl, there was no doubt. She had long dark hair, stood very straight and laughed easily. Mercifully she wasn't wearing a bow and from what Ben could see her body was thin and fit, like a dancer. She seemed to be the leader of her friends as everyone was turned to her in the circle and laughed and smiled as she talked. So far, Denny was outside the circle. They had looked at him but he hadn't been drawn into the conversation.

Ben was thinking it didn't look too hopeful for his friend when his focus was distracted by the music. There were outward facing speakers in the kitchen windows and to that point there had been a tolerable mix of New Wave and pop songs. But when Phil Collins came on he cringed and knew that he had to change the music before the dreaded Sussudio came on and made everything infinitely worse. It was the perfect job. Something he could do as Denny worked his magic.

As he prepared to go inside to find the source of the awful noise he saw his friend come back to the keg. He was holding three red cups. Sheila and one of her friends were now empty handed. Ben shook his head in admiration. "Well, he's resourceful," he thought.

He walked through the kitchen and followed the speaker wires to the living room where there was a turntable, CD player, and cassette player stacked on a receiver and amplifier. He began flipping through the albums and wasn't surprised at what he found. Not terrible but not great either. Just music that had been on the radio and MTV. Nothing interesting or different. Quite a bit that he didn't have in his own collection but nothing that was really compelling.

He found the best record for the party and was mildly irritated that it hadn't been added to the stack already. He returned the Phil Collins record to its sleeve, refraining from smashing it on the component rack and hiding the evidence deep in the yellow trash bag in the kitchen. Then he took New Order's Low-Life album, flipped it over to the A side and dropped the needle.

Immediately the drumbeat of "Love Vigilantes" kicked in, followed by the almost horn-like synth melody line. Bernard began singing the perky yet depressing lyrics as people at the party stopped in mid-sentence and looked towards the kitchen. Many began bobbing their heads up and down and back and forth to the beat. Ben looked across the yard at Denny who shook his head and smiled. He grinned back and shrugged his shoulders as he went back to the records to find other passable music to line up next.

He was in the mood for this sort of synth pop now. He found OMD and Pet Shop Boys and Erasure and decided the party would survive with these records.

A few people wandered in and out of the kitchen while he was there, but for the next hour he was flipping through records, sipping on beer and generally keeping to himself. He had just put on side A of OMD's Crush album, the simple piano chords followed by the bass line on "So In Love," when Billy came looking for him.

"Hey Ben, why are you hiding out in here?"

"I'm your DJ now. Haven't you noticed the music has significantly improved this last hour? Plus I'm a little tired and wasn't feeling too social. What are you up to?"

"Looking all over for you currently. How much have you had to drink tonight?"

"Not too much. Maybe three beers. Why?"

"I need you to drive home. Think you can manage that?"

"Probably. Why what's up?"

"I'm getting a little plowed. Wanted to be sure we had a designated driver. Sorry, I should have thought about it earlier."

Ben noticed that Billy was in fact slurring pretty badly and had a goofy grin.

"It's no problem. I'll do it. You have fun tonight. Here, give me your keys now so we don't have to fight about it later."

Billy handed them over, thanked him again, said he was a great friend and a fair DJ, and went back outside to join his friends.

This was turning into a weird night, Ben thought as he finished off his beer, resolving to not drink anymore after that one. He felt fine. Barely buzzed. He'd had three or four. It was hard to measure keg beer. Sometimes the cup wasn't empty when it was refilled. Sometimes it was filled two thirds. Other times it was to the rim. Anyway, he didn't feel drunk and certainly was less so than Billy.

And Denny.

Denny was still in motion in the backyard. Ben had seen him talking to Sheila and her friends. To swimmer friends and to some others. He was sometimes laughing and sometimes serious.

Right now he was whispering to a guy Ben didn't know. From where Ben watched he couldn't hear of course, but he was talking into the guy's ear. They were facing in different directions and both had relaxed expressions. They stayed like that for perhaps three minutes. Neither directly looking into the other's eyes. It was long enough that Ben had time to flip the OMD record to side B. When he returned he found Denny in the kitchen, on his way to the bathroom.

He came out after what seemed like a really long time, although Ben was kind of caught up in the music and in his own thoughts and in watching the people outside as he sat on the living room floor near the stereo, looking out the big window.

"Hey Ben, what's going on? Having fun?" Denny said, startling Ben out of his reverie.

"What? Oh, hi Denny. Yeah sure. Hey what're you up to?"

"What do you mean?"

"Who's that guy you were talking with out there?"

"What guy?"

"The one you were just talking to."

"In the john?"

"No, dumbass, outside. The guy in the black Guess shirt."

"Oh, that's Tom, just a guy I know."

"You guys were in it deep."

"Yeah so?"

"So nothing. Just wondering."

"It's nothing. He's just watching out for me."

"What's that even mean?"

"He's just making sure I'm safe. You can't be too careful man."

"Does he even go to school with us?"

"He did. Not anymore though."

"What're you worried about?"

"There's people watching me. Even here. I thought I saw someone at the house next door. Someone ducking behind that hedge over there."

Ben followed his finger to the neighbor's yard. On the other side of a six foot hedge was a concrete patio, surrounded by a row of low shrubs. It was dark but Ben seriously doubted that anyone could hide there. It was low enough that the person would have to be on hands and knees to not be seen.

"Really? Why would someone be watching you? Because of the meth?"

"Shhh... what's the matter with you? Keep it down."

"Whoa, simmer down. What's going on with you? Why are you so paranoid?"

"You don't understand how it is."

"Tell me then."

"It's bad, man. Getting the drugs. Selling them. The cash involved. There's some rough characters. These aren't college kids. They're mean people. Just in it for the money. They don't give a shit about you. Just getting paid."

"But why would someone follow you here?"

"I don't know exactly. It's just a feeling."

Ben noticed Denny's eyes. His pupils were noticeably dilated. But even stranger than that was how his left eye was twitching. Ben had noticed that before but it was much worse tonight

"What's going on with your eye?"

"Huh? Oh, I don't know. Maybe allergies or something." He blinked and kind of squinted hard in an attempt to stop it but as soon as he opened his eyes it began twitching again.

"Dude, are you okay? You seem a little jumpy. Maybe we should go. We do have classes tomorrow you know?"

"No, I'm good. You're right. We live in a little bubble right? College kids. Nothing can hurt us. Hey, did you see how long I was talking to Sheila? I really think she's falling for me."

"Ha! Okay, I'll believe that when I see it. I don't think she's fallen too hard since she left a little while ago."

"Wait, she did? But I was just talking to her."

"No, it's been a long time since you were over there. She and her friends took off at least thirty minutes ago."

"Hmmm. Well, we definitely made progress tonight. We had an actual conversation. I can't remember what it was about right now but it was amazing. It felt like we were alone out there. She looked incredible, huh? Did you know that Sheila's an interior design major? She understands all that stuff. Color, fabric, how rooms should be set up to be relaxing and efficient. I asked her if she'd design my dental office some day. Make it inviting and modern. No eight year old magazines and poorly framed photographs of sad looking flowers. No, something simple and clean. Miami Vice meets California dentist. "

"You talked about all of that?"

"Yeah sure. Why not?"

"You asked her to design your dental office in California?"

"Yes."

"In like 1995."

"Yes."

"And what did she say?"

"She said she'd love to. How about that? She'd love to! Now I just have to pass this semester. And I'm not sure I can wait ten years to speak to her again. I'll have to come up with another angle huh? So she really left?"

"She did."

"How do you know?"

"Um, because I saw her friend get out her keys and the four of them bodily leave the party."

"Dude, that sucks. I don't know what happened. I got to talking with that guy and lost track of time I guess."

"Guess so. Hey are you about ready to go? It's late and I think I've had about enough for one weekend."

"Just a little longer okay? We'll leave soon. Hey, isn't that your Anna out there?"

"She isn't my Anna anymore. Yeah. I saw her come in earlier."

"At least she's with girls."

"Yeah. It's still weird though. It feels like we shouldn't be in the same world anymore. Like one of us shouldn't exist. You know?"

"No."

"Just that we met and we were always together until suddenly we weren't. It was a strange thing. I'm not used to it yet. Being apart. But I know it's for the best. I wasn't truly in love. And I don't think she was either. Anyway, maybe I should go say hi. You wanna come?"

"No, that's okay. I'll let you two be alone. I need to talk to a guy over there anyway."

"We're leaving in fifteen minutes yes? Say yes."

"You got it. Fifteen minutes."

They went outside. Denny to the keg and Ben over to Anna who was talking to her friends and sipping from a Solo cup.

"Hey Anna."

"Hey Ben, how are you?" She said overly brightly.

"Good, so you know these people also?"

"Ben, we know basically the same people."

"Oh yeah, I forget sometimes. "

"How was your night on the streets?"

"Amazing! How did you know?"

"Denny told me. I'm really proud of you. That took a lot of courage. Were you able to see a lot? Was it all that you thought it would be?"

"It was incredible. I learned so much about how people live out there. They have to work so hard just to get a meal and a safe place to sleep, you know? These are real people. That's what we forget. Each homeless person is fully human with a personality, dreams and a story. It's so helpful to meet a few homeless people. A night on the streets would be good for anyone. Seriously. It's eye-opening."

"Well, I'm proud of you. Also, thanks for bringing Denny out tonight. I know this has been a rough day for him."

"What do you mean?"

She looked at him with surprise and then concern.

"So you didn't know?"

"Know what Anna? Tell me."

"His sister… This is the night she… This is the night she died. Last year."

She continued to look at him and seeing no click of recognition, only confusion, said, "He never told you."

"No."

"That's weird. But I know it's hard for him. I mean of course it is. He still feels guilty. Here sit down a minute," she said, moving over to the rock wall and looking over at Denny who was engrossed in a conversation with a tennis player.

She continued, "His sister was a year younger. They were good friends. Got along with each other better than most siblings. They had their own friends but also hung out together. They surfed several times a week."

"He told you all this? Where was I? I never even knew he had a sister."

"I don't know. I guess he needed to tell someone. Anyway, she died surfing. And he still feels guilty about it. About the circumstances. She'd been unhappy for some time. Probably depressed. She wasn't doing well in school. Had been in a bad relationship. Several things all at once- the way life always seems to work. And she just didn't care anymore. She hadn't wanted to surf or do much of anything for several weeks.

"So Denny pushed her that day. The waves were perfect and it was something that he thought she would love. Her kind of morning. She said no but he kept pushing until finally she relented.

"And they had fun. Caught some excellent waves. Surfed for nearly two hours, and wouldn't you know? Aren't tragedies always like this? They decided to go out one more time. And this wave… it was sensational! They both waited for it and then hit it just right. They got up within fifteen feet of each other and were really moving, skipping along the face of it. Denny saw her smiling. Really smiling for the first time in weeks.

"He didn't see her go under. He'd finished his ride and looked back and she was gone. Her board was there but she wasn't attached. He immediately began diving and searching. His heart was beating so fast. He was frantic. Diving and surfacing, screaming for help. And help came. Five other surfers began looking everywhere for his sister. They finally found her and got her to shore but it was no use."

"What happened?"

"Who knows? Head injury and drowned. Probably in that order. They did CPR. Took her to the hospital but she never regained consciousness."

"Oh my God. That is so awful. I can't believe I never knew about this."

"I knew he didn't tell many. But I guess I'm the only one he's told at TCU. It must be incredibly difficult to hold inside. And now today is the anniversary. I should've known he'd be here. How's he doing?"

"He's acting crazy. On speed I'm pretty sure. He's got this weird eye twitch and he's all over the place."

"You should try to get him home."

"That's exactly what I was doing right before I saw you. I told him fifteen minutes. Like he's my son or something. He is like a child tonight. Can you help me get him out of here? I need to round up Billy also."

"Who's Billy?"

"We came in his car. He made me the designated driver."

"You are? Are you okay to drive?"

"Sure. I've only had like four beers. I'm fine."

"Okay, if you say so. Let's start with Billy. Do you see him?"

They found him nearby. He was in no mood to leave though and convinced Ben to take his car home. He said he'd eventually get a ride from someone. Preferably the perky bowhead he was currently deep in conversation with.

Next they found Denny. Anna gave Ben a hug and rejoined her friends. It was poignant and friendly and laced with much meaning and yet none at all. Ben put his hand on Denny's shoulder.

"C'mon buddy, it's time to go."

"What? Go where?"

"Home. It's time to go. We have class tomorrow."

"But wait! Did you see that?" Denny said, looking up.

"What am I looking at?"

"The stars! Have you ever seen anything so amazing?"

"It's kind of bright here. I see like five."

"Yeah, but those five! Right there. It's Orion's belt. And they're like a thousand light years away. Light years! And we can see them. It's unreal. Magical. How's it even possible? And think how different they are now from the way we see them. We're looking at something that happened a thousand years ago. It makes our lives seem so unimportant. How can this time or place matter? I mean we're only a blip. An inconsequential blip in the long expanse of time. Not even a blip. A blipette. We're nothing. Our entire pathetic lives are completely and utterly meaningless."

"They mean something to us. And to the ones who love us."

"But why?"

"Because it's all we know. It's all we have. This moment. We don't even know how many moments we'll have. This may be our last one. No guarantees."

"You can say that again."

"Yeah, but it matters. It matters so much. Not really for ourselves. I mean, you're right. A few years of consciousness. Who really cares when we look at the full measure of eternity? But for others- the people we touch-it's everything. We have the opportunity to make an immeasurable impact in each other's lives. To relieve suffering. We can either spread love and acceptance and peace, or discord and fear and competition. It's an incredible responsibility and a priceless gift."

Denny looked at Ben. "She told you."

"Yeah, she did."

"I don't want to talk about it."

"We don't have to."

Denny looked at Ben and then away. He watched Anna for a few seconds then down at the ground in front of him. "I miss her every day."

"I'm sure you do. You'll always miss her."

"I haven't forgiven myself."

"It's not your fault."

"No, it's ok. I know it's completely my fault. I pushed her to get out there. She would've stayed safely in the house if I hadn't decided to surf that day. But even though I can't forgive myself, I know that she's ok. That she isn't pissed at me. I feel her and I know she's okay."

"That's really cool."

"Yeah… Hey are we leaving? I think I'm finally ready."

"Yes! Finally, let's go."

Ben winked and waved at Anna and he and Denny walked on the backyard lawn, opened the gate and came around the side of the house towards the front. The last song on the OMD album, 'The Lights Are Going Out', was playing and he thought briefly about going back to change the record, to give the party goers longer than the two minutes of music that remained. But then he realized how perfect the song was, how utterly appropriate and he left them, grinning just a little.

They found the car down the street, Denny still talking excitedly about the stars, and about Sheila, and about his sister, and about stopping for fries on the way home, about that place in Laguna with the best gravy fries, about how they were open late and how he and his friends would go there after night surfing and eat fries and drink coffee or milkshakes and how everything was so simple then.

21

Ben started the car and felt fine. He never once thought about having someone else drive or about not being perfectly capable of getting them home safely. He pushed in the tape and it was the very end of the Butthole Surfers' "Wichita Cathedral" and as they got to the end of the block it was Husker Dü's "New Day Rising" and he turned it up until the sound of that beautifully distorted Flying V guitar filled the car and the surrounding air, the pounding drum encouraging him to accelerate out of the neighborhood onto the main street, turning the corner fast, not squealing, not sliding, but still very fast, with some centrifugal force. Denny had stopped talking and was just looking ahead, listening to the music and lost in his own thoughts.

Ben was singing along. Sometimes the Bob Mould part, just the words "new day rising" over and over, the emphasis on the first syllable of rising. New day RISing. New day RISing… until it switches to NEW day rising at about the same time that Ben changed voices to sing the Grant Hart part. Just kind of harmonizing wordlessly at first and then holding the notes… riiiiiiiiiiiiiise. And goose bumps rose up as the song continued and he was lost in it, singing at the top of his lungs. And it felt like a new day. The song gained new meaning as they hurtled through the night, dawn only a few hours away. And Ben felt eternal and vowed to never sleep again, to never miss another second of life, there was too much to do, so many people to help, and so much to see and hear and taste.

He looked over at Denny who was drumming on his leg and looking ahead and then he glanced over for a second and smiled and nodded, like he could read Ben's mind, like he knew how important this night was, how the music was a soundtrack to their lives and their lives were meaningful and this moment would last forever. And for the last fifteen seconds of the song, when the drum beat sped along and it was either an incredibly fast down stroke on the guitar or maybe just long sustained feedback, and Ben's head involuntarily banged along to the beat so fast and so energetically, and then the drum stopped and the guitar continued, fading out over the next fifteen seconds, and it was then that Ben looked up just in time to see the curb.

He hit it straight on. The road curved to the right and the car didn't. The front tires hit the curb, exploding simultaneously like a gunshot, and then the back tires hit a split second later, another gunshot, plus this time there was another sound, a loud thunk from inside the car, coupled with an exclamation, "Ow! Shit!!" The car continued on, driving on the median for about twenty yards and then came back onto the road. Ben's reaction time was so slow that he didn't begin braking until he reached the other side of the road, the car now headed in the wrong direction into oncoming traffic. He finally got the car stopped, leaving one lane for cars to squeeze by. Mercifully there hadn't been anyone coming at this late hour.

Ben's heart was beating fast as he assessed the damage and tried to decide what to do next. His head hurt and when he reached up to touch the spot it felt wet and warm and blood began to reach his eye and his cheek. He looked in the rear view mirror and couldn't see a cut but there was blood, lots of blood.

And then he looked over at Denny. He was slumped against the door, his head also bleeding.

"Denny?" he said quietly at first, shutting off the radio which was now playing "Broken Home, Broken Heart" by Hüsker Dü, but it no longer mattered, nothing mattered anymore except Denny.

There wasn't an answer so he said it louder, and then again, and then again.

"Denny? Denny! Denny! Wake up. Dude, wake up. Are you okay? I'm so sorry. Oh shit, I'm so sorry."

Ben was shaking his shoulder but when he didn't get a response he stopped, turned off the engine and simply watched his friend, waiting to see if he was breathing. When he saw him take a slow, deep breath, and then when he finally thought to check his wrist for a pulse and found it to be normal and steady, he relaxed for a moment and looked around. His windshield was cracked where Denny had hit it. He hadn't been wearing a seatbelt. Ben worried for a second about Billy. About what he was going to tell him, about how he would come up with the money to repair the car. He didn't know the extent yet but was confident that it would cost more than the $220 in his bank account.

Next he began to worry about the cops. It wouldn't be long before someone found them. He felt very sober but wasn't convinced that a Breathalyzer would agree. Additionally he may have killed his best friend. He saw a horrible future of prison time and expulsion from school and he knew he had to get Denny awake and out of there. But what about his neck? He'd watched enough television to know he shouldn't move him without a collar.

It was as he was thinking about these things, as he was calculating the chance of getting Denny out of the car, protecting his spine, pulling/carrying him to safety somewhere (where?), getting away from the car before police arrived, that the decision was made for him. A car was coming south on Berry heading towards Billy's backwards-facing car. The headlights blinded Ben as it came to a stop about six feet away. They were still on as driver and passenger got out and came around. And Ben saw who the driver was and he was at once panicked and completely at peace.

"Hi. Are you okay? Ohmygod you're bleeding! And your friend? Mindy, can you go call an ambulance? I'll stay here with them."

Mindy argued briefly and then walked briskly across a large lawn headed towards the sorority houses where she could call.

"Hi, my name's Echo. I think we've seen each other around school, right? How are you feeling? What hurts?"

And Ben was speechless. Directly in front of him, leaning into the car through the driver's side window was the girl that he'd been dreaming about for weeks. He knew her face, her eyes, her hair, and now he knew her voice. It was the voice of an angel. Soft, a little higher than he had expected, compassionate, firm, and brave.

"I feel fine. My head's a bit sore. Right here."

"Eww. Don't touch it. It's bleeding... So, is your friend breathing?"

"He is and he has a good pulse. We need to get him to a hospital though."

"I know. Mindy's calling. We'll get him there. Can you get out of the car? Do your legs feel okay?"

"They do," he said, opening the door and crawling out, taking the key with him. "Thank you for stopping."

"Of course. It was the strangest thing. We were out on a donut run. I never eat donuts. Like never. But I had this strong urge to go out for a minute. We've been up studying and were finished and really should have just gone to bed. And yet here I am."

"Here you are."

A few more cars drove slowly by but no one stopped. They sat on the curb in front of the Accord to wait and as they did they saw a man come from the shadows across the street.

"Ben, hey, are you alright? I heard a crash and came this way. Sorry it took so long. Is that Denny?"

"James! I'm happy to see you! We're waiting on an ambulance. I think Denny's really hurt. This is Echo."

"Echo. Very pleased to meet you." He was close enough now to reach down and shake her hand. "Have you tried to move Denny yet?"

"No. I'm worried about his neck."

"He's breathing?"

"Yes, breathing. Has a pulse. But he hasn't moved. I'm really worried."

"We can probably get him into the backseat of your car, Echo. I could keep his neck stabilized while you drive."

Echo didn't seem to be taken aback that this man knew Ben and was offering to help in the crisis.

265

"Let's give them a few more minutes. Five. Okay?" she said.

And just then from the north came the ambulance and from the south came a police car. They arrived at the same time. Echo did the talking when everyone approached. Her smile, concerned voice, kind face, and decisive manner got everything moving. Denny was quickly and carefully moved out of the car and into the back of the ambulance, cervical collar in place. The police agreed to let them go with no charges filed. No investigation or Breathalyzer or sobriety test.

It was a small miracle.

James, Ben and Echo followed the ambulance to the hospital. Once they arrived Echo went with Ben to his room in the ER while James stayed with Denny, waiting alone in his room as the boy went for x-rays. He had cervical films and a CT of the head and James kept the others updated.

The doctor washed Ben's face while Echo held his right hand, standing next to him and speaking to him, distracting him with small talk. This is what Ben had dreamed of for so long. Not in an ER while he was having his face sewn up, but to be able to talk to Echo (oh how he loved that he finally knew her name) about music and movies and their families… it was their first date and as atypical and strange as it was, it was also completely perfect.

He received six sutures and nothing else felt bruised or broken. Looking back he wouldn't remember anything about the doctor or the lidocaine or the stitches. He would only remember Echo. Her shining eyes with the perfectly white sclera, even at four in the morning. Her tiny smile lines and the small dimple in her left cheek. He would remember her hair. Bowless and black and thick, the way she kept playing with it, sometimes putting it behind her ears, sometimes knotting it up on her head, sometimes twirling it around her fingers and dropping it in front of her right shoulder. He remembered what her hand felt like. It was warm, full, strong, and tender, with thin and surprisingly tiny fingers. All of his nerves seemed to be focused on his hand as their bodies met in that single point for those minutes, at once comfortable and electric.

These were moments that he would never forget and yet as soon as his face was repaired and the doctor left and their hands dropped away from each other his mind immediately went back to his friend.

"We have to find Denny. To see if he's okay."

"Yeah, I think he's this way."

And Echo led the way but they walked together, turning right out of the small room past the nursing station where they asked about Denny. One of the older nurses seemed to know who they were, how everyone fit together in the story, and she led them to a larger room and they found him there, lying quietly with eyes closed on a rolling cart. And after Ben had stopped watching Denny he looked over at James, who was sitting in a chair against the wall. He was leaning back on it, balancing on the back two legs and he looked at Ben and gestured to the right with his head and Ben and Echo sat down in the two remaining chairs and no one said a word for a really long time.

22

They eventually went home. After falling asleep in their chairs, after Echo went to find coffee and pastries for everyone, after talking to the nurses and then the doctor when Denny was moved to the neurology floor, after Ben called Denny's parents and they had begun scrambling to get a flight, they all felt like they needed a break.

The doctor said that Denny had a subdural hematoma and would require surgery that day but first he needed to get the swelling down with steroids and then some time needed to pass so that he could safely have an anesthetic. It would be early afternoon, so they could go home and shower and go to class, returning in time to see him as he came out of surgery.

They were preparing to leave when Ben thanked James.

"For what?"

"For being here. For staying with Denny while I was being worked on. It means a lot. So thanks."

"I heard that crash and I just had this feeling that I needed to check it out. Strange huh? I don't always come running towards trouble. Especially that close to TCU. Not really my scene."

"There are so many mysteries in life and I guess that's just another one. Something, some tiny wrinkle in the fabric of life alerted you. The amazing thing is that you responded. Most people would have shrugged it off."

"We're friends Ben. After the other night… well, that was amazing. You're something special."

Ben had told Echo a little bit about the night on the streets of Fort Worth. She said, "It sounds like you're both pretty special."

"I may have killed my friend so I don't feel very special right now. Scared and guilty, yes."

James said, "You heard the doctor, we can't worry quite yet. He's in there somewhere. His heart's working, his brain's functioning. Let's not panic okay? That isn't going to help anything. You two go get cleaned up. I'll meet you back here later Ben. I need to get away for a bit. I start feeling antsy and anxious when I'm inside building too long. You get used to fresh air."

"Yeah, I can understand that. Okay, well thanks again. I'll be back here by four. Maybe I'll see you then."

"Definitely."

Ben and Echo found her car and James waved as he walked through the parking lot and then in between two buildings. Ben waved back and got into the passenger side after Echo reached across to unlock it.

He was exhausted but really beyond the point where it mattered anymore. He felt like he hadn't slept in days but with the coffee and the sugary pastries and the chilly morning air and the bright sunlight and with the giddiness of sitting in the same car with Echo, with the sensory overload of seeing/smelling/hearing her, he was as awake as he had ever been.

They talked all the way back to campus, she drove surprisingly fast, not recklessly but with quick accelerations and lane changes, fiddling with the radio, drinking a morning Coke, laughing easily and often and generally bringing life and vitality to the much too short journey home.

Ben still felt like he was in a dream and didn't want to wake up. The fifteen minutes alone in the car with her, the four hours in the emergency room, the thirty minutes on the side of the road, all of these were, against all sense of reason, among the best moments of his life. He felt comfortable, at ease and at home.

When she let him off behind Tom Brown dorm he didn't want to get out. He was reluctant to break the spell.

"So… thanks. So much."

"You're welcome, Ben. I'll be praying hard for Denny. Call me if you need a ride back to the hospital okay? I'm happy to do it."

"I may do that. I've got your number." He had told her he had a ride but of course he didn't. He had possible rides. He was fairly certain that he could find someone to take him, but in fact he only wanted to be with Echo.

"Okay, seriously, call. I'm going to clean up and go to English then I'll just be in my room studying."

He was out, closing the door, wondering about the guy she had been with that day in the Snack Shack. He was waving, walking in the back of Tom Brown and opening the door to his room to find that his roommates were gone. He gathered his shower things, found clean clothes and headed to the bathroom.

Fifteen minutes later he was back in the room, hair clean, scalp stitches carefully avoided, wearing the same torn jeans and a fresh long sleeved polo shirt. A red and yellow striped one with padded shoulders. He put things away, slipped on his jean jacket and paused for just a few seconds to calculate how long it would take to get to class. He decided he still had ten minutes, so laid down on his bed to wait.

Three hours later he awakened to find Brian studying at his desk and Peter Cetera on the radio singing "The Next Time I Fall". It was a song Ben had heard entirely too many times without once purposely seeking it out. It seemed to be playing in the background everywhere he went. It was incredibly annoying even if secretly he had a tiny crush on Amy Grant.

"Good morning, Sunshine," said Brian. "Dude, you were tired. I've never heard anyone snore quite that loudly before. That was some impressive volume."

"You should have woke me up. I missed class. Slept way too long. How long have you been here anyway?"

"Long enough. You needed it. Where've you been anyway? Tim and I were this close to calling the cops. Or your mom. Or someone. We thought you'd moved to the streets permanently. Have you?"

"No, it was just a crazy night." Ben told Brian all about it, starting with the drive to the party, leaving out the drug delivery, and ending with the need for a ride back to the hospital. "I have to find notes from today's class and then get up there."

"Are you going to call Echo and ask her to take you? She sounds amazing."

"As much as I want to, I'm not. I'll try Steve or Marty first. I can get both notes and a ride if I'm lucky. That makes the most sense right now. I'll definitely call her soon though."

"You'd better," he said, turning back to his work.

Ben called Steve first, giving a Cliffs Notes version of what was going on. He immediately agreed to drive, saying he would be right there.

And he was. They returned to the hospital where Ben led the way to Denny's room, where they were in turn delivered to the surgery waiting room on a different floor. The space was crowded with chairs but devoid of people. There was a pot of old, burnt coffee and a few Styrofoam cups, a small television on the wall tuned to Jeopardy with the sound muted. Steve turned the volume up and they sat and watched and waited, answering the clues in the form of a question. Steve did better at elections and Ben cleaned up on the novel category and they both missed the Final Jeopardy question. The answer was the country that was tied for the longest average life span with Iceland. Steve thought it was Greenland and Ben said New Zealand and they both kicked themselves when they learned it was Japan.

They had just about decided to try the coffee when the surgeon came in. His paper mask was untied at the top and dangled down over his scrub top. He looked relaxed and kind.

"Are you some of Denny's family?"

"Sort of. Best friend. His parents are on the way."

"Yeah, I talked to them before we took him back. Okay, you can relay this to them and I'm happy to call if they would like. He's fine." He paused, giving it a moment to let it sink in.

"He's fine? What does that mean?"

"It means everything went great. We drained the blood from around his brain through two holes. He's starting to wake up already. He has every chance of making a full recovery."

"That's wonderful. Wait, holes? He has holes in his skull?"

"Yes, we had to drill two holes, each about the size of a dime, then carefully irrigate fluid through them until the clot was all washed out."

"Through his head?"

"Well, his scalp was pulled back. Listen, he'll be fine. He has some staples in his scalp, but otherwise looks the same. Not much worse than your forehead I might say. And the important thing is he's going to be okay."

"Sorry, I just hadn't thought through what was going to happen. Thank you so much, doctor. Thank you for your quick and competent work. When can we see him?"

"Soon. The recovery room nurses know you're here. Someone will come get you when he can have visitors."

And with that he left the two alone again. Jeopardy was over and the news was on. They watched in silence for a few minutes. Much of the national news concerned Ronald Reagan's recent confession that the US had sold weapons to Iran. It was a deal through Israel to help release hostages. It was confusing and not as exciting as the weather or sports but it seemed important and worrisome.

About the time the world news was over and the local version was beginning a nurse came to lead them to recovery. Down the hall and through a big set of double doors they found a big room with perhaps twelve bays but only three patients.

Denny was there, looking small and vulnerable. A pretty blond nurse with blue eyes and matching scrubs was sitting at the head of the bed on a high stool. She was charting but looked up when the boys arrived.

"Denny. Look, you have company," she said brightly.

And with that he opened his eyes. He looked at Ben and Steve and then back at Ben and then he smiled very slightly before closing his eyes again.

"Denny. Hey, it's me. How're you feeling?" Ben moved a little closer, tentatively leaning in to get a closer look. His friend's head was shaved and there were staples across his scalp. There was the very beginning of a scab, the coagulated blood starting to solidify at the lower edges of the incision. His head looked very white and his hair follicles were extremely and somewhat obscenely dark. There were sutures on his forehead where it had impacted the windshield. They were nearly the mirror image of Ben's who found himself lost in the wound. He was somewhat surprised when Denny spoke.

"Is he still here?" he said, opening his eyes very slightly.

"What? Who? Is who here?"

"Reverend Tilton. Did he come back?"

Ben's face changed from confusion to irritation to sadness in the time it took Denny to turn his head slightly to the right to find Ben's eyes.

"No. He isn't here. I'm sorry."

"I had the strangest dream. He was standing next to Jesus, His hands were out. Reaching. Like on TV, except there wasn't a TV there. And I was reaching for him but couldn't feel him there. Couldn't find his hands. I had this feeling that I was missing something, was supposed to bring something with me. Jesus was just standing there, smiling gently and kindly, silently watching us. And finally Reverend Tilton dropped his hands and turned and started walking away. I was so sad. Desperate for him to stay. He was moving back into the light and I wanted to follow him but I couldn't move."

Denny stopped talking and closed his eyes again.

"Really weird. Is that how it ended?"

"No. He left. Disappeared. And I was standing there crying. And Jesus put his arm around me. And I felt so warm and light. Like pounds of pressure had just been lifted from my entire body. Like I would float up, like I had no worries, no past and no future. That moment was all I had and it was perfect. I wanted to simply stay like that. His strong arm comforting me. But then he

275

whispered words that I couldn't make out. He wanted me to do something. I asked him to say it again. And he smiled and squeezed me a little with his arm and I felt this surge of relaxed and tranquil love and then I opened my eyes to see you two standing there."

"That's an amazing story. What do you think he said?"

"I really don't know. I've lost it. It's like on the tip of my tongue but I can't quite get at it."

"And what about Robert Tilton? How do you feel about all that now?"

"I feel like I've moved on. Like he couldn't give me what I need. He's a taker. Not a giver. I had my faith in the wrong person it seems. Maybe Reverend Tilton can bring people to Jesus, but I'm not so sure. And I don't need him to reach Jesus. He came to me personally and can come to any one of us. And he's free and easy and so beautiful."

"How're you feeling? I was so scared when you wouldn't wake up."

"I feel pretty good. A slight headache," he grinned at that. "How long was I out? What day is it?"

"Same day. Monday. It's like six in the evening."

"What? I have no sense of time right now. It feels like only a few seconds have passed, and yet like it's been weeks since I've seen you. Mondays suck."

"You were really out. I thought you were dead."

"I'm not dead."

"Nope. Thank God. I'm really sorry. I shouldn't have been driving. And when that song came on... I've just so sorry."

"Don't worry okay? I was a mess too. Remember? I've been a mess for a long time." And with that his eyes closed once again and he was silent.

Steve and the nurse had been standing and listening but not speaking. She spoke now.

"Wow. I don't think I've ever heard such profound first words before. Usually it's something like 'When's surgery going to start?' or 'Can I have some coffee?' or 'Are you married?' Not a detailed near-death experience."

"Yeah, that was freaky. I didn't even know Denny was religious," said Steve.

"Me neither. Not until last night. I guess he'd become obsessed with this televangelist. The guy really got to him. And his bank account. But maybe his dream is real. Maybe he'll realize what a scam artist that guy is."

"Do you think he saw Jesus?"

"I think he experienced something very profound. There's much that we don't know about this world and the way our brains work. And don't forget that someone was probing and scrubbing on his cerebrum. I imagine that creates some strange reactions. But, I like to leave room for mystery. So yeah, I believe he definitely met Jesus."

They all watched him rest for a few more minutes, talking quietly to each other as the nurse went to tend to a new post-op patient. When it became apparent that Denny was going to sleep awhile, or at least drift in and out, they decided to return to the waiting room.

"I'm going to stay here tonight. You can go back home," Ben said.

"I can stay. It's not a problem."

"No, go. I'll be fine. Maybe you can get me tomorrow morning?"

"For sure. I can be here at like seven thirty to get us to class on time."

"That would be awesome. Truly. You've been a good sport. Thanks for driving and spending part of your day here."

"Thank you for letting me. It's a great gift to be allowed to help another. And I'm here for you okay? Anytime."

They shook hands and Steve left as Ben settled in to wait. Once Denny was moved to a patient room he could hang out there but in the meantime it was television and outdated magazines.

He settled into a worn brown and orange cloth upholstered chair, with a pattern carefully calculated to not reveal its many mysterious stains, slumped down with a six month old coverless People magazine and quickly fell asleep.

It was nearly nine when he awakened enough to remember where he was and to muster the motivation and energy to fight his way out of the chair and to the nurse's station where he discovered that Denny had been moved back upstairs. He found the room and entered as the nurse was doing her hourly neuro check, determining that Denny still in fact had all of his senses about him.

"Hey, you still in bed?"

"Yeah, it's not like me huh? I'm about done with this place though. When can you bust me out?"

The nurse looked back as she left the room saying, "There'll be no busting out sweetie. You're going to be mine for a few days at least."

They waited for her to leave before Ben said, "No, we're busting you out. Soon."

Denny smiled. They sat quietly for a few minutes before he said, "My parents are on the way. They called from DFW."

"Good. It'll be nice to see them huh?"

"Yeah, it will. I feel terrible about them coming though. My dad hates leaving the restaurant. He didn't even come to move me in."

"Oh, right. Well, you can blame me. It's not your fault."

"We're in this together, my friend. And you know what? It may turn out to be a blessing. Who knows? I was on a bad path, that's for sure. Not a sustainable one. Maybe I needed a good whack to knock some sense into me."

"I pray that something good comes from this. You're amazing Denny. A great friend. You have so much energy and passion and you can do anything. You can be a dentist or a surf instructor or CEO of a huge non-profit. Anything. For now though you should probably rest. Until your family gets here anyway."

Denny closed his eyes and pretty soon his parents arrived. They were concerned, loving, nurturing and worried. Ben greeted them and explained and apologized and they all shook hands and hugged. The nurse let them break the rules this once, allowing all three of them to stay in the room after hours, talking and catching up and telling stories and remembering and planning and dreaming. It was well past midnight before Denny's dad and Ben left to sleep in the waiting room, leaving his mom to sit alongside her son, so very thankful that he was alive.

23

The next morning he peeked in on Denny, making sure that his mom was awake with him, and that he had breakfast and was comfortable. Steve picked him up right on time. He went to class, showered, studied, and rested and then got up the nerve to call Echo, asking if she would take him back to the hospital.

And when she agreed, and sounded so sweet on the phone, so concerned and friendly, he felt his heart expand and a small knot of excitement begin to form in that place where the pain had been not so very long ago. He had no expectations. Only hope.

She picked him up and they talked all the way to the hospital. Her dark, smiling eyes were like magnets, keeping him turned in his seat as they traveled through the Fort Worth streets. He learned she was from Santa Fe and her parents were artists and free spirits and lived outside of town where they had peacocks and chickens and goats and where she and her sisters had been encouraged to question and dream and explore. It explained much about the ease in which she lived. The comfortable acceptance of people and events. The way she had stopped to help and was so calm and competent, never doubting that all would be well. Her peace was contagious, as was her smile and excitement about the smallest things.

She pointed out the Botanic Garden on the way and said it was her favorite place in the city. Beautiful and serene. They promised to go together sometime and that, right there, that small, spontaneous plan gave Ben such a strong sense of purpose, a future that felt as important as graduating and going to medical school, as writing a novel, as caring for the poor and forgotten in the world. He knew that going to the Botanic Garden with Echo, sitting on a bench and contemplating the beauty of a hosta, of simply existing next to each other in the same space and time, their lives intersecting in that moment, that was something to live for.

He also knew that this short ride to the hospital, this fifteen minutes, a mere .000036% of an eighty year life, would be ingrained completely into his brain, in a way that was unbreakable, the neural connections reinforced and stabilized countless times over the remainder of his life.

And when they arrived at the hospital and had checked on Denny and had sat with him for awhile, watching television and talking and laughing with him, giving his parents a chance to go out for a bit, and then when they returned and Ben and Echo discovered that they also were hungry and decided to eat in the hospital cafeteria just this once, just to say they had, they resumed their conversation and it was magical and eternal.

They were talking about James, wondering if he would return like he said he would and whether they should try to go find him.

"That's so cool that you two have become friends. Not everyone would do that, you know."

"Well they should. I feel like everyone is important. Each one of us is fully human and loved and has something to teach, something to contribute to the common good, the life that we all live together."

"Me too, Ben. I remember when I was much younger, back in Santa Fe, I saw a man digging through a trashcan, I thought maybe he'd lost something. I asked my mom about it and when she told me that he was looking for food I couldn't believe it. I had no way to process that. No context. And when she told me that he was homeless, that he didn't have a place to sleep where he felt safe and dry and warm…well, I cried. I remember just sobbing. I couldn't understand how someone could not have food or a home. He didn't look a lot different than my dad."

Ben laughed at that. "Really?"

"Well, it's true. My dad was a hippie. Long hair, didn't bathe very regularly. He wore old, handmade and second-hand clothes. This guy was probably better groomed than my dad. So it was really difficult. I've never been hungry, always had more than I need. Anyway, it's what led me to want to become a social worker."

"That makes a lot of sense. It's amazing that it all stemmed from a single moment. It's extremely noble."

"It's not noble at all. But I wanted to help. To somehow make a difference and to provide resources to people like that, so they don't have to dig through trash for food. Your opportunity to help's even greater. Doctors can provide hope to so many."

"Yeah, that may be true. But certainly being a doctor doesn't guarantee that social injustices will be addressed. I would venture

283

to guess that most people become doctors for the job security, the personal challenge, the prestige and the money."

"Oh, you may be right. You seem different though. In the few discussions we've had so far."

"Yeah. I'm different," he said, smiling a little.

"No, really. Hey, do you want the rest of this?" she said, pushing the remainder of her pizza and cherry pie slightly towards him.

"Of course I do," he said, starting with the pie, finishing it in three bites and then shaking a thin layer of red pepper flakes onto the remnant of her pizza slice.

"It's so easy to become homeless," Ben continued after finishing his meal and hers. "I mean, what's incredible is that there aren't even more. The deck is stacked against so many people."

"I'm afraid you're right. The prison system. The dominant culture. The lack of medical and housing support…"

"Yeah, all of it. For instance the minimum wage. It's three thirty-five an hour and hasn't changed since eighty-one. Multiply that by forty, assuming people can actually get a full time job knowing that many minimum wage employers only hire part-time workers, and you get what? About a hundred and thirty bucks a week. It's less than five hundred a month after taxes. Where can you get an apartment and utilities and transportation and food for five hundred dollars a month?"

"Nowhere. You can't. A person would need a roommate or at least two full time jobs."

"Right. I would even argue that if a person was homeless, paid zero for housing and utilities they still couldn't make it on five hundred a month. Food and buying a bus pass ok. But what about health care? What about child care? It's not possible. They're still going to need public assistance of some kind."

"I'm learning that's true. And the Reagan administration is working as hard as it can to make it more difficult for the poor. "

"They need people like you to help."

"I wish that wasn't true," said Echo. "That everyone could receive a fair wage and not need subsidized housing or food stamps. It's getting worse and it'll continue to worsen until enough people stand up to say that there is enough for everyone. Enough room for housing. Enough food. Enough medical care. Enough love. Churches and charities can't do it all. It'll have to be a change of culture. Something big. Like Doctor King and his poor people campaign."

"Right. There's definitely enough to go around. That's the problem. It's cultural. It's consumerism. It's competition and greed. Why do we always have to strive for more and bigger and better? Why do we have to feel more important than other people? To receive special treatment? I'm not one bit more important than James or any of his friends on the street. Or than poor people in Delhi or Lagos. It's all luck and grace and good nutrition and parents that loved us."

"True."

"Now, I haven't been to church much lately but I've read the Bible enough to remember the beatitudes. Are you familiar with them?" Ben asked.

"I am. My mom's Presbyterian but we didn't go to church as a family. I went with a friend some though and really enjoyed being there. I love the beatitudes. They teach such humility."

"Yeah, I wish I could remember all of them right now but it's where Jesus is teaching people how to live. About how being on the bottom is how we come closer to God. Blessed are those who are gentle and humble and whose hearts are clean."

"And the peacemaker and those who hunger and thirst for righteousness. I'll bet we could find a Bible somewhere in this hospital."

"Great idea. We should definitely do that. It's right before the Sermon on the Mount. Matthew five. But yeah, can you imagine if more people followed those teachings? If we worked for the common good instead of for ourselves and our friends and family? If we took people into our homes and really funded alcohol and drug treatment programs? If we actually rehabilitated and forgave wrongdoers instead of ruining their lives by locking them up and forgetting about them, and then setting them up to fail after release? What if we took responsibility for everyone in the country? Not just the white males. Not just the pale, moneyed people. Everyone. What if we sacrificed something for a fellow human being? Not a handout or a tiny donation from our abundance. But actually sacrifice something. Until it hurts a little."

"You're on a roll but I like it. I think the same way. It's so frustrating when the solution is simple. People are too greedy to see it."

"And if they do see it they reject it as idealistic, expensive, dangerous, naïve or some other dismissive comment. What can we do?"

"Well, I think this conversation is a start, Ben. It helps me to discuss it out loud with another person. And then talking to others. Voting. We get to vote now. How cool is that? Many young people think the way we do. Inclusive, forgiving, hopeful… so just talking helps. And then working towards a career that helps others and keeps us engaged in the world. All of these things are useful."

"Well said. So, let's recap what we've learned. Number one, sharing is good. Number two, long term planning and attention to the less fortunate is also good. And number three, you like cherry pie but not enough to eat a whole slice. Number three is the most important tonight. Thanks again for giving me the rest of it."

"Well to be fair, you did buy it."

"True, but still, you could've eaten it all. And yet you didn't. And you shared it with me. That's like in my top ten ideal girlfriend characteristics."

Echo laughed and they finished their sodas and they put away their trays. They continued to talk as they headed towards the exit.

In the hallway a worker was singing and mopping the floor. In a rich, warm voice he warned them to be careful because it was slick and he pointed to the dangerous area. They stayed close to the far right wall, cautiously placing their feet in such a way that they didn't slip.

"Have a blessed day," he said as they passed and made their way down the corridor. He resumed his song as he mopped, "It is well... with my soul.... It is well, it is well with my soul." His voice resonated off the walls and created a sound much larger than should have been possible.

"That was beautiful! Don't you feel we were a part of something really special?" Echo said as the reached Denny's room.

"It was magical. I had goose bumps when he started singing again. I can still feel it inside of me."

"Me too, what a gift he is. Isn't it amazing what a simple act like that can do for so many?" she said, smiling. And they would have continued talking but Denny's parents jumped up as they entered, and the moment passed.

Denny was awake and grinning as his friends entered.

"What were you two talking about out there? You look like you were sharing secrets."

"Nothing really. Just about how rich and wonderful and surprising life can be," said Ben. "How are you doing?"

"Good. Fine. I honestly feel great. The doctor came by. He said I could probably go home tomorrow."

"That's wonderful!"

"Yeah. No football for a while. Or slam dancing. But hopefully not much worse for the wear. I can't thank you two enough for everything. You saved my life."

"Well, right before that I almost killed you, so I don't really feel like a hero."

"We were both messed up. But James, Echo, and you got me here in time and I'm fine. So thank you," he said again, looking at both of them. "Did I miss anything in class today?"

"Not much. That biology test is coming up. I'll talk to him if you want."

Ben's dad spoke up. "I called the school earlier today so they know what's going on. It sounds like he'll get a chance to make up anything he missed."

"That's great."

"Shouldn't you be studying? I'm seriously okay. And my parents aren't going home until Thursday."

"You sure?"

"Yeah. Go. There's no reason for all of us to fail."

"You're not going to fail."

"I know, I'm exaggerating. Go. We'll talk soon."

"Okay, I'll be back tomorrow. And I'll call in the morning."

Echo leaned over and hugged him, saying, "Goodnight Denny. I'm praying for you. Constantly."

She left and Ben looked back at Denny with a look that said, "Don't even think about it. She's mine."

Denny smiled back with a "Relax, I know, I know" expression.

24

It was on the way back to campus that she said it. It was like she had been trying to find the right time. Although they had talked nearly constantly since meeting it hadn't come up. Perhaps she was weighing the pros and cons, waiting to get to know him a little better, wanting to be sure he wasn't a psychopath or just after her beauty, someone who would use her like others had in the past. Not that she'd dated many but still, the price of beauty was having to fend off men (and women for that matter) of all sizes, shapes and political ideologies. Whatever the reason, this was the moment she asked, just as they were passing Ol' South, right when Ben had finished a long diatribe on the absurdity of the death penalty.

"Hey, have you heard of Charis Ministry?"

"I don't think so. What is it?"

"Well, it's two things really. It began as a feeding ministry. Kind of a soup kitchen but better. I'm sure that James knows about it. It's Monday nights at an old church near downtown. They feed probably two hundred people every week. Good food too. Casseroles, veggies, bread. They give everyone a vitamin C tablet."

"That sounds pretty cool. Maybe James didn't tell me because it's on Mondays. We spent the night outside on Saturday. Have you done it yet? Helped serve?"

"I have. A few times. It's great. Very well organized. A girl in my sorority told me about it. She's from Fort Worth and her youth group had helped before. We went together and it was really fulfilling. But here's the part you'll love... They have a small free medical clinic as well."

"Really?"

"Yeah, I checked it out. They also use social workers to help with health benefits and housing issues. So after a couple of weeks of serving food I switched to the clinic side. It's so amazing. Difficult and heartbreaking. But vitally important and necessary."

"What kind of patients do they see? Do you know?"

"Yeah I do. It seems to be just general medicine. Some kids but mainly adults. Problems that homeless people with no money or health insurance have to deal with. Asthma, diabetes, high blood pressure, mental health issues, spider bites, burns, alcoholism... just everything other humans have but much of it's untreated. On the streets they see patients in Sunday School classrooms. Nothing fancy at all but somehow they have medicine and supplies."

"Do you think a pre-med college kid could come watch or maybe even help?"

"I do. The two doctors are really cool. I've seen other volunteers there."

"Then we should do it. Definitely."

"How about tonight? I know you must be really exhausted so it's okay if you don't want to."

"You had the same amount of sleep as I did. Yeah, let's do it. What time?"

"We should leave by six. I can pick you up."

"No, let me come to you this time. I'll meet you outside your door a little before six."

"Great! Oh, I'm so excited. My friend couldn't come tonight so this is really perfect." Her eyes were wide, shining and happy as they pulled up to Tom Brown once again and Ben got out of her car, again regretting the fact that it was only a fifteen-minute drive from the hospital. He had never felt such easy comfort with anyone. How was it that they met less than two days earlier? Perhaps those looks that they shared at Sound Warehouse and the Snack Shack had begun a process that had then percolated and flowed along. Maybe it had begun even earlier, before they had even consciously seen each other, maybe they had sensed each other as they passed in the cafeteria or from far away on the school grounds or across the football field. Surely they had passed without knowing it. Was that enough to start some mysterious connection? A continuum that led to that moment at Billy's car when Echo stopped to see if she could help?

He was thinking about all of this. He couldn't get her out of his mind. Her voice, her thick dark hair, her kindness and the way she looked so deeply into his eyes. The way she lifted her chin and looked up and to the right when she was thinking, her milky white and flawless sclera…it was all so mesmerizing. He remained lost in all of this for several minutes, until the phone rang. It was Billy asking if he could come over to bring that mix tape. He said sure of course and when Billy arrived Ben apologized and asked about the car and offered to pay for the damages.

"Well yeah, I think that's the way it works my friend. You break it, you buy it. It goes on your insurance. You'll just pay whatever the deductible is. You really did a job on those tires. How fast were you going anyway?"

"Pretty fast. I'm not sure. I think I hit it just right."

"You must have, to pop three tires like that. Really impressive. So Denny's okay?"

"Yeah, it appears so. The wreck may have actually knocked some sense into him. He seems more focused now. Like he wants to get back to school and salvage the semester."

"Well, it helps that the drugs have worn off."

"True. Maybe that's it. We'll see what happens when he gets home."

"Which is when?"

"Hopefully tomorrow…Sorry about your car again."

"No problem. It's really just the windshield and the tires. It's supposed to be ready by Friday."

"Cool."

"Oh, here's your tape."

"Thanks," Ben said as he took it and shoved it into the right back pocket of his Levi's. "I don't think I'm giving this to James after all."

"Why not?"

"I just have a negative association with it now. It's what we were jamming to when we crashed. I blame Hüsker Dü for what happened," he said, mostly kidding.

"You can't blame the band. You would've found something on the radio to sing to. You were in that kind of mood. It's just as much my fault for giving you the keys."

"No, I thought I was okay to drive. Obviously not. But I think I'll make James a more mellow tape."

Billy laughed saying, "Don't be too hard on yourself. Don't forget, we're kids. We're allowed to make mistakes. Everything's fine. It's how we develop wisdom, right?"

Ben smiled. "I like that. Thanks for being so cool. Let me know when you need the money okay?"

"Sure, have a good one."

Ben was touched by Billy's kindness and then later by Brian and Tim as he spoke with them and then studied with them and later still went to dinner with them. They were good roommates. Not great but he definitely could have done worse. They were nerdy and goofy and innocent and made him feel blissfully young for a moment as they talked about television and their families and elementary schools and those lazy summer days on bicycles exploring the neighborhood without cares or fears. It was a great hour, at once typical and rare and he treasured it as he headed back to Tom Brown.

Echo was waiting when he ran to his room and peeked through the blinds to see her blue Colt. He grabbed his jacket and rushed down the hallway and through the double doors in the back and then slowed down, trying to look cool as she smiled and he got into the car, buckling in and handing her a cassette.

"Here, have you heard this before?"

She looked at the cover, flipped it around to see the songs, removed the Howard Jones cassette from her car's player and pushed in Ben's tape.

"Big Star? No, but let's try it. Tell me about it okay?" she said, backing out of the space.

"Gladly," Ben said, smiling. "In the early seventies Alex Chilton and Chris Bell put out three of the best records of all time. This is Radio City, the second one. My favorite is the third one, Sister Lovers, but it's pretty dark and slow so I thought we should start with this. There are so many perfect pop moments on here. You know that Bangles song, 'September Gurls'? That's actually a Big Star song."

"Really? I love that song."

"It's towards the end of the tape. We'll get there. So, how've you been? Did you get anything done?"

She said she did. That it was a productive afternoon. And they talked and shared and experienced Big Star together and "What's Going Ahn?" would forevermore be one of their songs. They would both remember that drive, where they were when the song came on, the feeling that they had at that moment, the anxious excitement of new love and new experiences. And entirely too quickly, like they had been teleported, they were at the church and they parallel parked on a side street, careful to avoid the scores of people spilling out of the parking lot and sidewalks into the streets, their dirty and layered clothing in muted colors, taking on the hue of the surrounding buildings and pavement and parking lots.

They entered the church through a side door, greeting the security guy and Echo led Ben downstairs to show him where the meal was served. There were twelve long tables, each with twenty place settings and chairs, empty and ready for the guests to arrive. There was a big kitchen and food was being brought to the front and there were probably thirty volunteers, some preparing the room, others talking to their friends and still others standing quietly and taking it all in.

She introduced him to the couple that had founded the project. They had a patient kindness in their eyes and were gracious and grateful for Ben just as they were for all the volunteers. Even though it was busy and soon to be chaotic he felt like he had their full attention for those moments. He could feel the open and inclusive compassion that he'd always been searching for. They were very different from each other. He was tall and direct and had a thick distinctly Texan accent. She was soft and had an easy intelligent spirituality. But they seemed to fit together like two halves of a whole and appeared to have a singularity of purpose that was evident even during the brief introductions.

And then they were upstairs meeting one of the doctors. Dr. Powers, but went only by Jane, had long straight thick grey hair, wore faded but colorful flowing clothes and carried a faint scent of patchouli. She invited Ben to tag along as she saw patients and wasn't at all like his pediatrician or the general surgeon he had shadowed that time in Kansas City. She was unhurried and personable and asked questions and waited for responses. She asked about living situations and about family and seemed to know many details about her patients' lives. And if she didn't know something she asked.

So by the time a forty-five year old homeless woman with four teeth, entirely too many wrinkles but an easy smile had finished seeing Jane for a refill on her blood pressure medicine, she had shared a tremendous amount of information and had taken away advice and reassurance and assistance far beyond what she would have received in five appointments with a doctor at a private clinic. It was a priceless encounter and it was all free.

Ben's eyes were opened and his heart was filled as he saw this doctor's compassion and the extent of her sacrifice. Although she would never call it sacrifice. It was her calling and her joy to care for the poor. These people had little to no access to health care. Every place else seemed to require medical insurance or cash or lengthy applications and complicated instructions. Jane was able to provide everything with volunteers and donated supplies and charitable giving. Ben discovered that she was divorced and lived on very little, driving a rusted out Saab and working at an inner city clinic during the day to make enough money to support the free clinic.

Echo had been in a different area, triaging patients and discovering their needs. When they rejoined each other at the end of the night they exchanged stories, the conversation continuing in the car and during the drive home. And as they continued to sit in the parking lot he told her about an old lady with infected spider bites on her legs and arms and she told him about a young guy who was drunk or on drugs or schizophrenic or all three, who needed to talk and did so in a disjointed confused agitated and at times violent manner but it felt like he simply needed to let it out to someone who would just listen for a few minutes without arguing or judging. They wondered whether it was possible to feel helpless and optimistic at the same time. Because they did. How could they let these people return to the cold dark streets and yet still be inspired by the strength and humor and intelligence and faith of every single person they met?

"I don't want to go in," he finally said, taking a breath and pausing to look her in the eyes.

"I don't want you to," she said, also slowing down and noticing the music and the night.

"This has been amazing."

"Yeah, Charis is an incredible project huh? It's so needed, unfortunately."

"It really is. But that's not entirely what I meant. This whole thing. All of these conversations and the driving around. The cafeteria and this talk. I'm taking it all in and I'll save it for later. There'll be days that I'll need to remember these moments. Difficult times."

"Are you planning to have hard days?"

"There'll always be hard days. They can't be avoided. No matter how careful we are and especially if we live bravely, things will fall apart. And I am fully aware of that. Just as I'm fully aware that these moments with you, right here and right now, these will be among the best moments of my life."

She was quiet for a moment, trying to decide what to say.

"Really?"

"I'm being completely honest. Think about it. We're eighteen and everything is new and possible. We're so blessed and this is utterly magical."

And then the Big Star cassette that had been playing in the background during the conversation, flipping over and repeating twice during their time together that night came to the last song on the second side. It was "I'm in Love With a Girl," and the moment was flawless as she seemed to lean forward just a little. And instinct took over even before Ben had a chance to think about it. Before he could overanalyze or stop it. His mind went blank and all he saw were her gigantic dark hypnotic eyes that seemed to fill his entire field of vision and then her thick soft lips, how the top one curled up just a little and the bottom one was full and pink and she licked it just slightly with her tongue which was two shades lighter, as he leaned forward and she came to meet him in the center of the car, looking also at his eyes, then lips. And it wasn't awkward or uncomfortable or require much adjustment in their seats as they kissed and then as their tongues lightly touched. It was like they had been waiting for this all their lives as an electrical shock traveled from their tongues and rapidly through their bodies, spreading and multiplying from that tiny contact point until it reached every extremity and their middle and every possible exit point and yet it didn't exit, it remained and built to such a level that they felt like they were incandescent, absolutely glowing in that dark car on that shining night.

It wasn't a long kiss, perhaps ten seconds, but as they pulled away, breathless and speechless, they knew that their understanding of the world had changed.

They looked into each other's eyes, silently searching for an explanation where none existed nor was required. They were at once on fire and calm, every nerve alert and every cell in their bodies focused on each other. Everything else had faded away. The car, the music, the school, the night, their future, and their pasts. There was only this one perfect moment.

They continued to study each other's eyes and lips while attempting to breathe. And as they drew near again as if by gravity or electromagnetic force and once again their lips met and once again their entire lives were focused on the contact point between them, Ben's right hand reaching under her hair, cupping her neck and the back of her head with his extended fingers, gently pulling her even closer, they realized that this is what they had been waiting for. She for him. And he for her.

There was no way to calculate the odds of finding each other among the millions and billions. The universe had taken care of that. The important thing was that it had happened. Here they were in a car, in a parking lot, sharing a kiss that was an ending and a beginning.

And once they finally had to come up for air, separating reluctantly, still hungering and thirsting for more, knowing they would never get enough of each other, not if they spent every remaining moment of their lives together, Echo finally spoke.

"Ben."

Her voice, the way she said his name, was the most beautiful sound he had ever heard.

"Echo."

They were silent again. He was absorbing her face, her expressions, every muscle twitch and hair adjustment and tiny line, the curve of her eyebrows, the line of her nose, and her soft golden neck with the faint scent of almond.

"I feel like we should…" she said, trailing off.

She tried again a few seconds later, "That was…"

"Yeah," he said. "I know."

"I'd better get home. Thank you Ben."

He laughed a little. "Thank you, Echo. This was an amazing night. In every way imaginable…"

He wanted to say more. The emotions and words were all dammed up, tenuously being held back. He knew that now wasn't the time or the place to spill everything, all of his feelings and hopes and dreams. It was too soon. It had been one kiss. How could they create a life from one kiss? He struggled with the question but knew in his soul that they had. And that there would be time for everything. For all the words. For all the emotions. Time for another kiss. And for so much more…

So in the end he kissed her once again, looked her in the eyes, holding them with his and said, "Goodnight Echo. I can't wait to see you again."

He smiled and she smiled, her dark eyes shining and he got out of the car and floated inside.

It was two weeks later. Denny was home and was more focused than he had ever been. He had studied and caught up with all that he had missed while hospitalized. And pretty soon his grades began to recover as the next round of tests went well and as he put more effort into homework and projects. His goal was to finish as strongly as possible for the next semester and then switch majors. He had met with his counselor and together they had worked out a plan. Denny had decided that dentistry wasn't for him after all, that his talents fit better with business. People. Sales. Entrepreneurship. He dreamed now of returning to

Laguna and starting a nonprofit to help with the homeless there. Veterans benefits, help for addicts, job training, housing, he wanted to give back. He'd been a part of the problem these past few years and now wanted to be part of the solution.

Ben felt a resolve and a singularity of purpose that he hadn't previously seen in Denny. This career choice seemed much more in line with where his heart was. He had all the time in the world to change his mind, to further define a plan. They spent lunch and some study time talking it over and Denny certainly was at peace.

Monday night Echo and Ben went to Charis as had quickly become their habit. They arranged their days to make time for the clinic and for each other on those evenings.

The patients and the volunteers and the experience had varied the two prior Mondays and this week was no different. With Dr. Jane he saw a lady with a horribly infected and purulent toe. She didn't remember what had happened to it. Stubbed it? Dropped something on it? Froze it? She wasn't diabetic but was a heavy smoker so surely a vascular problem of some kind. Ben loved hearing Jane think through this out loud, loved being a part of the medical team. They soaked her foot, carefully washed it, removed a small amount of dead tissue, all that she could tolerate, and rewrapped it. She was relieved and thankful, saying all that had been done at the ER was a cursory glance and a prescription for pain meds.

"I'm not a drug addict."

"I know Lydia," said Jane.

"You people are a godsend. Thank you so much," she said, looking first at Ben and then at Jane.

"It's our pleasure," she said. "Make sure you take all of the antibiotic. And keep your foot clean and dry."

"Oh I will. I'm a good patient."

"You really are. And we'll be out to see you on Friday to change the dressing again. Can you meet me about seven on that concrete slab? You know, the one on Lancaster by Speedy's where we met last time."

"I'll be there."

"And you know we'll try to be on time but can't control everything, so wait for us."

"I will. Thank you. Have a good week."

And as Lydia's friend pushed her wheelchair back down the hallway towards the warm well-lit fellowship hall where the fragrant food was being served, Ben nearly teared up. That was how he pictured a medical interaction should be. As fellow human beings. Care and empathy on both sides. Jane wanted to help Lydia. Not just by healing her painful foot, but by helping her live a less painful life. And Lydia wanted to be a good patient, to keep her foot clean. Maybe she would even quit smoking some day. As people regain dignity they regain the ability to participate in society in a meaningful positive manner. Every time love is shared, love also grows and multiplies in a mysterious way.

There were other patients that night, and with every visit the sum seemed greater than the parts. Long discussions where a few words could have made the diagnosis, conversations when orders would have sufficed. Ben thought of the Parable of the Sower. That the usual method is to toss the seeds out and hope for the best. There isn't the time, and the emotional cost is too great to care too much. But here the seeds were lovingly planted in rich, warm soil. They were watered and tended. They were supported and encouraged and given just the right amount of attention, knowing that growth and life are miracles that can't be created, only loved.

It was a really busy night. One of the rare times that Jane had to turn people away. It usually and miraculously worked out. The number of patients that wanted to be seen and the time allotted for them matched up. Not today. So Jane and Ben were busy examining what they thought was surely their last one of the night when a volunteer handed him another history form. He glanced at it as Jane continued to talk and teach. James Kennedy. Remove stitches. Nothing clicked and he looked back up.

Shortly they were ready for him and as the parlor door opened and Ben's old friend James walked in he felt a surge of concern, relief, and happiness. He hadn't heard a word from him since that night at the hospital.

"James!"

"Hey, what's up?" not outwardly shocked to see Ben here.

"What do you mean what's up? Where have you been hiding? Are you okay? Let me see your hand."

Jane looked on with some interest but let Ben take the lead as he took James' right hand. It was swollen compared to the left and had the fading remnants of a bruise, yellow and green discoloration at the periphery of the hand. Just under the fourth and fifth knuckle there were seven black sutures, the wound was crusty and red but the incision was intact with no drainage. Both hands were dirty and cracked from life outside.

"What did you do?"

"Nothing. Hit a guy."

"Why did you hit a guy?"

"He pissed me off."

"Where have you been?"

"A lot of questions. I'm fine. I'm back now. Thanks for taking these out," he said as Ben carefully pulled up the end of the suture with a forceps and got underneath the knot, cutting it with the tiny scissors.

"Sorry. I'm glad to see you."

"How's Denny?"

"He's fine. Actually he's great. It's a miracle."

"Wow, that's amazing. He's back in school and everything?"

"Yeah, can you believe it? How are you really?"

"I'm okay. There're some days I don't remember much but I'm back on the wagon now."

"Hey do you want to go to dinner? We're about done here. Echo's around too."

"Yeah, I saw her. You do know that they serve dinner here right?"

"Oh yeah, I actually forgot. I never see it. Okay how about coffee?"

"Sure, let's do it."

The three went to a dingy diner around the corner, a place that Ben had ridden by several times before and yet had never noticed. They found a booth and Echo slid in first with Ben next to her. She put her purse and jacket to her left, up against the wall, which meant that she and Ben were touching. It felt intimate and natural, like their hips had been together forever.

James told his story. It was one of falling and rising, failure and forgiveness, a story that he had lived scores of times and would continue to experience as he struggled with himself, with his past and with his fear of the future. Ben and Echo listened and understood and felt the same way. At times life would become too heavy, too big for one person. James knew he needed others, needed to share the load, that he carried too much. It is one of life's truths that community is not a luxury. It's a necessity. That what is too heavy for one person, what crushes and stresses and gnaws at and squeezes that place in the abdomen, below the stomach, deep inside, causing physical pain as real as pancreatitis or a perforated viscus, if shared with others, by becoming open and honest with trustworthy friends, healing can begin. It doesn't happen instantly. And the wound remains fresh and can be reinjured startlingly fast. But developing and nurturing friendships is the only hope. James knew it and Ben had begun to realize it.

And they talked and shared and drank coffee with plenty of milk and sugar and promised to always be friends no matter what happened. To hold each other with care and to carry each other's loads. It became late and everyone began to feel the night so they shook hands and hugged and parted at the door, James disappearing into the dark.

On the way home Echo and Ben told stories and reflected and got to know each other by the topics and opinions and thoughts that were shared. And their relationship deepened and spread and grew in all dimensions. Those initial faraway glances had led to this moment as inevitably as the sun rises and sets, as the monarchs flitter south, and as the music they were listening to at that moment would forevermore bring forth bittersweet memories of love and limitless potential.

And when they got back to Ben's apartment to find that his roommates were blessedly and inexplicably gone, they finally kissed and touched and loved and explored and discovered and appreciated as if this was the only moment that mattered. And it was.

Epilogue

It was only a few days later when they were in the drive-through at McDonalds, three cars back from the menu. The person at the window seemed to be taking awhile but it was okay. It was Steve's jeep. Marti was next to him and crammed tightly and joyfully, half sitting and half standing in the back were Ben, Echo, Denny, and Sheila. Sheila had finally given in to Denny's persistence when he explained that he had nearly died and that she had almost missed her chance to get to know him. And for some reason that worked and they were both glad it did.

The last rays of sunlight were igniting the distant high clouds. Red, orange, and yellow, the colors began at the horizon and extended up the width of a hand if one were to stretch it out and try to measure. The oblique angle to the light created a cinematic effect that was too beautiful for words.

There was beer and there was laughter and the air was crisp and clear and Ben had goose bumps as U2's Unforgettable Fire CD in the car's player faded from "4th of July" to the first unmistakable guitar sounds of "Bad". And it suddenly became not only a memorable moment but also a holy one.

Everyone in the car noticed. They all had their own thoughts and yet all realized that this was special, like a Polaroid. It instantly and permanently was imprinted into their minds, just like the time they had all seen the song performed the summer before last, the band playing it at Live Aid before an audience of hundreds of millions of rapt and silent and even tearful fans, Bono pulling a girl from the endless crowd, holding her close and everyone feeling that embrace.

They were all in love. They were in love with each other, with the music, with the gorgeous North Texas late afternoon, with youth and health and gigantic hearts and emotions. It was the excitement of being free. Of having limitless potential and yet knowing that all that mattered was the moment.

And they began to sing, no one knowing the exact lyrics, but feeling Bono's passion, and as poor as their imitation was, no sound more perfect had ever been created. Their voices rising and falling, Ben's arm was around Echo's waist, partly to be as close as possible to her, partly to keep from falling out of the topless Jeep. They both felt an exchange of energy, continuous and powerful and eternal. And no two people had ever been more in love.

Life is made of moments. A far-reaching knotted rope of individual memories that extends on and on from our earliest pre-conscious experiences until our minds finally begin to fail. As carefully as we plan, as comforting or disturbing our memories, all we have is the present moment. It's something that eighteen year olds know intuitively and appreciate wordlessly. Mindful and self-aware, each fleeting and constantly dawning and culminating moment is precious and at once eternal and ephemeral. God is in the present. Our spirit nudging us towards each other and ultimately towards the mystical body of God. We are all as infinite as the atoms that make up our fleeting existence.

And in that Jeep, singing U2 quietly and then at the top of their lungs, voices cracking with emotion, matching Bono note for note, they were wide awake. And the sun was still shining and everything was still possible and all six of them knew that this moment would never come again. And Ben and Echo looked into each other's eyes, goose bumps rising on their arms and on their legs, as they looked deep, glimpsing eternity for those few seconds, and they couldn't detect a trace of sadness, only joy. Only beauty. Only love. And every song was still about them.

Also by **Brandon Pomeroy**

"A spiritually thought provoking and thoroughly engaging novel."
-Newell Williams, President of Brite Divinity School at
Texas Christian University

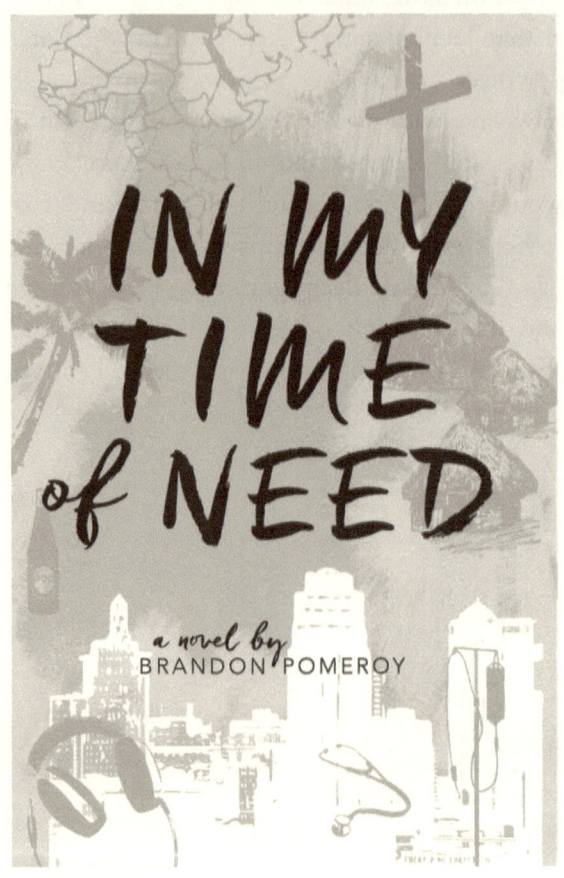

In My Time of Need is an unconventional love story that takes
the reader from Kansas City to Central America and East
Africa. Filled with grace and humor, it is a spiritual journey
that is as universal as it is meaningful.
Available now at Elpidapress.org and Amazon.com

About Elpida Press

In our busy lives, when we are only able to see things superficially and quickly, when information comes in headlines, tired quotes, and filtered photos, when everything seems fragmented and temporary, and when our actions are motivated by fear rather than hope, Elpida Press provides an alternative. A non-profit publishing company unsatisfied with the status quo, we are committed to love and reconciliation. We are on the lookout for skilled artists and writers to work with. As a non-profit we are also dependent on your kind donations. Every little bit helps as we strive to be part of the solution, carefully mending and repairing what has been nearly torn apart.

Please visit our website and follow us on Facebook.

Elpidapress.org
Facebook.com/elpidapress